Quick, Quick, Slow

SAN DIEGO AFTER DARK
BOOK ONE

JESSA LEADS

Published by Smart Sauce

ISBN: 979-8-9942102-1-5 (ebook)

ISBN: 979-8-9942102-0-8

For HY,
for loving me through
every turn, every stumble, every dance.

Playlist

These songs are part of the story, setting the pace of connection, the rhythm of desire, and giving voice to emotions where words fall short. Listen to each song as they come up in the story, or enjoy as a playlist. I hope you dance!

Baile Inolvidable – Bad Bunny
Valió la Pena – Marc Anthony
La Llave – Grupo Latin Vibe
Ven, Devórame Otra Vez – Bembé Orquesta
Anacaona – Cheo Feliciano
Todo Tiene Su Final – Willie Colón & Héctor Lavoe
Micaela – B-Side Players
Otra Oportunidad – Jimmy Bosch
Cali Pachanguero – Grupo Niche
Tú con Él – Rauw Alejandro
Fallarte Nunca – Ralphy Dreamz
Would I Lie – Cubaneros
¿Dónde Se Fueron? – Ozomatli
Pégate – Ricky Martin
Aguanile – Marc Anthony
Aquí Traigo Mi Montuno – Ismael Quintana
La Cura – Frankie Ruiz

Apple

Spotify

Chapter One

Apparently, booking a one-way ticket across the country doesn't magically make you brave. It makes you tired, overdressed, and alone on a sidewalk in downtown San Diego.

Gia tugged at the hem of her black slip dress and stared down the block like courage might show up in heels and a blowout. But there was no sign of her cousin. Just a buzz from her phone.

NIKKI

I'm so sorry! One of my athletes got hurt during the race. Heading to hospital now. Not sure how long we'll be. I swear I'll make it up to you, Gia. LOVE YOU and so happy you're here!

Gia sighed. Her thumb hovered over the message, tempted to reply with a list of dramatic emojis. Instead, she scanned Fifth Avenue for something that might wake her up. Casa Sevilla stood behind a bold red awning and wrought-iron railings, glowing like a portal to another world. From inside, a flamenco guitarist's melody drifted into the night like an invitation. *Come in, Gia. Something's waiting for you.*

She wasn't ready. Not for this city, its music, or the version of herself who would walk alone into a moody slice of Spain hidden in the heart of San Diego's Gaslamp Quarter.

However, she hadn't traveled three thousand miles to play it safe.

Gia stepped through the threshold into the night that changed everything.

The room was lit by low-hanging chandeliers and flickering candles tucked into wall sconces. Tables of dark wood stood beneath paintings of matadors. Garlic, saffron, and roasted seafood drifted through the air, stirring her appetite.

At the front of the restaurant was a narrow stage with a guitarist, palmas, a cajón player, and a vocalist in an elegant crimson flamenco dress. Her voice was raw with emotion as she sang over the guitar's wail, getting louder and louder until suddenly the music stopped completely. Silence stretched into suspense until the singer struck her heel against the floor. Percussion surged back in with claps and pounding footwork loud enough to rattle the floorboards. Gia startled, then laughed at herself.

She ordered a spicy margarita, a twist on her usual classic. A few minutes later, the server dropped off a plate of fresh halibut and shrimp ceviche, citrusy and loaded with garlic and onions. Gia mused that one of the underrated perks of flying solo was eating whatever she wanted. No sharing. No Italian food for the hundredth time. *Take that, Miles.*

As Gia savored the last bites of garlicky seafood, something caught her attention near the entrance. People entered the restaurant, but none of them waited to be seated. A couple dressed in cocktail attire stepped inside, barely glancing at the dazzling performance before veering toward a narrow staircase tucked along the side wall, half-hidden in shadow.

Then came a group of three women. Their voices sparkled with excitement as they made a beeline for the stairs, not the hostess stand. Each one dressed for the spotlight. A tight tube dress on the first. Black spandex leggings and a sequined halter top on the second. A slinky catsuit on the third that covered every inch of her tanned skin, yet left nothing to the imagination. They all wore sandals. Plain, squishy, beach-day flip-flops. Not what you'd pair with clubwear.

That's when Gia noticed each of them had a drawstring bag tucked under her arm. Dancers. No question. Those bags likely held suede-soled, strappy ballroom high heels. No committed dancer would ever wear their dance shoes outdoors.

Curious, Gia flagged down her server, a brunette with sun-streaked hair and the carefree attitude of someone who spent half her life on a surfboard.

"What's happening downstairs?"

"Salsa-bachata night."

That was not what she expected from a flamenco-themed restaurant. It wasn't even nine p.m. yet.

"You missed the lesson, but the DJ plays until one a.m."

"What happens at one?"

"The club closes, along with most of downtown."

"Seriously?" Back home, people didn't leave their houses until eleven. Not that she had visited nightclubs recently.

"Yep. You should check it out."

Gia gave a polite smile in response. Dance wasn't part of her life anymore.

She returned her attention to the flamenco dancer and let the memories of her college dance studies flood her mind. The memory of the cool studio floor pressed against her bare feet. She could still hear the soft scuff of dancers gliding over Marley too. Back then, her body moved without hesitation or apology. She was fully alive. It was another lifetime, though. Before she understood what it would cost.

Gia wished her cousin Nikki were with her as planned, but she knew if she didn't take the opportunities when they came up, she might lose her nerve altogether.

She wiped her fingers on her napkin, took a last sip of her

spicy margarita, and walked over to the stairs. Time to follow through.

As Gia stepped down the creaky steps, the muffled beat of congas replaced the chatter from the restaurant. Her heartbeat matched the pounding of the drums as she got closer. When she reached the bottom, heat and music hit her like a tidal wave. It was a full-body assault on her senses.

The basement nightclub was a world away from the moody, candlelit dining area upstairs. The low ceiling trapped the air with the smell of spilled tequila and citrus. A bar stretched along one side, bottles glowing amber beneath neon lights, while the rest of the room belonged to the dance floor.

And the dance floor was beautiful chaos.

Gia watched the ever-shifting kaleidoscope of dancers, their bodies spinning and pressing close, then breaking apart with the drama of a steamy love scene. She recognized the track playing: Bad Bunny's "Baile Inolvidable." The song was everywhere lately, but here, it hit different. Sounds of percussion and brass instruments pulsed through the air, entered her body, and poured into her bloodstream like warm honey. The piano solo's ebb and flow, a playful tease before the beat's return, seemed to taunt and invite.

"Baile Inolvidable" carried a sense of nostalgia and longing that went straight to Gia's heart. All the dancers seemed to experience the same thing. With every drumbeat, horn trill, and shift in melody, they moved in harmony, turning the music into something you could see.

Gia recognized the lead-and-follow of partner dancing. Leaders started the movement; followers responded. Each couple was bound in choreographic conversation. The key was knowing the language and rules of the dance.

Rules wasn't the right word, Gia mused, because salsa was neither rigid nor rehearsed. If anything, the room rippled with freedom. When was the last time she had experienced something like this? In college. In dance class. Maybe Miles hadn't been entirely wrong...

She pushed the thought aside. She'd drifted away from the staircase, but was still observing like an outsider. She didn't know anyone or speak the language of salsa, but, consumed in the heat of this basement party, her body yearned to move. Her earlier training taught her to execute choreography alongside a partner, not to *follow* one in an unscripted social dance.

Someone brushed past her, a man in a crisp button-down, sleeves rolled up, his forearm grazing hers as he spun the woman in his arms into a turn. He moved with the grace of a ballet dancer and the intensity of a matador. Gia rubbed the spot on her arm to soak in the sensation. Then her eyes landed on his partner.

High cheekbones, sun-kissed skin, a dancer's body sculpted by years of training. Her hair was pulled back into a sleek dragon braid, preventing it from whipping her dance partner as she spun what looked like a hundred seamless revolutions. The only thing that shone brighter than her emerald eyes were the glittery straps of her heels. Even her gold tube dress glittered as she moved, each turn a display of curves and long legs.

They danced within a razor-thin slot, moving forward and back along the same invisible line. His feet marked the rhythm in crisp, precise steps, leading her with subtle shifts of weight, hand placement, posture, and tension. She responded, following his signals with whip-like speed and feline grace.

Gia's chest stirred with admiration, longing, and a hint of desire.

On the second beat of the music, he stepped forward, slicing into the space between them. She moved back on her right foot, hips echoing the percussion in fluid figure-eights. On five, he pivoted to open the slot, his torso angling to create room for her to walk across. She strode through it, each step a brushstroke skimming the floor. He set her up for a turn with a smooth twist of the wrist, sending her into a triple spin that unwound with breathtaking speed.

Their connection stretched and retracted like elastic, never tense, always alive with possibility. She floated into an open break, shoulders rolling in sync with the percussion while her wrists and fingers carved graceful arcs in the air. She danced at a professional level but scaled for the social floor.

Gia leaned forward, drawn into the current that swirled around the two dancers. Her hands twitched at her sides, itching to move, to mimic the dancer's styling. But her feet wouldn't budge. They were cemented to the floorboards. The dance invited her body, but it refused the call.

The song's climax pulled her from her thoughts as the energy in the club peaked. Then, like a tide receding, the crowd dissipated to the edges of the floor.

Gia remained frozen near the staircase, unsure of what to do next. She was so mesmerized by the dynamics on the dance floor that she missed the handsome stranger standing in front of her.

"Care to dance?"

Gia blinked. The room shifted as if someone had nudged the lens of a camera from a panoramic view to a sudden close-up. Her gaze snapped from the crowd to the man standing in her personal space. He was in his mid-thirties, tall and lean, with a simple charm in his manner. He wore a tight black T-shirt, designer jeans, Adidas Sambas, and an aquatic cologne. Understated yet stylish.

Gia glanced back at the dance floor for one more glimpse of the woman with the dragon braid, but the couple had vanished. New partners already claimed the spot where they had danced seconds ago. When Gia turned around, she realized the man was waiting for her response.

"Oh. Um. No, thank you... I don't know how to salsa."

His smile deepened, warmth flickering in his smoky eyes. "No worries," he said, undeterred.

He extended his hand, palm open. Her gaze lingered on it, caught by the quiet weight of the gesture. It seemed symbolic, as if taking it meant stepping out of her safe corner of observation into the vulnerable light of being seen.

"I'm Dom. I teach the beginner's class before the club opens.

I make sure new dancers have fun." His voice was friendly. "We'll take it slow. Promise."

Wow, that was quite a line.

To Gia's surprise, Dom didn't say another word. Instead, he held her gaze and tilted his head toward the dance floor. His eyebrows raised the silent question: *Well? Are you ready?*

Her pulse quickened. *This is why you're here. To feel a spark again. Don't think. Just move.*

A part of her screamed, *Say no. Stay safe on the sidelines.* Yet another voice, the one that had uprooted her East Coast life and brought her here for the summer, whispered, *Say yes.* That voice was louder.

She took his hand before she could second-guess herself.

As he drew her into the frame, Gia's muscles tensed. Her brain tracked everything. She marked where his hands were, how close he stood, where his eyes landed, and whether she looked awkward. *Oh my God, I look so awkward!*

"Mirror my steps. Let your weight shift when mine does."

Gia concentrated on the weight transfer, the push-pull of his lead, and the rhythm of the song. She noticed with relief that he didn't monitor her body or stare into her eyes while they were this close. He wasn't evaluating or judging her. Instead, he focused on their partnership and connection, as if he knew how much room she needed to find her footing. The music curled around them, and the tension in her chest loosened as they danced. Not a grand release. Just a tiny crack. Her jaw unclenched. Her shoulders dropped half an inch. For the first time in years, Gia slipped back into her body like it was a home she'd abandoned. She was no longer floating somewhere above, viewing from a distance. It was terrifying, wonderful, and right.

When the music ended, Dom released her hand and smiled. He gave her a nod of acknowledgment, and his eyes sparkled with amusement. "Okay, maybe it's your first time with salsa, but you've definitely danced before."

"Yeah. Well, thanks for taking it easy on me."

He arched a brow. "I didn't."

Gia stood up taller. She couldn't suppress the giant grin plastered across her face in response.

"Are you visiting San Diego?"

"Kind of. I'm here for the summer. From New York."

"Nice! New York has the best salsa scene. Where's your favorite place to dance out there?"

"Oh, um, no salsa. I minored in contemporary dance in college, but I don't really dance anymore. Except at the occasional wedding." She winced at how ridiculous that last part sounded.

"Well, obviously, dancing never left you. Listen, leads notice when I partner with someone new, especially when she can follow." He tilted his head toward the sea of dancers under the lights. "You won't have trouble finding partners for the rest of the night. Hope I see you here again!" He gave Gia a quick wink and walked over to what appeared to be a line of women waiting for a turn with him.

Dom guided his next partner to the center of the nightclub. She wore jazz shoes, unlike the other dancers in high heels. The woman approached with stiff shoulders and downcast eyes. She barely closed her hand in his. Her feet shuffled into position, weight unsettled, as if she might bolt at any moment. However, once the music started, she seemed to get her footing. With each count, her steps found their way. By the second half of the song, a hint of confidence peeked through like sunlight through sheer curtains.

Gia smiled to herself, realizing she probably had looked the same moments before.

With his new partner, Dom's lead was gentle, encouraging, attuned to exactly what she needed. Every touch was an invitation. He was so light on his feet, it was almost otherworldly. He seemed to hover above the floor, as if the ground didn't dare to hold him down. Dom was an angel, Gia thought, equal parts grace and power, guiding his partners through a private little heaven right there in the middle of a crowded dance club.

Gia wasn't ready to leave or sit down, so she wandered to the bar to watch more dancing.

A slower, more sensual song began. The lead guitar traced a delicate melody while the rhythm guitar added syncopated strums with a gentle swing. Underneath, the bass rolled in steady like a heartbeat. The music pulsed in counts of four, lifting on the fourth beat. The sound was lush and hypnotic...bachata.

Gia watched the dancers move with ease, their steps simple. They shifted side to side, tracing a small rectangle on the floor. Right, together, right, tap... left, together, left, tap. Each tap landed with a suggestive hip accent. Some couples danced with light, flirtatious energy in an open position with intricate turns. Others leaned into the music's sensual pull, moving with slow body rolls, dramatic dips, and a frame so close there was no space between them.

Gia swayed to the rhythm, shoulders rolling, hips catching that lift on every fourth beat, until a deep voice interrupted her reverie.

"Bachata?"

Gia turned and found him, tall with smooth features except for a jawline that could cut glass. He was at ease, but his presence was impossible to miss. His hand extended toward her in a silent invitation.

This wasn't salsa, where the steps offered moments of flair and flourish, a chance to play and pull back. Bachata was intimate and languid, every movement as seductive as a dark secret.

Her hand hovered, not quite within his grasp. She could say no. Avoid the sensation of butterflies fluttering low in her belly. And yet...when her fingertips finally brushed his, her body moved before her brain could protest.

"I should warn you, I have no idea what I'm doing."

He responded by pulling her close, his frame closing around her like parentheses.

Her every nerve lit up with sensation. The nearness, the press of his chest against hers, the subtle brush of his leg as they swayed together in rhythm awakened something deep inside her. Her body craved the intoxicating closeness of the embrace and the electric thrill of the music taking over. She honed in on the exact location of each inch of skin touching this handsome stranger.

He led with subtle shifts, a weight change, a hip nudge, a soft signal of intention. Instinct guided her response.

The steps were straightforward: side, together, side, tap, repeat. The bachata rhythm provided only enough time to feel. There was no time for thinking.

As the music swelled, he transitioned to an open hold, keeping her hands in his, but now their arms stretched wide to the sides, creating a sudden distance between their bodies. Her skin ached for the heat and steady burn of contact. She wanted it back.

When he pulled her in again, his chest, hips, and breath aligned with hers. His scent filled her lungs with salt and spice. With his leg between hers, her thighs instinctively pressed together, awakening a hunger between her legs she hadn't known in far too long. The music and their bodies in sync teased every nerve awake. *All this from dancing with a stranger?*

The song's last notes struck just in time. She turned and rushed to the outdoor seating area, grateful for the cool breeze.

Her pulse raced from the connection in the dance and from everything that followed. It was as if someone had flung open all the windows of her heart at once, and now a thousand butterflies were swarming out and through her chest, wild, chaotic, desperate to break free. They beat against her ribs, fluttering up into her arms, making her fingertips tingle. She shook out her hands as if she could scatter them into the air, but they only multiplied, a beautiful, maddening storm of winged creatures inside her.

"You okay?" A woman's voice asked. "You were flying out there. But now you look like you're trying to shake off your wings."

Gia jumped in surprise as the dancer with the dragon braid walked outside, fanning her face with her hands. Gia chuckled at her own startle, shaking her head back and forth.

"I think I broke some internal fuse. My nervous system short-circuited or something."

She looked up to face the woman. Gia felt safe confiding in a stranger she'd never meet again, so she spilled her guts like she was talking to her childhood best friend. "I haven't danced in years. I didn't realize how much I missed it."

The dancer nodded, holding space.

"It's like I've been living outside of my body. Where did that part of me go?" She paused, tears welling up in her eyes. "What if this was just a fluke?"

"It wasn't. But even if it were, you danced tonight. That's not a fluke. It's a thread you can follow."

Little by little, the wild swarm inside her calmed, the butterflies back at rest, and Gia regained her grounding.

The woman squeezed Gia's hand. "I teach a beginner's class on Wednesday nights. Friendly group, fabulous style," she said with a wink. "Why don't you swing by and see if you like it? I'll keep an eye out for you and make sure it's your speed."

"You teach here?"

"Not here. I have a studio in North Park called Ritmo Latino. I performed here earlier tonight."

"Wait, you're a flamenco singer too?"

"God no. I can't sing for shit. My partner and I danced after Dom's intro class."

Gia laughed, and some tension melted from her shoulders.

"I'm Camila, by the way."

"Gia."

Camila's smile deepened, warm and easy. "Nice to meet you, Gia. Come to the studio next Wednesday. We're starting a new series. Total beginner."

Gia gave a nod. "I will definitely...think about it."

A couple walked outside, laughing and chatting, a reminder that this was a social scene and not a sanctuary. Camila gave Gia one last smile before slipping back inside and into the music.

Gia turned her attention to the couple, each one dabbing sweat from their foreheads. Their flushed cheeks told the story of how much they'd been dancing tonight. Gia wanted that for herself. She missed the rush of every part of her being awake.

Still, taking a salsa class at this point in her life seemed like crashing a party after the music ended. Awkward. A little desperate. Besides, she had left dance for good reason.

She'd already said yes to two dances tonight. That was a brave thing. Did she need to sign up for a whole series of classes?

Salsa and bachata stirred a part of her she kept muzzled for years. Some things, once unleashed, refused to be caged again. She wasn't sure she was ready for that. Not yet.

<h1 style="text-align:center">Chapter Two</h1>

You can't live off the memory of screaming fans. At some point, you have to find a new rhythm that doesn't break your body.

Sebastián jogged to the edge of the turf with his whistle in hand. He moved with the confidence of a pro accustomed to hearing entire arenas chant his name, but his knee pulsed with each step. The pain wasn't loud, but it was loyal. It haunted him like a quiet ghost of the life he had before.

Across the field, the rookie striker flubbed the trap again, sending the ball skittering a yard too far. Sebastián inhaled through his nose. Not irritated. *Invested.* That's what he told himself.

"Set your feet!" he called out. "Don't chase. Control it."

The player adjusted, this time cushioning the pass. It landed with a satisfying thunk.

Sebastián nodded once. Not bad. He kept walking, one hand on his hip, eyes tracking each player's movement, though his mind drifted. He liked drills. They had shape and logic. He enjoyed coaching too, but it didn't reach the part of him that still craved the rush of the game. The roar of the crowd, the sting of cold air in his burning lungs while sprinting across the field, that final breakaway goal in overtime.

Sebastián pivoted too fast, and a bolt of pain shot through his knee. He swallowed a wince and cursed himself for forgetting his brace.

"Pressure!" he barked at midfield. "Hunt the ball!"

A midfielder lunged, intercepted the pass, and spun out clean. That was a good note to finish on, so Sebastián blew his whistle to mark the end of practice.

"Alright, bring it in."

They jogged over, and he met them with nods, shoulder taps, and flashes of praise.

"Thanks, Coach Solano!" Some rookies spoke to Sebastián with a reverence that made it clear they'd grown up watching him score goals on ESPN.

It was a good job. He liked the players. It wasn't Major League Soccer or La Liga, where he used to play, or Copa Libertadores, like the clubs his dad supported, but they *crushed* their competition. The Breakers were the top-ranked professional arena soccer team in the U.S.

Sebastián appreciated the opportunity to train these guys, but every fiber of his body yearned to be on the field in the middle of the action, savoring the rush of the play. He missed the stadium lights, the pressure, the split-second decisions that required instinct. It still lived inside him. Just... unreachable now.

The head coach clapped a hand on Sebastián's shoulder. "You've got a gift, man. Ever think about taking a full-time coaching position?"

Sebastián offered the smile he'd practiced in the mirror. "Of course. Definitely."

He meant it. At least he wanted to. He needed to believe he did.

He glanced at his watch.

Shit.

The Ritmo Latino studio was a forty-minute drive from Frontline Arena, so he was already late. He moved faster than he should've without his knee brace, tossing his duffel into the back of his car and peeling out of the parking lot with one hand still towel-drying his neck.

A notification from his sister lit up his phone.

CAMILA

Advanced class tonight @ 7:15 pm. Need you
to help teach!

"Hey Siri, text Camila that I'm on my way!" He turned the volume up on his favorite playlist as he drove south on the 5. No matter what happened, salsa was there. It was the one constant in his life.

At the next red light, he reached for his knee brace on the passenger seat. He pulled it on like armor. It was lightweight, flexible, and necessary to manage half the pace he used to keep before the injury. He flexed his foot on the brake, rolled his neck, and headed toward the studio.

Forty minutes later, Sebastián stepped into Ritmo Latino. The advanced class had already started. The saucy blend of instruments that distinguishes salsa music replaced the noise of the outside world. It was warm with so many students packed into each session, despite the air-conditioning and huge ceiling fans. Camila was mid-demonstration with the group, correcting someone's frame while cueing the next song from her smartwatch.

Sebastián walked in like he belonged. The veterans glanced his way to nod hello. Newer students always did a double-take. One lead stretched taller, taking up as much space as possible. A follower smoothed her hair and adjusted her sports bra for maximum impact. Another pointed and whispered to a friend, half in disbelief and half in awe.

Sebastián knew they still looked at him like a legend, and he tried to live up to his reputation. He just hoped they didn't notice how much he relied on his knee brace these days. He smiled at the group and gave them a friendly salute.

Across the studio, Camila caught his eye in the mirror and winked. "Yes, Sebastián Solano has entered the building. For those of you who are new, he's my brother, but you probably already knew that. He'll help demo some of the partnerwork today."

Sebastián stepped into the corner, kicked off his trainers,

and slid into line beside Andrés and Daniel in the back row. Both danced on Ritmo Latino's pro-level competitive team. Daniel, Camila's new partner and the company's principal lead, was taking advanced classes to learn the follower's role. Camila was shaping him into the strongest dancer possible, which required him to understand how it felt to be led. It also meant he'd be able to teach both roles and cover for Camila when needed.

Andrés, the team's resident badass, spent his days battling Southern California's notoriously brutal fire season and his nights owning the dance floor as a scene-stealing salsero. Salsa was his release valve, a way to breathe after the anxiety and "always on" nature of his work, which he never talked about. Andrés dropped into classes whenever his schedule allowed, no matter the level or style of dance. Sebastián loved how Andrés could turn even the most mundane rehearsal into a comedy set.

Neither Andrés nor Daniel looked at Sebastián with starry eyes anymore. They were more like brothers now.

"Look who decided to grace us with his presence," Andrés said, clapping him on the shoulder.

"What's up, guys?" Sebastián greeted them.

"Big day today, huh? What did you think of the team?" Daniel asked. "Did the Breakers live up to the hype, or are you there to whip them into shape?" The underlying excitement in his tone was impossible to miss.

Sebastián smiled, but before he could answer, Camila's voice floated over the music like a melody. "Let's talk soccer after warmups, gentlemen."

"Yes, ma'am," the three of them chimed in unison, drawing laughter from the rest of the room.

Sebastián flowed through the warmup with precision, each movement economical and exact. A smile played at his mouth, the tell of someone who loved the work required to obtain mastery at something physical.

Camila wove a few of their rehab drills into the routine, without calling it out. Extra conditioning disguised as choreography. He met Camila's eyes in the mirror with a silent nod of thanks. She winked back before shifting into the next sequence.

Camila clapped twice, signaling a transition. "Okay, let's move to partnerwork. Leads to the left. Follows on the right. Sebastián and I will show the pattern. We'll practice with our current partner and then rotate to new people every few minutes."

After the demo, Camila and Sebastián joined the leader and follower groups. Sebastián's partner was Sabrina, a social dancer who took advanced classes for fun. With long limbs and razor-sharp styling, she always seemed to slice through the beat rather than dance to it.

Her brows lifted the moment their hands met. "So I get you first?" She lowered her head to stare up at him through her lashes, a slow smile tugging at the corner of her mouth. "Lucky me."

Sabrina added extra flair to the turn, letting her body ride the momentum, her blonde hair fanning about her. She held his eyes as long as she could before the spin pulled her around. With each rotation, she snapped her gaze back to his, steady and sure, like a tether. Her half-smile told him she enjoyed every point of contact: his fingers skimming the curve of her waist, the firm anchor of his other hand in hers, and those green eyes glued on her.

He appreciated the private moment they shared in public and let her know with a subtle body roll as she completed her turn. He meant to tease her with the sexy gesture, dancing it just out of reach.

"Okay, Solano," she sang under her breath. "I see you."

Eight eight-counts passed in that electric space dancers live for, the zone where great timing and expert skill dissolve into pure chemistry. The kind that makes people stop and watch.

The next rotation came, but Sabrina didn't budge.

"Let's rotate!" Camila repeated.

Sabrina made no move to leave Sebastián's arms.

"Girl," Camila said, with a smirk this time, "he's not yours all night."

Sabrina shrugged. "Just making sure the bar's set high."

Her tone was light, but the message was clear.

Sebastián chuckled, dipping his head in a small, amused bow. As the rotation carried him from partner to partner, Sebastián tuned in to each one like a musician adjusting to a new instrument mid-song.

With Paula, a nervous dancer who had never taken the advanced class before, he softened his frame. His lead became gentle, almost whisper-light, inviting rather than directing. "Thanks, Sebastián," she said when their turn finished.

"Thank *you*," he replied as Camila called, "Rotate!"

His next partner was Daniel, who was practicing the follower's role tonight to help with his future teaching. Sebastián strengthened his frame to match Daniel's weight and grounded energy. He challenged his friend with a triple spin in place of the double everyone else was doing and added a few directional changes, knowing Daniel could handle it. They grinned through the exchange, laughing when they stumbled through a funky footwork pattern and recovered in perfect unison. It was about pushing the edge of skill and having fun.

"Making me work today, Sebas!"

"You're killin' it, D." He added with a teasing tone, "Always a pleasure, cariño." And along the rotation he went.

Then came Ava, all elegance and grace, with arms like ribbons. All she needed was space. Sebastián opened up the frame, giving her room to breathe and extend. He spun Ava out into the double turn, then anchored her, letting her finish the phrase with styling all her own.

As the rotation continued, Sebastián adjusted his lead, lighter here, firmer there, always attuned to the person in front of him. He'd danced with most of the women in nightclubs or at parties, so he remembered how each one moved, what made them feel confident, what made them glow.

That quiet generosity set him apart in a scene full of overly confident men. It didn't hurt that he had the physique of an athlete in peak condition, with the rhythm of two salsa legends flowing in his veins. Calling Sebastián charismatic was like describing a jalapeño as slightly zesty. Technically accurate but also wildly misleading.

Sabrina kept glancing at Sebastián, her gaze lingering longer each time until the rotation brought her to his arms again.

As Sebastián led her through the pattern, Sabrina grazed her hand across Sebastián's chest slower than necessary. Then came the subtle bite of her lower lip, like punctuation at the end of a dare. Her hips did all the talking, describing to Sebastián exactly what she wanted, throughout the dance.

Sebastián took a measured step back, eyes flicking from her parted lips to the blonde hair that reached down to her tailbone to the flash of hot pink on her manicured toes in her stiletto heels. He let out the faintest breath, shook his head once, then offered a polite nod as the music faded.

Off-limits.

Camila left no gray areas on that topic.

"Hook up with anyone in the social scene if you want," she'd said one night last year while he helped her close up shop. She swept the dust and laid down her rules at the same time. "Have fun, do your thing. But don't mess around with the women in my studio unless you're serious. It takes a hell of a lot to get these dancers to Ritmo Latino level, and I'm not risking any more walkouts over bruised egos or broken hearts. Besides, you've got all of San Diego to choose from."

Fair enough. He respected her too much to make things messy. Besides, she wasn't wrong. Dancers got emotional. The moment someone caught feelings, and it didn't go both ways, everything got awkward. Fast. In partner dancing, it was too easy for the line between connection and attraction to blur.

He'd learned that lesson the hard way. During his first month in San Diego, he'd let those lines vanish. Three dancers, a few drinks and too much chemistry. He thought it was just one night of fun, but they wanted to keep it going. What started as a hot night turned into weeks of jealousy and whispered drama on the studio floor until all three of them finally walked out. Camila had been furious.

On the bright side, the "off-limits" rule created the space for genuine friendships to form. Over the past year, the studio grew to be a second home, a place where he could show up, sweat, and connect without pressure. He never needed that more. His closest friends now were Andrés and Daniel. He was pretty tight with Amber and Luna, who were also on the pro team. And of course, he and Camila were closer than they'd ever been. That meant something. More than he let on. Especially for a guy who still missed the soccer brotherhood that had once been his entire world.

Sabrina was dance floor dynamite and a knockout in bed if she moved anything like she did in her heels, but she wasn't dating material. She wanted the status boost of dancing, or more, with Sebastián Solano. Son of salsa royalty. Millionaire pro athlete. Local legend. Her gaze said to him, *I want to be seen with you,* not *I want to see you.*

For Sabrina, his name was interchangeable with any other celebrity's. She craved the spotlight that came with proximity. Sebastián knew that look all too well. He got it in locker rooms, during matches, and in more than a few VIP sections. He loved women and thrived on the attention. His career had offered no shortage of enthusiastic invitations, and he enjoyed the perks. Frequently. He wasn't a saint, and he didn't pretend to be, but casual had its place, and it was outside of Camila's studio. Besides, lately, the shallow thrill wasn't cutting it anyway.

As the class wrapped, dancers peeled off the floor in pairs and groups, swapping shoes for Reefs or Uggs and laughing as they headed for the exit. Daniel and Andrés waved goodnight as they passed him.

"Let's get a beer this weekend. I want to hear about your new gig," Daniel said.

"Yeah. After rehearsal on Saturday."

Sabrina offered one last glance, but he kept his eyes on the mirror.

"Stay a few minutes?" Sebastián asked his sister as he walked over with a water bottle in hand.

Camila didn't even look up. "You mean for actual work, or to brag about how gracefully you turn down my dancers these days?"

He smirked. "A little of both?"

She waited until the last dancer left before facing him. "Before we stretch, let's practice that new combo from tonight. You're favoring your left again."

Sebastián bent and straightened his leg, testing the joint. "I wasn't favoring. I was... strategically adjusting." Camila raised her eyebrows in response.

"Adding sabor?"

"You're full of shit. We'll take it from the top."

With only his sister in the room, the energy softened from performance mode to honesty. No pressure. No curious students waiting to see how a famous ex-athlete tackled basic technique and rehabilitation exercises. He could let loose and be honest about how much it took to make it appear effortless. Just like when he'd first limped into the studio two years ago with nothing to prove and everything to relearn. Like when they were kids. Except now Camila was the one helping him reach.

He taught her how to ride a bike on her fifth birthday, how to throw a right hook in case he wasn't around to put a bully in place for her, and even how to follow when they danced salsa backstage during their parents' concerts. These days, she corrected his balance and coached him through rehab drills as if it were her mission. When your sister happens to be the top salsa pro and dance therapist in Southern California, rehab starts to look a lot more fun. Besides, it was the doctor's orders.

They worked through the combination at half speed, and Camila paused often to adjust his lines, shift his weight, and re-center his balance. Her cues were precise but never clinical. She knew how to keep things light and playful.

"Nice. Much cleaner," Camila said mid-sequence. "Still landing like a sack of bricks, though."

"I am bricks. Muscle mass." He shrugged, deadpan.

"Excuses, excuses." She rolled her eyes. "You were quicker on your feet as a scrawny ten-year-old."

"Yeah, well, ten-year-old me didn't have thirty years of fútbol in his knees."

They laughed. Then she tapped her phone and queued up their favorite: "Cali Pachanguero" by Grupo Niche.

The song filled the space, bright and familiar. Cali, Colombia, was their parents' hometown, a city known as the world's salsa capital. The melody always brought them back to their childhood visits there and to memories of dancing with cousins at family parties while trying to keep up with their grandparents.

"Little extra motivation," she said with a shrug, "for your ancient joints."

"You're lucky I need you."

"You're lucky you have me."

"Ain't that the truth, Cami." He teased her whenever he had the chance but always made sure she knew how much he appreciated her. Same as when they were kids.

They moved through the rehab exercises with quiet focus. This was work no one clapped for. There were no lights here. No chants and no cameras. No scoreboard lit up with his name. A stadium full of fans singing "Solano, Solano, Solano" was music, power, and belonging. Without it, he wasn't sure who he was. For now, all he could do was show up every day, stay in the arena through coaching, and, most importantly, rehearse with Camila. That was the only way to get a microscopic fix of competing and performing for a crowd, two things he held on to like a lifeline.

Camila sang the lyrics as she danced.

For the first time all day, his knee pain went quiet.

Chapter Three

Her cousin's artisan-style house in Bay Park was pure Nikki. Restored and modernized, it sat on a quiet street complete with a lush garden and a sunlit patio just big enough for a dining table and two yoga mats. The location was ideal, close to La Jolla, Pacific Beach, and Mission Bay, with quick freeway access to major athletic facilities. Nikki worked as a physical therapist and performance coach for triathletes and pro athletes, so she needed that convenience. Lucky for Gia, it also meant beach views in every direction, perfect for long runs or aimless walks.

Gia took her laptop outside, keeping quiet so Nikki could sleep in. She opened her computer to check her calendar and figure out how to space her meetings, interviews, and writing for the next week. The first thing she saw was Miles' schedule. Delete. No need to ensure their schedules aligned.

She reached for her phone and paused. Her wallpaper still showed a brunch photo from one of their regular spots. Time to change that, too. She wanted something lighter and new. Gia searched her camera roll, then changed course and opened a browser instead. *Dirty Dancing.* She could quote every single line. It was her favorite movie since she was a kid, and she'd never admit how many times she'd seen it. Gia found the final lift within seconds. Baby soaring with Johnny, strong and steady beneath her. Perfect. A reminder to take up space again.

Next, she opened Instagram out of habit. The algorithm delivered instantly: a happy couple, a blurry sonogram, a growing bump, a swaddled newborn. Milestones she was supposed to be chasing. She locked her phone and turned it facedown. No more reminders that she wasn't "on schedule."

Gia returned to her laptop and typed "salsa dance shoes." The screen filled with images of strappy heels in bronze satins and soft leathers, suede soles made to glide across hardwood floors, and descriptions that promised "elegance and control" or "flawless spins." She clicked through one shoe after another, her pulse ticking up a notch.

"Somebody pinch me! You're really here!"

Gia squealed and bolted from her chair, throwing herself into Nikki's arms. They spun in wild circles, laughing and clinging to each other like little kids.

"I missed you so much!" Gia said, tears spilling before she could stop them.

"Oh no, don't you cry, Gia Mia!" Nikki impersonated their grandmother's voice as she wiped her cousin's cheeks.

"You started it, Nicoletta," Gia replied, exaggerating their grandmother's Italian accent.

Gia squeezed tight before pulling away to sweep her gaze around. "I can't believe I'm actually here! Your house! It's perfect. So you."

"Right?! I love it. Still unpacking, but getting there. Home-ownership in San Diego is no joke. I'm just glad you said yes to moving in for the summer! This is going to be the best four months of our lives."

"Timing couldn't have been better. Thank you for giving me that push. Feels good to be on the opposite coast."

"Oh, I can imagine." Nikki grabbed Gia's hand and led her to the kitchen. "You probably need some downtime, but you won't disappear here, babe. Not on my watch."

Gia tilted her head as if to question what her cousin meant, but they both knew.

Nikki continued. "I'm crazy excited you're here. But what the hell? So left field of Miles. I want to hear what happened, but... wait." She stepped back to give Gia a once-over, top to bottom. "You look amazing. Maybe too amazing. How are you holding up?"

Gia gave a shrug that aimed for breezy. "Oh, you know... when all your long-term plans get upended overnight, it makes you rethink pretty much everything." She looked down into her mug, avoiding Nikki's eyes. "I'm not ready to unpack it yet. All I know is that San Diego is the right place to start fresh. At least for a while." She lifted her chin, meeting Nikki's gaze. "Thank you for having me."

"It doesn't have to be just for a while, you know."

"Thank you. Really. But the publishing firm wants everyone to be close enough for regular meetings in New York. I'll need to go back eventually. In the meantime, I've got some time to reinvent myself. Prove I'm not as boring and predictable as certain people might think."

"Well, it really doesn't matter what *certain people* think. That said, I am more than happy to help you explore beyond boring, predictable stuff! Babe, we haven't been single together since the holiday breaks in college. So, what's first? Or did you get a head start while I was at the hospital? Dang it! I can't believe I missed your first night!"

Gia smiled in return. "Don't sweat it. We have plenty of time to make up for it!"

"Yes! Let's catch up over breakfast. We can walk down to Mission Bay and grab a bite somewhere. I'll show you your new digs."

"That sounds perfect."

"And I want to hear about whatever you got into last night. I'm so sorry I wasn't there. Such shitty timing with Brian. Poor guy."

"Bike accident?"

"Yup."

Of course. Nikki's world was full of cyclists, runners, and swimmers. That was why she stayed in California after college. There was always someone training and always someone recovering.

"Are you still working with triathletes?"

"Yeah, and I've got a few opportunities with the local professional teams too. Exciting."

"Like the Padres?"

"The soccer teams. San Diego Power FC started a couple of years ago. It's a women's club. They're *amazing*. Rumor is we're getting a men's team soon, too. Oh, and Frontline Arena just opened in Oceanside. The Breakers play there. It's arena soccer. A little different from what you're used to. The Condors G League basketball team plays there too. We're definitely hitting a few games." Nikki bit back a laugh. "You'll enjoy the view. I always do. Sometimes I even forget to look at the scoreboard."

Nikki had a weakness for muscle-bound athletes and didn't try to hide it. Unlike everyone else Gia knew in their age bracket, Nikki was on no timeline for a wedding, white picket fence, or baby. She'd get around to settling down once she'd sampled the population and had her fill. It was the opposite of Gia's "safe" plan, which collapsed in on itself anyway. Perhaps Nikki's approach had more merit than Gia gave her credit for. Her cousin's dating stories were her guilty pleasure. They were reckless, pleasure-driven, and nothing she'd ever dare do herself.

"Grab your shoes," Nikki said. "Let's eat."

Gia slipped on her sandals, feeling lighter than she had in ages. She was grateful for a sunny day, a new city, and time with her bestie.

Nikki and Gia took off through the neighborhood, coffee tumblers in hand and pep in their steps.

"So, what's on your San Diego bucket list?" Nikki asked as they turned a corner.

Gia gave a mock groan. "I don't want to jinx anything. I can't say it out loud."

"Say what?" Nikki grinned. "That you've been Googling salsa shoes like dance porn?"

Gia stopped in her tracks. "How—"

"Girl, I *know* you." Nikki pointed her finger at Gia as she sipped her coffee. "Also, I saw your screen this morning when I walked outside." She shrugged, all innocent mischief. "I love this for you. And for me!"

They'd danced side by side through childhood and high school. They were on the same teams, attended the same studios, and spent the same long nights hot-gluing rhinestones to costumes before competitions. After graduation, their paths diverged.

Nikki headed to California. She studied kinesiology at the University of California, San Diego, and minored in dance. After college, she always found a way to dance. West Coast swing, salsa, tango, and lately, bachata. Nightclubs, socials, backyard parties with live bands. She lived for it. Her job kept her body in motion, but dance was the movement that lit her up.

Gia stayed on Long Island. She also minored in dance but ditched it her junior year.

"I don't know," Gia said. "My feet are rusty as hell. I haven't *really* danced since college. The random night out. Weddings. After tequila."

"Yeah, but it never left you. Gia, you've never been as happy as when you were dancing. I understand why you walked away, but maybe enough time has passed that you can stop denying yourself."

Gia absorbed Nikki's words. She expected her cousin to push her. That's what made this move so necessary.

"Well, on that topic, you'd be very proud of me. Yesterday I went to Casa Sevilla."

"Oh yeah? I love that place. It was salsa bachata night, right?"

"Yeah. I must admit it was...pretty hot."

Nikki raised an eyebrow. "Did you dance?"

"I mostly watched...but I danced a salsa with the teacher and a bachata with some random guy. It was fun. But honestly? I kinda freaked out afterward."

"What do you mean?" Gia rarely talked about dancing, let alone did it.

"Like an internal meltdown," Gia said, shaking her hands at the thought of butterflies rushing through her body again. "But it also lit me up. Does that make any sense?" She took a deep breath, still caught between elation and panic at how she'd jumped in without knowing what she was doing, somehow loved it, and then spiraled out.

"Maybe I'll take a class. Just to try it."

"You totally should!" Nikki cheered, then caught herself and lowered her voice so she didn't scare her cousin off. "San Diego has an amazing social dance scene. Everyone thinks SoCal is all surf, yoga, and ultramarathons. It totally is, but we have nightlife too! Salsa, bachata, zouk, kizomba, swing..." Nikki's voice shifted from playful to earnest. "One of my good friends owns a dance studio in North Park. I joined her training team when she first got started. Camila is like... if Beyoncé and a Dominican auntie had a baby."

Gia stopped her cousin mid-stride. "Wait. Did you say Camila?"

"Yeah. She's a trained dance therapist, so we used to work together a lot. Then she opened a Latin dance school, and it blew up. Now she's always teaching, performing... doing all the things. You'd love her. Everyone does."

"I might have met her last night." Gia let out a dramatic sigh. "She walked outside for air and into my meltdown. She was really cool about it."

"Yup. That sounds like Camila."

"She invited me to try her class next week. Start of a new series or something. I'm thinking about it."

"Go! I'll even come with you." Nikki lit up. This was something she could help with. "Camila's the real deal. A world champ, choreographer, general badass. Her studio's gorgeous, too. And her brother, Sebastián Solano, started cross-training and teaching there, so it's been getting a ton of attention lately."

Gia nodded in acknowledgment.

"Sebastián Solano," Nikki repeated.

Gia stared at her, waiting.

"You've never heard of him?" Nikki blinked. "Seriously? Nothing?"

"Nope. Should I?"

"He's kind of famous, babe. How have you never heard that name? Sebastián's been in like a bazillion Adidas ads." Nikki sipped her coffee before continuing with a smirk. "Used to play soccer, trained in Colombia, played on a Spanish team, then in L.A. to be closer to his family. He's basically San Diego's David Beckham. But he looks more like Cristiano Ronaldo... with longer, wavy hair and a *Colombian* accent. Oh, and did I mention he can dance?"

Gia laughed out loud. "I am now motivated to learn salsa just for the partner potential."

"Totally valid motivation." Nikki added with a softer tone, "Hot guys aside, taking a class would be good for you. It's fun. It's healing. We haven't done this together since high school. What, ten years?"

"Twelve." Gia gave a mock groan. "But who's counting besides my lower back?"

"Exactly. You writers spend way too much time hunched over a laptop. You need to move."

"Hey, I run every day. That counts."

"Sure. You can keep your runs, but this is different. New city, new rules. You said you wanted out of your head and into your body, remember? Dance is the way. This is your sign."

Gia didn't respond right away, but the resistance was already fading. She liked the idea more than she cared to admit, and doing it with Nikki by her side felt like coming home.

They grabbed breakfast at a neighborhood cafe with outdoor seating and a view of the Pacific. It was a casual spot where people wore Birkenstocks with flashy metallic buckles and carried natural rubber yoga mats slung over their shoulders like accessories. Nikki ordered a turmeric latte and a power protein burrito. Gia stuck with a cappuccino and a fresh muffin.

Afterward, they walked the long way home through Mission Bay, taking the sidewalk that curved along the water. Paddleboards and kayaks glided by while jet-skis raced. They passed a cleanup crew dismantling the last bits of the event setup from yesterday's Ironman race. Metal barricades leaned against a truck bed, and someone in a volunteer shirt swept stray confetti into a dustpan.

"I'm off," Nikki said once they returned to the house. "I've got three patients this morning, and it's all knee work."

She kissed Gia on the cheek, tossed her cup in the dishwasher, and collected her gear. "Let's do dinner at home tonight. I'm cooking."

"You're what?" Gia asked in disbelief.

"Yep. Growth and new things this summer, right?" She winked at Gia as she closed the door behind her.

Gia poured herself a glass of green juice and set up at the backyard bistro table with her laptop. She had work to do. Before heading to San Diego, Gia worked out a compromise with her manager. She would handle a project for a key client, and in return she could shift to part-time hours for the summer. It was the first choice she had made in a long time that felt like it was truly for her.

In a few days, she had a client meeting with Eli Maddox, a San Diego-based tech founder who'd hired her to ghostwrite his memoir. In his early forties, with a charismatic TED Talk voice, he was a startup visionary with bold ideas and a goal to have his journey told as a hero's arc. The head of publishing had recommended her, and Gia jumped at the opportunity to shape his story through that lens.

Gia was used to video interviews, so the chance to meet Eli in person was a rare treat. It had been a long time since she'd met a new client outside the glow of a laptop screen.

She should start by reviewing Eli's presentations on YouTube to study his work and his communication style. Instead, she typed Marc Anthony into the search bar. The opening bars of "Valió la Pena" filled the patio. *It was worth the pain.* Or *it was worth it.* Her Spanish was rusty. The bass hit first. Then came the trumpet riff that all but dared her to keep from moving.

Gia picked up her laptop and carried it into her bedroom, where the mirrored closet doors lined an entire wall. They reflected her barefoot silhouette, hair tousled from the beachside walk, juice still in one hand. She set the glass down and turned up the volume.

Gia let the beat sink into her shoulders, then roll down her spine. She danced the basic step: quick, quick, slow, quick, quick, slow. Barely moving at first, she shifted her weight from foot to foot and then leaned into it once she found the groove. The memory of salsa's hip motion and Dom's lead echoed through her body.

She remembered the feminine styling that Camila added to her dancing. Gia lifted her arms overhead and let her hands glide down her sides. She slowed her fingers at her bust, her waist, her hips. Since high school, these were the curves that drew the wrong attention. They were the ones teachers told her to "neutralize" on stage. Too much bounce, too much distraction. Not the shape judges wanted to see at auditions.

She looked at herself now, twelve years later. Her eyes were a little less bright and her posture a little less tall. She overdressed despite the heat of late summer. Her layers looked less like fashion and more like armor. What if she could shed all that? She wouldn't be dancing for a score anymore. Or for a place on stage or in a company. Not for toxic directors on a power trip. Just for the pleasure of being back in her body. For herself.

The song ended. Gia stood still and tried to pinpoint when it had all changed, when she had become disconnected from her body and from movement, but there wasn't one dramatic moment. Over the years, it had been a quiet, gradual retreat.

There were the teachers, the criticism, and that judge at her last audition, which she still avoided thinking about. Trading dance for writing had kept her in a creative lane. Most days, that was enough. However, as her career progressed, she spent more time behind her desk and less time moving her body or interacting with people. Then came the pandemic, and her work went fully remote. Days blurred together, marked by Zoom faces, takeout dinners and most meals eaten over her computer. When the world reopened, her industry didn't, and neither did she.

Writing had always been mostly solitary, but now the research, interviews, client meetings, and brainstorming could happen through a screen. Anywhere, anytime. It was a whole new level of flexibility and isolation.

Miles witnessed everything. For a while, his steady presence had been a comfort, but twenty-four-seven togetherness strained even the strongest bonds. He told her once, toward the end, that she was disappearing. That he could still see her, but couldn't feel her anymore. That she was watching life instead of living it. He believed she wanted more, and he was right. He also knew she'd never chase it unless something forced her to move. So he moved out.

A summer in San Diego was supposed to be her answer to that. She was looking for massive disruption to her routine. A reconnection with herself. A discovery of anything that might help her come alive again. She didn't want to spend her life writing other people's stories. She wanted her story to be worth telling too.

Less thinking. More moving.

Less isolation. More connection.

Less ghost. More main character.

With these thoughts swirling into a tornado, she began pacing the room, arms pinned across her chest.

What if I walk into Ritmo Latino and look ridiculous? Too stiff. Too nervous. Awkward as hell. Surrounded by twenty-two-year-olds who are fearless and loose-limbed, hips unburdened by years of sitting at a desk?

Her pulse quickened at the thought. She felt equal parts panic and yearning.

Gia opened the sign-up page for Camila's salsa class and reread the description:

Beginner-friendly. No partner necessary. Just bring your energy!!

She had energy. Somewhere. Buried under more than a decade of deadlines and career goals.

She increased the quantity to two. Nikki offered to go, and without accountability, Gia would find some excuse to bail at the last possible second. *Register.*

A confirmation page popped up: *Your spot in Beginner Salsa Class with Camila Solano is confirmed. See you on Wednesday!*

There was one thing left to do.

She clicked back to the salsa shoe website. A pair of bronze Latin ballroom shoes drenched with rhinestone accents caught her eye. They were strappy, high-heeled, and unapologetically bold. Gia imagined they sparkled like jewelry under the lights. Probably a bit too much. She added them to her cart anyway, along with a pair of jazz sneakers like she wore in college, and paid for rush shipping.

Dancing again wasn't the story she'd come here to write, but perhaps it was the one she needed to try.

Chapter Four

Gia's Lyft dropped her off on a colorful street in North Park, San Diego. Murals wrapped around buildings, and string lights hung above the outdoor patios of homes and restaurants. A musician played a saxophone outside of a dive bar with a chalkboard sign that read "Taco Tuesday, Every Day."

Ritmo Latino stood out on the block. While neighboring storefronts flaunted colorful art and lively displays, the dance studio kept its secrets behind frosted windows. From the sidewalk, you could only see the blur of bodies moving across the floor. Golden light poured through the glass door, spilling onto the pavement like a pathway to discovery.

Gia walked in and scanned the room for a sign of Nikki. When she didn't see her cousin, a flicker of nerves crawled up her throat. She swallowed it down and found a bench where she could change her shoes.

There were about thirty people in the class, a mix of bodies including tall, short, curvy, lean, and everything in between. Most men stuck to jeans and t-shirts, while a few dressed it up with slacks and rolled-sleeve button-downs. Women wore sundresses, flirty skirts or sleek leggings, and hair styled to say, *notice me.* The unspoken dress code was clear: show up as your best self, or at least the version hoping to attract love or a score for the night.

Gia was in her usual monochromatic uniform from top to bottom—a black t-shirt and straight-leg yoga pants, with her hair pulled into a simple ponytail. She reached for her jazz sneakers, but as she went to slip them on, Miles's voice echoed in her head.

You're disappearing.

With a flick of annoyance, she tossed them into her bag. Instead, she slid her feet into the new glittering ballroom shoes, a flash of risk peeking from the hem of her pants. It was a baby step, but it still counted.

Despite being a beginner class, it was a mixed crowd. Some moved naturally, their bodies already in sync with the music. Others, like Gia, looked more uncertain about what they had gotten themselves into. The studio seemed to be a place where experience and age didn't matter. Attendees spanned generations, the opposite of classical dance classes or mainstream nightclubs.

Gia overheard one of the other girls stage-whispering to a friend as she nodded toward the front of the room. "Look at her. Total icon."

Gia followed her gaze to where Camila took her place to start class.

Her outfit was minimalistic yet sexy; a plum-colored sports bra with delicate crisscross straps in the back and matching high-waisted leggings that hugged her frame. She wore skin-toned ballroom heels embellished with gems. They looked a lot like Gia's new shoes, only much taller. Camila's fingers and toes were bright gold, like the championship trophies that lined the front desk and Ritmo Latino's logo. She moved as if she were aware of how each part of her body looked and made sure it was worth watching.

Her smile was sharp enough to kill and warm enough to make you laugh, depending on her intent. Right now, it was somewhere in between. Her eyes told everyone she was about to push them to their limits, and they would love every second.

Nikki appeared out of nowhere and slid into line next to Gia. "Sorry I'm late. Friggen traffic..." she said, slipping into her East Coast accent.

A loud clap at the front of the studio redirected focus before

Gia could respond. Camila scanned the room. When she recognized Gia, she gave her a warm smile and a quick wink. Then her eyes went wide, and she broke into an ear-to-ear grin. "Nikki! What?! So good to see you here, babe!" She turned to the class, beaming. "You're all in for a treat tonight. Say hello to one of my dearest friends and one of my very first dancers!"

Nikki grinned, gave a beauty pageant wave to the other dancers, and blew a kiss to Camila.

"Okay, everyone. Welcome to beginner salsa," she said, addressing the broader group. "We're going to dance on1. That means we step on the first beat of the music. You may have heard of on2, also called mambo, or New York style. The rhythm feels slightly different. On2 dancers step on the second beat. It aligns with the clave and percussion rhythms, but we'll save that for another class. Today, we keep things simple and start with on1."

She walked to the front center of the room and faced the mirror. From that spot, the mirror showed both angles at once— her face from the front so she could talk to the students through her reflection, and her body from behind so they could follow her movements. "Okay, everyone, imagine there's a straight line on the floor right in front of you. We're going to step onto that line. Left foot forward on one, the first count. Step in place with your right foot on two. Then bring your left foot back together on three. Hold on your four. Right foot steps back on five. Your left foot steps in place on six. Close your right foot back to the center on seven. Hold on eight." She demonstrated as she spoke, fluid and graceful. "That's your basic step. And we will repeat it a lot because we want this in your muscle memory. Whenever you get lost or unsure what's next, always return to your basic step."

The class followed, some more confidently than others, but the nervous laughter was already giving way to concentration.

Once the group seemed to have the steps, Camila clapped her hands, drawing their attention again. "Great start. Now let's make it look like salsa and less like marching. I want you to bend your knees a little. Just soften them. When you step, press into the floor. That pressure will naturally push your hip up on the opposite side."

She exaggerated the steps. "This is where that yummy hip motion comes from, the one that makes salsa so sexy. It's not about swishing your hips like you're hula-hooping. It's the weight transfer. Your hips react to your feet pressing into the floor, and that ripple moves through your body. Mírame."

Camila turned sideways so the class could watch her profile as she danced through the basic steps of salsa. Her shoulders rolled in opposition to her hips; the motion was hypnotic, effortless. "See what's happening here? Shoulders and hips are moving in opposite directions. This is called contrabody motion. It makes salsa a full-body dance, not just the feet and arms, but everything working together. Everyone ready to try the basic step with the weight transfer? Let's put it to music. Here we go." She teed up "La Llave," by Grupo Latin Vibe, and the dance began.

"Alright, dancers, we're going to add some more steps. Follow me. Ready...and..."

Gia followed along, picking up the movements quickly. Her training in contemporary dance might not have prepared her for salsa's rolling hips and grounded weight shifts, but it had given her muscle control, balance, and fluidity. She would adapt.

At first, she had to dictate the moves in her head while she danced. As the rhythm picked up speed, she stopped thinking for a moment and let her body lead.

"Okay, you've all got the steps. Now I want to see *sabor*! That means *flavor*, people! Make it yummy!" Camila shouted over the music. "Que rico!"

They moved through the combination again. Basic step, side basic, right turn, basic step, Suzy Q. Once the pattern was in their bodies, the uniformity disappeared. Each dancer embellished it with their own personality and style. Some added sharpness, like they had something to prove. Others kept it smooth and grounded, letting the rhythm roll through their hips and shoulders. A few dancers improvised their own arm styling or tossed in a head whip for attitude. One guy threw in an exaggerated, cheeky shoulder shimmy that made the people around him giggle.

A few women stood out as experienced dancers, adding sophisticated flair to every step. There was nothing basic in what they were doing.

Right as Gia got the hang of it, Camila clapped her hands again, signaling a transition.

"Find a partner! Everyone, make two big circles. Leaders on the outside, followers on the inside."

Gia searched her cousin's face for an anchor as nerves rippled up her spine.

"Don't overthink it." Nikki shrugged her shoulders. "It's a beginner class. It starts simple."

Gia stepped into the inner circle to join the followers. To her surprise and relief, Camila took a spot in the leaders' circle, directly across from her.

"I got you," she whispered to Gia before addressing the rest of the group.

"Nikki, can I borrow you to show the pattern?" Camila held out her hand to Nikki, who was happy to step in as Camila's partner. Camila showed a simple choreography: basic step, cross-body lead, back to basic, and then a right turn. Nikki added arm styling, running her hands through her hair during the turn, a move that turned a simple spin into something more like flirtation. Gia was impressed but not surprised.

"This little combo can fill an entire song and never get boring because you add different tension, timing, and style to it. Simple moves, when executed well, are really fun. Let's give it a go with slower music." Camila used her smartwatch to start the next song. Bembé Orquesta's rendition of "Ven, Devórame Otra Vez," played, its sensual rhythm filling the room like a warm invitation.

"Thanks, love." Camila air kissed Nikki's cheek before passing her to a partner in the leaders' circle. Then she walked back to Gia. "I'm glad to see you. Ready?" Gia nodded and let Camila lead her into position.

Camila guided Gia through the pattern twice. Once Gia could

follow the combination on time, Camila placed a hand on each of Gia's shoulders and met her eyes in a quiet transfer of confidence. "You've got it. Gorgeous. Now keep going." With a louder voice, she addressed the room. "Here we go, people. Rotate!"

Each dance lasted about a minute before Camila asked the group to change partners, and the leaders moved to the next follower in the circle. The steps were simple enough, but Gia had to stay fully tuned in because everyone danced and led a little differently.

Her first partner was a gentle, anxious man in his early fifties. He wore a tucked-in polo and orthopedic sneakers, and his cologne carried a hint of nostalgia, like everyone's favorite uncle at a wedding. "Hi, I'm Joe," he offered before he took Gia's hands, his palms slightly clammy.

They fumbled through the first few steps, out of sync and unsure. His lead felt like tentative nudges rather than a direction, but he studied how Gia responded to it and tried to figure out how he could better set her up for each move. Gia softened her frame, made herself extra responsive, and offered encouragement with her smile. She sensed how much he wanted to get it right.

On the second pass through the pattern, something clicked. Joe's spine lengthened, his shoulders relaxed, and his lead became clearer. When he executed a basic turn and Gia spun without faltering, his face lit up.

"We did it!" he said with quiet delight.

Gia smiled, warmth growing in her chest. "You're a natural," she said, and meant it. Perhaps not technically, but in spirit, and that counted for something.

"Rotate!" Camila called.

They released hands, and Gia gave him a parting smile.

Gia's next partner looked like he'd stepped out of a beach resort. He had tan skin, effortless hair, and a casual designer outfit that said I woke up like this... after a lot of effort and prepping. He smelled of leather layered with vanilla and offered a wink instead of a hello.

"I'm Ray."

"Gia."

From the first count, Gia could tell he had training. Precise timing, a confident style and beautiful technique. Everything was in place, but something was missing.

Ray kept scanning the room, smile aimed more at the mirrors than at her. His posture never wavered, but his presence did. Gia felt like a prop in his performance, a rehearsal dummy for whatever show he thought he was starring in. She followed without issue because he made it easy, but there was no give-and-take or push-pull. It was more of a showcase in motion. Gia noted to herself: *Strong technique doesn't always mean good connection.*

"Cambien de pareja. Rotate!"

Gia barely had time to catch her breath before a tall, sandy-haired wall of muscle with a grin built for trouble stepped in front of her.

"How's it going? I'm Andrés," he said, offering his hand like they were about to take the stage instead of run through a beginner's pattern.

"Gia."

"Ready to fly, partner?"

Andrés' energy was equal parts goofball and athlete. The moment he took her in his arms, Gia sensed the difference of what it was to dance with someone who knew what he was doing. Every step had an intention. Nothing looked forced. He turned every move into play and celebration. In this tiny moment with him, Andrés made her remember why she fell in love with dance in the first place, so many years ago.

"Here comes the turn," he whispered, like it was a surprise plot twist.

Gia laughed, letting the rhythm carry her through the spin. With Andrés, she didn't have to think. He provided pressure when she needed direction, then loosened to let her find her own space. Their footwork clicked, their timing synced, and for a moment it felt as if they'd rehearsed this a hundred times.

When Camila called "Rotate," Gia stepped back breathless, not from exertion, but from delight.

"Damn," she said with a laugh. "That felt really good."

Andrés gave her a dramatic bow and grinned. "The pleasure was all mine," he replied before moving to another partner.

When Gia looked up and locked eyes with her new partner, her breath caught, like that suspended moment right before an ocean wave crashes on you and pulls you under.

His face belonged on a billboard. Sculpted cheekbones, a strong jaw softened by a playful mouth, and a smile that seemed to be lit from within. Waves of dark hair fell to his temples, framing sun-warmed olive skin that glowed beneath the studio lights. His green eyes traced her with open curiosity, like she was a puzzle he wanted to solve.

Broad shoulders and a tapered waist made her pulse spike before she'd even taken a step. The atmosphere shifted around him, charged and magnetic, like the room had tilted toward him somehow. The scent of him hit next: clean ocean air, a whisper of citrus, grounded by woodsy and warm cedar. She inhaled, and her senses lit up.

It was absurd. One look, one breath, and she was completely, overwhelmingly, obsessively aware of him.

Then, his hands found their places on her body.

His right hand slid to her back, firm and deliberate as his palm landed just beneath her shoulder blade. His fingers were hot through the fabric of her top, like a spark pressing through to her skin.

His left hand captured hers. Slightly calloused, a textural contrast to her own, it hinted at stories she hadn't heard and experiences she hadn't lived but now wanted to explore.

"Ven, Devórame Otra Vez" suddenly seemed to swell around them, the female vocalist's voice dripping with hunger and longing. Gia's pulse quickened to match the sounds of countless percussion instruments. Desire and curiosity mingled in her chest. *What is happening?* Gia asked herself, intoxicated.

He started dancing. Following him was effortless, like breathing.

He went beyond the pattern Camila had taught, but with his

clear lead, Gia had no problem keeping up. He wasn't dancing to the counts they learned either. Instead, he improvised with the beat of the clave, with the piano and then with the lyrics. Every step was woven seamlessly into the song like a bespoke choreography made just for them in this moment.

Her gaze dropped to his mouth. He was singing under his breath. Such full lips. What would it be like to press hers against them? Would his kiss taste as sweet as the temptation he breathed into the space between them? Like late summer and bad decisions that felt too good to regret?

His fingertips skimmed down her spine, initiating a body roll, guiding the motion, and leaving a trail of goosebumps in their wake. There was tension in his frame, as if he were holding something back too. One tiny lean forward and they'd be past the point of no return. She was already surrendering to it...

"Rotate! ¡Cambien de pareja mi gente!"

His hands released her. It was over.

Was that real?

Did I hallucinate the whole thing?

Gia tingled with sensation everywhere he'd touched. *No, it was real.*

His voice was deep. Amused. A little teasing? "You don't dance like a beginner."

She blinked, trying to remember how words worked. "Thanks. It is, though. My first salsa class. Yeah."

He tilted his head, studying her. "Most people don't catch the details in the music that quickly. You did."

"That's generous. I was just trying to keep up with you."

He stepped a little closer, still not touching her, but undeniably in her space. "Maybe that's why it was so good."

Gia narrowed her eyes, half-suspicious, half-intrigued. "Good? Pretty sure I was three beats behind."

"You weren't behind. We just stopped dancing On1 pretty quickly."

Her stomach dipped. "I don't know what that means."

"Camila taught the choreo On1," he said, his smile tugging at the corner of his mouth, "but you followed me when I switched to On2. Most beginners cling to counts like a lifeline." His voice dropped, almost a confession. "I should have led On1, but I couldn't help it. That song makes you want to break the rules."

Her lips curved before she could stop them. "So, the song made you do it?"

"Maybe. Yeah. And you. "

Before she could think of a response, her new partner let out a pointed cough, making it obvious he was done waiting.

"Thanks for the dance," her one-song romance said and moved on in the rotation.

She exhaled hard, rolling her shoulders like she could shake the daze out of her body. *Get it together, Gia. It's just a dance. A ridiculously hot, distracting salsa, but still, just a dance.*

She watched him take the hand of a pretty dancer who was undeniably sure of herself. She lifted her chin as his palm pressed against her shoulder blade, her spine lengthening in response to his lead. When he guided her into a turn, she followed as if they had danced together a hundred times before. When he pulled her into a closed position, she laughed, her head tilting back, her smile wide and easy, making Gia wonder if their connection went beyond dance. Or maybe capable leads had that effect. This one just happened to have a body carved like Cristiano Ronaldo, a Colombian accent that could melt butter, and a way of moving that made a basic step feel suggestive. *Right. Of course. This has to be Sebastián Solano.*

She glanced around. Other women were watching him too, tracking his movements with barely hidden interest. His shirt clung to his sculpted torso, forearms flexing and veins tracing down to hands that knew exactly where to land. He was easy to watch.

He danced from inside the music, as if rhythm lived in his bones and blood. Gia couldn't help but think of that old saying: if a man can dance, he's probably amazing in bed. No doubts there. He certainly knew how to listen with his body. She wiped the back of her neck, her pulse still racing from the exchange.

Gia turned to face her next partner, flashing a polite smile, but beneath it, a quiet disappointment twisted low in her belly. Another beginner. Not the billboard model, who moved like warm honey and made her body respond before her mind could catch up.

Camila clapped her hands together to mark the end of the lesson.

"Great class, everyone! Did you have fun? Sí o yes?"

The room erupted in a mix of Spanish and English, voices overlapping in chorus.

"Alright, dancers, bring it in! I have a few announcements to share. The training team starts next week. If you're serious about leveling up fast, that's your gateway. It's also the first step to our advanced teams. If you've ever considered performing or competing, take this as your sign from the universe."

That got Gia's attention.

Besides work, her calendar was a blank canvas. She didn't know anyone in San Diego except Nikki, who, thankfully, loved dance, music, and pretty much anything active. She'd be up for salsa nights. Perhaps this was a way to find her tribe.

Dancing again, not just for fun, but with purpose, sent a thrill through her. It was like a second chance with your first love. The one that got away. For Gia, it was always dance. You don't say no to the universe twice and expect it to keep offering.

"Sooooo, what did you think?" Nikki asked as she took Gia into a closed position and led her into an inside turn.

"I kinda loved it," Gia responded as she tried, and failed, to lead Nikki through the same turn.

They laughed as Camila walked over and joined them.

"Nikki! It's been forever. To what do I owe this fabulous surprise?" Camila wrapped her in a big hug.

"Camila! Girl, I miss you! Incredible class as always." Nikki stepped back and held an arm out towards Gia. "This is my cousin and bestie, Gia."

"We've met." Camila turned to Gia with a warm, knowing

smile. "I'm so glad you came. No push from your cousin, I'm sure."

"Push? Me?" Nikki said, feigning innocence. "Never."

Camila raised a playful brow, then refocused on Gia.

"You've danced before. I can tell. You move like someone who's trained. Seriously trained."

Gia stood a little taller. "I minored in modern dance in college. Lots of bare feet and tortured metaphors. I was obsessed with Alvin Ailey. Almost auditioned for a regional company in New York during my junior year."

"Almost?" Camila asked, tilting her head.

Gia gave a small shrug. "Yeah. I ended up switching majors. Thought I should go for something more practical." It wasn't the complete story, but it was enough for now. She felt grateful Nikki didn't add anything, although she felt her cousin's eyes on her the entire time.

"Anyway, thank you for keeping an eye out for me tonight. I really loved your class."

"Well, salsa loves you back. You picked it up fast."

Gia's smile spread across her face. "Coming from you, that means a lot." She paused, then took a small breath. "I heard you mention a training team. I'd love to learn more. I'm in San Diego for the summer, and honestly, I can't think of a better way to spend it than dancing again."

Camila's eyes lit up. "Absolutely. Sundays, ten to noon. You'll level up fast. The class moves quickly, so everyone practices outside of rehearsals, but you'll meet people who are down to train during the week. Plus, you have your cousin, who's pretty flashy on the dance floor." Nikki shook her shoulders at the girls in response.

"Maybe you can get her to come out more often," Camila said to Gia as she gave Nikki a nudge with her elbow.

Gia nodded. "So...the team. What level is it?"

"It varies. It's more a matter of intensity and pace. There are some beginners, but they are committed. A lot of them use it as a launchpad to join the advanced teams or compete. And yes, you'll perform occasionally. There's no disappearing into the back row."

Camila leaned in, lowering her voice just enough to feel like she was letting Gia in on a secret. "If you're serious, come check it out this weekend. It's basically salsa bootcamp. Technique, drills, stamina, the whole thing. But more important than any of that, you'll need to go social dancing. A lot."

Gia tilted her head. "Why's that?"

"Because otherwise, it's just choreography," Camila said. "We teach steps and technique in class, but real social dancing is where it clicks. When you ditch choreography for social dancing, you have to stop thinking and start feeling."

Nikki chimed in. "You don't know what your partner's going to do, and they don't know how you'll respond. That's the magic. The best dancers aren't the ones who've mastered an impressive routine. They're the ones who can create something beautiful in the moment, even with strangers."

"And trust me," Camila added with a knowing smile, "once you get comfortable, and you will, you're going to fall in love."

Gia let that sink in. It sounded exactly like what she needed.

Camila waved her hand across the room. "We go out all the time. Come with us. Both of you," she continued, looking at Nikki. "Nik's got my number. Think about it."

On the other side of the studio, Sebastián leaned against the mirror-lined sidewall, taping his knee while half-listening to Daniel's ramble about the Breakers' last soccer match.

"So, are the rumors true?" Daniel asked, bouncing on his heels. "Is Paredes going to retire this year?"

Sebastián gave him a wry look. "You think I'd tell you that?" He shook his head no, making it clear that the Breaker player would not be retiring. "I can't say a word."

"Got it." Daniel grinned. "You know, I bet you like having

someone around who appreciates your insights, not just your fame or your abs."

Sebastián laughed out loud, smoothing the last strip of tape down across his kneecap. He glanced up and caught sight of Gia again.

She stood near Camila and Nikki, posture long and upright, one foot slightly in front of the other like a ballerina. Her brown waves were pulled into a high, messy bun. A bead of sweat rolled down her neck, catching the light as she tucked a loose strand of hair behind her ear and nodded at something Camila said.

Most beginners walked into Ritmo Latino with some version of the same cocktail: wide eyes, uncertain feet, and an edge of either nervousness or bravado. You could read a lot in how someone carried themselves.

There was a quiet poise about her: the way she held her frame, shoulders back and neck elongated, like her head was suspended from an invisible string. A dancer's posture. She didn't move like someone who'd taken a few classes or flirted with social dancing in nightclubs, but like a woman who once spoke dance fluently, as if it had been her first language.

Camila was gesturing wildly now. She was clearly in recruiting mode.

Sebastián's brow ticked up. Camila didn't throw herself at just anyone. There must be something special about this new dancer.

"Hey," Daniel elbowed Sebastián. "You good?"

Sebastián blinked. "Yeah. Sorry. What were you saying?"

Daniel followed his gaze, then chuckled. "Ah. Nevermind."

Sebastián rolled his eyes. "It's not like that."

Daniel grinned. "Sure."

Across the room, Camila laughed at something Gia said. Her laugh was loud, full-bellied, and genuine. That warmth said it all. Gia was already part of the inner circle.

And if Camila wanted her, Sebastián would see a lot more of her.

He shifted his stance so he could get a better stretch through his leg, but his gaze lingered. The memory of their brief connection danced through his mind. There'd been a beat mid-song when he felt her lock into the rhythm like a key turning in a long-forgotten door. Her shoulders dropped, her breath changed, and her eyes came alive.

She danced like she had put a part of herself away a long time ago and was just now brave enough to open the box again. He knew that feeling. Hell, he'd lived it every single day for the last year.

Goosebumps rose along his arms. Watching someone come back to themselves through dance was mesmerizing. He wondered if he had looked like that in Camila's eyes when he first came to the studio after his injury.

"Sebas, Daniel," Andrés said, shouldering his bag. "Drinks?"

Sebastián glanced again at Gia, her hands now gesturing mid-air as she explained something.

He smiled to himself. "Nah. I'll hang around. Help Camila close up."

Daniel gave him a knowing look. "Such a good brother."

"The best," Andrés added.

Sebastián didn't answer, but the grin that tugged at the corner of his mouth said more than enough.

As Gia pulled on her jacket, ready to leave, Sebastián approached the ladies. He glanced from Camila to Nikki to Gia, clocking that his sister had roped someone, maybe both of them, into something.

"Careful," he said, eyes on Gia. "You might get hooked."

The line was tossed out casually, but the way he delivered it sounded more like a promise.

Camila rolled her eyes. "Well, you would know."

"Good to see you, Sebastián," Nikki said.

"Hey, Nikki. The Breakers are looking sharp this season, right?"

"Well, they've got the best coaches in SoCal," she replied.

He chuckled. "And the best physical therapists, too."

"No argument here." Nikki laughed.

Camila gestured between him and Gia. "This is my brother, Sebastián. He trains the pro team and covers my classes sometimes, too. And hopefully," she added lightly, "he's helping with a few co-director duties until I find someone permanent." She cut Sebastián a wide-eyed look, as if daring the idea into existence. Sebastián just shook his head, smiling, as if verbally refusing would make any difference.

"And this," Nikki cut in, grinning, "is my cousin, Gia. Fresh off the plane, new to San Diego, ready to sample all the city's... goodies."

Gia rolled her eyes.

Nikki only smiled wider. "Word on the street is she's about to become your training team's next breakout star."

"Wow. Subtle introduction. Guess I'll just go ahead and live up to *all* that." Gia's eyes went wide as a flush of embarrassment warmed her cheeks.

Sebastían smiled and shook her hand. "Gia, the girl with the perfect timing. Pleasure to meet you officially."

Camila interrupted before her brother could say anything else. "Well, I hope we'll be seeing both of you in class more often. Nikki drop in whenever you want. I'll try to keep Daniel from cornering you about sports stats."

As Nikki and Camila chit-chatted and hugged goodbye, Sebastián stepped toward Gia, closing the space between them again.

"I'm glad you're coming back," he said, with a smile that stretched up to his eyes. "It would be a shame if we don't get to dance a full song."

Gia tilted her head, smiling back. "Do you say that to every beginner you rotate through in class?"

Sebastián's smile deepened. "Nope. Only the beginners who aren't really beginners."

"Is that why you were improvising instead of following the choreo?"

He gave a little shrug, his eyes never leaving hers. "It's always more interesting when you don't know what's coming." The glint in his eye made it clear he was feeling her out. "You can tell a lot about someone by how they respond."

Gia's fingers tightened around her bag strap as she forced herself to hold his gaze.

"And what did you learn about me, then?" Her tone sounded like a dare.

He held her gaze for a moment longer than necessary, as if debating how much to say. "That you don't like being caught off guard," he said finally, his voice low, almost private. "But even when you are...you're absolutely graceful. You move like a trained dancer."

"Good answer."

"But I think you're capable of more."

"Oh? And what do you think I'm capable of?" The question came out sharper than she intended. A man speculating about her potential always made her bristle.

His eyes sparkled. There was no challenge and no judgment in them. Just a flicker of mischief.

"Not being caught off guard. Loving social dance. Making this all a bit more...fun."

That earned him a quiet, amused laugh.

"I guess we'll see," she said lightly, though her heart was pounding. He was flirting, and she was so out of practice.

"I'm counting on it. Hopefully, this was just a...warm-up."

Gia had promised herself this summer was about saying yes to anything that made her feel alive again. Sebastián Solano seemed like one hell of a yes.

Camila leaned against the front desk, idly buffing her nails with her thumb as she watched her brother close the door after Gia and Nikki had gone.

"You're so obvious," she said lightly, not even looking up.

Sebastián frowned. "Obvious about what?"

Camila raised her eyes and arched a brow. "About her."

"Oh, yeah?"

"Don't play dumb with me, Sebas. You've got that look you get right before you do something impulsive. Like pursue one of my dancers."

He let out a low laugh, rubbing the back of his neck. "Relax. I'm not pursuing anything."

"Mm? Really." Camila's voice dripped with skepticism as she crossed her arms. "And why's that?"

Most beginners either froze up or melted in his hands. Gia wasn't intimidated or star-struck. She didn't even seem to know who he was. It had been a long time since he danced with a stranger, someone who brought no expectations or assumptions based on his career. Sebastián couldn't stop replaying the feel of her in his arms, how she moved like she had her own music, and he'd just tuned into the station.

"Timing's all wrong," he muttered finally, his smile slipping as his gaze drifted out to nowhere.

Sebastián joined Camila at the desk, leaning back against it beside her. He ran a hand over his jaw, his expression dark and unsettled.

"She's new here. You know how that goes. She needs to dance with a bunch of people, feel out the scene, before she even thinks about..." He trailed off.

Camila tilted her head, narrowing her eyes. "Thinks about what? You? Since when do you care what someone's figuring out? That's never been an issue for you before. Or for them, for that matter."

He smirked faintly. "Boss' rules, right? No flings with your dancers." He said it as a joke, but the laugh that followed was dry and empty. Then his voice dropped, quiet and serious. "And I've got nothing else to offer right now."

Camila studied him for a long moment, the playful teasing gone from her face. When she finally spoke, her tone was soft and careful.

"Sebas, are you sure this *timing thing* is about her?"

He didn't answer, just let out a breath and gave her a faint shrug that said more than words ever could.

"Come on," he murmured instead. "I'll help you lock up."

Nikki and Gia walked down the street to a quiet bar, where the air smelled of hops and citrus, a signature scent of San Diego as a craft beer capital. A mellow Bob Marley song played, providing a welcome contrast to the rush of energy they'd left behind in salsa class.

"Okay, first of all," Nikki said, leaning forward across the table. "How are you going to act like you haven't danced since college? You still move like you were born for it. Camila was all over you. Sebastián *wanted* to be all over you. Not too shabby having the attention of both Solanos on day one." Nikki shimmied her shoulders at Gia.

Gia filled a glass for Nikki and handed it over. "You forgot to mention that Sebastián is a walking GQ cover. Unfortunately for me, it was just a dance. But *damn*." She dragged the last word out for three syllables.

Nikki let out a laugh that practically echoed. "Just a dance," she repeated, her tone dripping with disbelief. "Gia. Please. I was there. If that was *just a dance*, then I need to reevaluate my entire love life. I mean, I've danced with Sebastián before. He's amazing. He makes every follower feel like the only one in the room. Everyone knows that. What I saw with you two was different. You didn't even stick to the choreography. You just..." Nikki made a wave with her hand, searching for the word. "You went into your own little world. Don't try to tell me you didn't feel *something*."

Gia took a long sip before answering, stalling for time. "You mean apart from the fact that his arms are basically sculpted out of marble? Yes. I definitely felt something."

Nikki arched a brow knowingly. "Say more words..."

Gia set her glass down and ran her thumb along the rim.

"Okay, it was super hot. But. I think, maybe I was just caught up in the dance itself. It's been so long. My body literally missed it."

Her mind replayed the way his hand had pressed into her back, the weight of his gaze, the sound of his voice when he told her she surprised him. Her skin still tingled from where his fingers had been.

She couldn't stop thinking about what he'd said as she left: "This was only the warm-up." No, that hadn't felt like just a dance.

Nikki pointed at her. "See, I *would* believe that, except I saw your face when he touched you. And your face right now!" Nikki fluttered her eyelashes.

"You are so dramatic."

"Am I?" Nikki's eyes gleamed. "Or was it *intense*?" she added in a deep, breathy tone.

Gia lifted both hands as if she were confessing. "Tonight was just a dance. That's the story, and I'm sticking to it."

"Mmm-hmm. You keep telling yourself that. We've *all* tried to tell ourselves that about Sebastián. There isn't a woman in this city who hasn't been *a little* wrecked after dancing with him. And if she's lucky, a little wrecked after *dancing* with him."

Gia froze, her hand tightening on her glass.

"Yeah, I imagine he gets around, huh?" Gia said lightly, though a bit of intrigue and a sharp twinge of caution danced in her chest. "What's his story? He's a former soccer pro turned salsa dancer?"

"Not exactly. He's a retired soccer player, and he's always been a salsero. His parents are Antonio and Rosa Solano."

Gia stared at her with a blank expression. "And...?"

Nikki's jaw dropped in mock offense. "Oh my god. How did you grow up in New York and never hear of Antonio and Rosa? NY is, like, the mecca of salsa. The birthplace of the Fania All-Stars?"

Gia blinked at her.

"Héctor Lavoe?" Nikki prodded.

Gia kept staring.

"Willie Colón?"

Nothing.

"Celia Cruz? Queen of Salsa?" Nikki flung her hands up. "Azúcar?"

Gia bit her lip and mouthed, "I'm sorry."

Nikki clutched her heart dramatically. "I've failed you as a cousin. Seriously."

Gia let out a laugh despite herself.

"Anyway," Nikki said, recovering her composure. "Camila and Sebastián's parents grew up in Cali, Colombia, another salsa mecca. They're pretty famous salsa musicians, so Camila and Sebastián have been dancing since before they could walk."

She leaned back in her chair and added casually, "Even when he was playing pro soccer, Sebastián would drop into Camila's classes whenever he was in town."

Nikki tilted her head, eyes narrowing slightly, like she knew more than she was letting on. "After his injury, he rehabbed here, moved to San Diego full-time, and started helping Camila at the studio. Now he helps train the advanced dancers and competes with the pro team when they need a sub."

She took a sip of her drink. "He took a coaching position with the arena soccer team in Oceanside a few months ago, so I'm seeing more of him at work. Lucky me."

A sly grin tugged at her lips. "He's all beast mode when he's training. Super intense and incredible to watch. Off the field, he's a blast. Bit of a playboy. Walks into a room, picks the prettiest woman, and ruins her for all other men."

Gia scoffed. "What, he hypnotizes them with his fancy footwork?"

"That's the sound of someone who's never lost herself in a salsa song and a lead that knows what he's doing. Don't worry, you'll understand soon."

Gia felt heat rise in her cheeks but kept her tone cool. "Have you ever been with him?"

Nikki laughed, loud. "Me? Please. I've got access to *all* the hot athletes in San Diego, so his celebrity isn't a big deal to me.

Besides, I'm really close with Camila. That would be weird. And if I had to pick one guy at Ritmo Latino?" She grinned. "It'd be Andrés. All. Day."

"He was there tonight, right? Seems like a lead who knows what he's doing." Gia teased. "And jacked, to say the least. Is he an athlete, too?"

"Firefighter. That can dance. Need I say more?"

Gia laughed so hard she almost spat out her beer. "It's good to know some things never change. Anything ever happen between you two?"

"Nope, our paths don't cross that much. I hadn't seen him in forever until today...and whew, he did not disappoint. Those arms? Built like he carries people out of burning buildings for a living. Oh wait, he does." She smoothed out her hair and folded her hands together as if about to say something more serious. "Just saying, I wouldn't mind a little fire drill with that one." She burst into laughter. "Couldn't resist. Too easy. But still true."

"Well, like Camila said, start going out socially with them more often. Maybe you can get some of that Andrés all day."

"Not a bad idea, actually."

"Okay, *new topic*." Gia straightened up, changing tone. "What do you know about the training team? You said you've done it. What's the deal?"

Nikki leaned back, swirling her glass. "I did it when Camila first started teaching. Mostly to help her get it off the ground. It's like salsa bootcamp. Fastest way to improve. Nobody's dabbling. They all want to level up and get out of beginner classes as fast as possible."

She paused, then added with a little smile. "It was fun back when I did it, and it's only gotten better. I've seen them perform a few times recently. They're good. Really good."

Gia hesitated. "I don't know. I just started—"

"And you're already picking it up." Nikki finished Gia's sentence. Then she added, more delicately, "It would be a welcome distraction from everything that happened with Miles..."

"Still not ready to talk about that." Gia cut her off.

"Besides, what better way to meet people?" Nikki quickly pivoted. "Might as well get *really* good at salsa while you're here. When you go back home for visits, you'll be able to keep up with the scene out there. Take some classes with Eddie Torres and the greats."

Gia looked at her cousin with a blank face.

Nikki gaped at her in mock horror. "Are you *sure* you're from New York? By the end of this year, you'll be the *only* salsera from New York who knows nothing about salsa in New York. We definitely need to fix that before you go back."

"Alright, come on. Long Island isn't the same as Manhattan." Gia shook her head, laughing at herself. She never expected to stumble into this new world, yet it felt as though she'd been waiting for something like this to wake her up. And the best part? She had Nikki to share it with.

"Okay," Gia said, "I'm in. I'm going to text Camila about the training team now."

"Yeah, you are." Nikki cheered her on. "Plus, if you are hanging around the studio, you'll get more time with Sebastián..."

"Oh my God. *Not* why I'm doing this."

"Sure, babe. Keep telling yourself that. You're the only woman in San Diego not attracted to Sebastián Solano."

Gia opened her mouth to argue, then closed it with a sigh. "Oh, I'm attracted. The man is obviously...

"Hot in a way that makes therapy inevitable," Nikki finished.

"Yes, but..."

"Exactly the kind of man women write entire novels about and then pretend didn't ruin them," Nikki offered.

"No. Well, yes, but, oh my God, stop it Nikki!"

"Okay. Sorry. I'm listening. You were saying."

"Sebastián is obviously all those things but I'm not here for flings. I've been single for all of five minutes. I was with Miles *for years*, Nikki. I was expecting forever. Instead...well, you know. This is supposed to be my year to reconnect with myself, with people who actually matter. You, for starters. The last thing I need is a rebound. Besides, I don't do hookups. I never have."

"I get it. I'm just saying maybe something light and fun wouldn't kill you. Maybe the best way to get over one partner is to let a new one take the lead. You know...a little 'quick-quick-slow' back at his house. Honestly, Sebastián seems *built* for that."

"Wow, are you giving me dating advice or sex choreography?" Gia shot Nikki a look of mock outrage. "Although... dancing is basically a shortcut to happiness, right? So maybe it wouldn't hurt."

"You mean dancing with Sebastián Solano?" Nikki arched a brow. "Or *dancing* with Sebastián Solano?"

Gia let out a squeak and slapped her hands over her face. "Both?! All the above? Ugh, delete this conversation from existence."

Nikki whooped, tapping her glass to Gia's. "A toast! To Sebastián! The man, the myth, the reawakening!" They dissolved into laughter, then let their talk wander through the salsa-scene gossip: the dancers to know, the ones to dodge, the festivals and competitions worth the trip.

Gia lifted her beer and swallowed the cool bitterness like it might smother a flame that was already out of her control.

Chapter Five

Gia shook her head. Eight years. She'd let eight whole years slip by without this. When she reached Ritmo Latino's door, the emotion hit her hard, like running into a lover she had never gotten over. Dance *was* her first love. Today, she was finally ready to let it back in.

Gia arrived ten minutes early at the training team rehearsal so that she would have extra time to stretch. When she walked into the packed studio, she realized everyone else had the same plan.

Last week's beginner class had been in this same room, but with an entirely different atmosphere. Today, there was no chatter, no playful flirting, no one laughing through a clumsy turn. Dancers stretched across the room. Water bottles stood in neat rows along the wall, while duffel bags lay open with shirts and towels within easy reach.

Everyone looked polished in sleek athletic wear. The women wore fitted tanks, high-heeled suede-soled shoes, and leggings that fit like a second skin. Even the "casual" dancers dressed in coordinated sets paired with crisp trainers.

Gia glanced down at her own outfit—black running leggings and a loose t-shirt. She tugged at the hem of her top and tied it in a knot at her hip as she took it all in.

The music hadn't started yet, but the team was already moving through footwork patterns. A few couples ran partner-work sequences in the corner. No one made small talk. No one scrolled on their phone.

Gia spotted Sebastián up front, barefoot, talking to a woman Gia recognized from the pro team. A few advanced dancers were spread throughout the room. She had seen them on the studio's YouTube videos. They each had sharp lines, fast spins, and tons of energy. Now they were warming up right next to trainees like her, perfecting the basics with laser focus.

"Alright, team, let's go," Sebastián called out. "Camila is out today, so you're stuck with me." No complaints there.

Gia gravitated to the back row, directly behind a tall, lithe dancer in red leggings and a cropped top. She fixed her eyes on the floorboards, then on the head of the dancer in front of her. Anywhere but in the mirror. Her reflection loomed at the edge of her vision. Her old thoughts threatened to come back. Too much here, not enough there. She avoided the mirror and focused on the woman in front of her instead.

The choreography was faster than Gia had anticipated. Basic steps, yes, but not how she learned them in the beginner class. Here, they danced On2. Mambo timing. Followers stepped back on the second count instead of the first, dancing on the clave beat. This was a whole other level of musicality. Sebastián didn't call out the footwork. He demonstrated it and expected everyone to keep up.

"Again," Sebastián called out, voice sharp but encouraging. "Mark the steps. Feet first. Then flavor."

They repeated the pattern what seemed like a hundred times. By the end, Gia's shirt clung to her back. She could see why most of the women wore sports bras or athletic tops, and she would remember for next time.

"Okay. Everyone's got it. Now let's lock in that contrabody motion. Watch me."

There was no mistaking the athlete in Sebastián. He was a wall of lean muscle, compact power, a physique shaped by years of disciplined training and refined by rhythm. He wore a dark, fitted shirt, already damp at the chest, that showed off sculpted arms and a V-shaped torso. His joggers clung just enough to show the lines of his legs as he moved. He was barefoot, unlike the other guys in suede-bottomed, Cuban-heeled dance shoes or crisp, clean trainers.

"If you simply step forward, you're missing the heartbeat. In salsa and mambo, contrabody motion is the natural rotation of the upper body in opposition to the lower body. It creates balance, fluidity, and expression. It travels through your legs, into your hips, through your chest, shoulders, and arms. Full-body movement where every part of you is moving. It's the difference between looking mechanical versus connected to the music." He performed the basic step with exaggerated contrabody motion to emphasize his point.

Sebastián rolled his shoulders back and let his torso twist, one side driving forward as the opposite hip followed. The motion was slow and seductive as it flowed through his whole frame.

"This is what makes salsa sexy. Your body never moves in pieces. It moves as one. Every part connected, each complementing the other, creating a rhythm that runs from here—" he slid a hand across the front of his hips, "to here—" he motioned to his chest, "and out through every step, every reach." He exaggerated the movement in his legs and arms until the ripple was unmistakable. A handful of dancers laughed nervously.

"Now, when you move with your partner like that...it feels like magic."

"Are we sure he's talking about salsa?" one of the other girls in the back line whispered. Another dancer fanned herself in response.

Sebastián turned sideways so everyone could see from that angle and slowed everything down.

"Let's practice our basic step a few times and repeat the pattern with a focus on body movement."

Midway through rehearsal, the room was a sauna, but no one

complained. No one took a break either. Even the seasoned dancers, who could've coasted, pushed hard to perfect their technique.

Sebastián told them to take five minutes before starting partnerwork. The dancer in front of Gia reached for a towel, wiped her forehead, and swapped her crop top for a dry one in one fluid motion. Gia saw three other guys do the same. She made a mental note to bring a towel. Her shirt was already clinging to her back.

Gia's calves ached. Her ponytail stuck to her neck. Despite the exhaustion and overwhelm, a spark danced inside her chest. She craved this intensity and the thrill of trying to keep up.

As Sebastián moved past her row, he slowed just enough for their eyes to catch.

"Hey, Gia. Looking good."

She was almost sure he meant her dancing, but the warmth in his tone and that sexy smile made her stomach dip harder than she cared to admit.

"Pair up with your partner from last week," Sebastián told the team. "Gia, since you're not partnered yet, you've got me. Come on up."

Her breath caught mid-step. She hadn't expected Sebastián to be leading class tonight, let alone dancing with her right there in front of a room full of people, most of whom were leagues ahead of her in skill and experience.

As she made her way to Sebastián, a wave of heat rose up her neck. She could feel the eyes on her and some downright hostile.

"Oh, really? The new girl gets Sebastián? That's cute," someone stage-whispered behind her. She didn't see who said it, but a few dancers nearby snickered, and one of them, the tall, lithe brunette she'd been following earlier, arched an eyebrow at Gia in the mirror.

Gia's stomach clenched. Her t-shirt, already clinging with sweat from the drills, now felt suffocating. Every step toward Sebastián felt like wading through syrup. While her mind scrambled through a dozen retorts she'd never say out loud, she forced her chin a little higher and walked to the front of the space.

Sebastián didn't seem to notice the tension moving through the group, or if he did, he didn't show it. His easy smile met her as she approached, his hand already extended, ready to guide her into position.

"Let's warm up with the choreography we went over last week."

Gia gave him a look, half panic, and half plea, that said, *You know I have no idea what the choreography is, right?*

"Don't overthink it. Just follow me. We'll walk through it, and once you've got it, we'll run it with everyone else."

Then he stepped into a closed position, his hand settling on her shoulder blade, guiding her into his frame like she belonged there.

A memory struck hard and unexpectedly: Miles, standing in their apartment, his voice cool and final. "You're not really here, Gia. Not with me. Not with this life."

The words had gutted her then, but now she wondered if he'd been right all along because in this moment, everything inside her lit up, fully present.

Sebastián counted, "Hold, two, three, hold, six, seven," steadily and patient, his body moving through the sequence. He offered verbal cues occasionally, but his lead did most of the talking. His frame was so clear that missing a step was almost impossible. Here and there, he scatted syllables, verbally drumming the music to keep the beat.

Gia settled into the rhythm, the nerves melting away as her body tuned to his. In his arms, she was sure-footed and fluid, as if she'd never left dance at all.

The choreography, which might have taken hours to learn in the beginner class, landed within minutes under Sebastián's lead. The more she gave herself to the dance, the more time unraveled, leaving nothing but the pulse of the music and the press of his hand at her back.

"Beautiful," he said, offering a nod of approval. "Let's run it with the group."

Sebastián called out to the room. "Alright, everyone, let's run it together. Make sure you can see yourselves in the mirror." He tapped his phone, and the notes of Cheo Feliciano's song "Anacaona" began, rolling an ethereal vibe throughout the studio. The dancers formed two lines facing the mirror, with each couple staggered so everyone had a clear view of themselves. Gia stood front and center next to Sebastián.

In Sebastián's arms, Gia was exactly where she needed to be. He was so attuned to her that he seemed to know what she needed before she did, offering a gentle give of his hand when she needed to catch up on the timing, or the faintest resistance when she rushed ahead. Sebastián was in constant conversation with her body, asking and responding, shaping the dance with her. Their connection made everything else in the room blur.

Partner dancing was a world apart from anything Gia had known. In her previous training, power came from the choreography she controlled. Here, she gave up that control, and somehow that surrender unlocked emotions she hadn't expected.

What surprised her most was how liberating it was to be tethered. It felt like someone else was carrying the weight of the decision so she could sink into the music and give into creativity. It seemed contradictory for a woman who'd fought so hard to own her power to give it up, even for a moment. Yet on the dance floor, it didn't feel like loss. It felt like freedom.

With every step, her confidence grew until a quick spin snapped her out of her thoughts. She missed the beat, landed wrong, and collided with the couple beside her, heel grinding down on someone's toes.

The lithe brunette yelped.

"Oh my God! I'm so sorry," Gia blurted, face blazing as she stumbled backwards.

The brunette sucked in a sharp breath. "Watch it!" Her glare slid past Gia to Sebastián, then back again. "I know you're a beginner, but you're dancing with *Sebastián Solano.* The least you can do is pay attention."

Heat rushed to Gia's face. "I am—I was—" The words tangled, useless.

The dancer gave her a slow once-over, unimpressed. "Then maybe try harder." With that, she turned to her partner, dismissing Gia like she wasn't worth the air she was standing in.

What am I even doing here? Panic bubbled under her skin. *I'm embarrassing myself and him.*

Before the sting could settle, Sebastián's voice cut clean through the music. "Vanessa, that isn't how we do things here." His gaze swept the studio but landed squarely on the brunette. "We support each other. Everyone was a beginner once."

The brunette turned and looked at Sebastián in disbelief.

The room went still. A few couples shifted awkwardly, eyes down.

Sebastián softened, turning to Gia. "You're fine. Keep going. Mistakes are part of the process."

He started the song from the beginning, and the dancers picked up the choreography again. Gia's chest eased only because he'd given her something solid to hold on to.

As the class wrapped up, a wave of applause and easy chatter rolled through the studio. Gia drifted toward the edge of the dance floor to grab her things and check her phone. There was a text from Miles.

MILES

Gia, Nikki posted a photo of you two dancing in a studio. Fun to see you at it again. You look happy.

Her stomach tightened. The words were harmless enough, but the message underneath wasn't lost on her. Before the knot could settle, Sebastián's voice cut through the noise.

"Gia," he said, his eyes still sparkling. "What did you think of the class?"

"I didn't realize how much I missed dancing. It's been a long while," she admitted. There was a level of vulnerability in her voice that surprised even her.

"I get that." His tone matched hers, without the charm he used when addressing the group.

They stood there for a moment, looking at each other. Surprisingly, it wasn't awkward. If anything, the silence held a pull. A shared curiosity. Gia didn't want to share a word about the doubt creeping in her chest, so she broke the quiet with the first thing that came to mind. "Do you teach the training team a lot?" The second it left her mouth, Gia cringed. *Wow. Smooth. Very original. May as well have asked if he comes here often.*

He laughed like he heard the pickup line in her comment too. "I cover classes when my sister needs it. So, no, not the training team very often." He paused, then added with a tilt of his head, "But...I always make time for private lessons. If you happen to know anyone interested."

Gia narrowed her eyes. "Do you say that to *all* the new girls?" She gave it a teasing, sing-song lilt, pointing a finger at him.

That earned her a flash of genuine surprise, like he wasn't used to women calling him out or tossing the ball back at him. His smile returned, wider.

She laughed, half embarrassed and half flattered. "Aw. It must be exhausting, being every woman's fantasy in here."

He leaned in slightly, lowering his voice so their chat felt private. "Fantasies aren't usually laughed at by new students." His grin widened even more. "I actually liked it."

Her chest warmed. Her pulse stuttered as Nikki's voice played in her head. *If being next to him feels this good with lots of people around, what would it be like to 'quick-quick-slow' with him... alone?* It was too easy to imagine those hands guiding her hips, his eyes fixed on her like no one else existed. *Don't go there. Just dance, Gia. That's all this is.*

She summoned a smirk, aiming for breezy confidence. "So, you like a woman who isn't easily impressed. Unfortunately for you, I am kinda blown away. Not with the soccer legend thing... sorry." She gestured toward the dance floor. "But with how you make this feel possible. Like I could actually find my way back into dance. Tonight was...really good for me. Thank you. I needed this." The words hung between them, heavier than she had meant.

Sebastián's grin softened, the tease fading from his face. He looked at her as if he understood she'd handed him something fragile. "My pleasure," he said quietly. "Literally."

"Have a good night, Sebastián. I'll try to be less impressed next time I take your class."

"And I'll try to be more impressive."

Chapter Six

Camila didn't make polite suggestions. She made declarations, and this one was simple: Everyone from Ritmo Latino showed up for the studio's annual summer kickoff beach party held on the first weekend in June. No excuses.

Gia had no intention of arguing. A beach day with the entire dance company was the perfect chance to meet the full cast of characters she'd only glimpsed across the studio floor and maybe catch another moment with a certain man-shaped plot twist in a fitted tee.

Pacific Beach was everything the movies promised about Southern California. The boardwalk stretched wide along the sand, alive with movement in every direction. Wheels ruled the scene. Roller skaters glided by, dancing to the music playing in their earbuds. Retro bikes and cruisers wove through the crowd. Scooters zipped past while bikini-clad walkers took their time to see and be seen.

Beyond the boardwalk, the ocean was a shifting stage. Surfers paddled out, dropped in, wiped out, and then did it all over again. The lineup was a mix of locals, who carved through the waves like second nature, and tourists, who wobbled on rented boards. The occasional surf pro made the whole thing look like a game. A crowded patchwork of sunbathers, families with coolers, and volleyball games covered the beach. Countless footprints marked the endless flow of people moving between the sand and the surf.

When Gia found the group, Camila was bouncing between towels and shouting orders like a general in flip-flops. "Volleyball in ten. Sunscreen or suffer. Someone better have brought the speaker!"

Standing barefoot in the warm sand, Gia caught herself smiling at nothing in particular. Just happy. She was glad she'd come to the party and grateful she was in San Diego for the summer. For once, she felt included instead of invisible. It was a sharp contrast to the version of her that used to spend most evenings on her laptop, holed up in her home office. Remote work had offered convenience but slowly blurred into isolation, made worse during and after COVID, when solitude stopped feeling like freedom and more like exile. Today, though, she was outdoors, the sun on her face, the breeze in her hair, and in the company of talented dancers. Life was good.

Gia scanned the Ritmo Latino group for Nikki, who was stretched out on a towel beneath a hot pink umbrella.

"Gia mia!" Nikki waved her over, sunglasses perched on her head. "Took you long enough."

As Gia dropped her chair next to her cousin, she leaned in and whispered, "Okay, am I crazy, or is everyone on this beach ridiculously fit? Is a chiseled body some West Coast entry requirement?"

"Most of these people are competitive dancers," Nikki said, raising an eyebrow.

"No, I mean *everyone* on the beach," Gia gestured east toward the boardwalk and west to the ocean. "Look at those surfers, for God's sake. It's like a *Sports Illustrated* casting call out here."

"It's America's Finest City for a reason." Nikki shrugged, rubbing sunscreen onto her sculpted legs before passing the bottle to Gia. "Here. The sun is way stronger than back East."

Gia slathered on the lotion as she scanned the group sprawled across the sand. "So... give me the scoop. Who's who, and what do I need to know?" Gia knew the dancers on the training team, but this was a rare occasion when the entire company was in one place.

Nikki sat up straight, always up for sharing the tea. "Okay, well, you remember I mentioned Andrés a while ago," she said, nodding toward the tan guy in red board shorts stretching like he was warming up for the Olympics. "Firefighter. Absurdly strong. Hilarious and super chill." Then, with a mischievous grin, she cupped a hand over mouth as if telling Gia a secret, and she didn't want to risk anyone reading her lips. "He's off limits in case I didn't make that clear already."

"Oh, crystal clear, Nikita. Don't you worry," Gia joked back. "He is definitely sponsored by some kind of protein powder, right?"

"Right?" Nikki laughed, then tilted her chin toward Camila's partner. "That's Daniel. He's the quiet genius type. PhD student in computer science. He's basically a future doctor of algorithms or something. Totally brilliant, on and off the floor." She leaned in a bit. "He's the new principal dancer. Camila's been pouring a lot into him this year, getting him ready to compete with her next season. Big shoes to fill, but he's holding his own."

Gia squinted as Daniel adjusted his glasses and dabbed sunscreen onto his neck. "He looks so serious. About to defend a dissertation or something."

"Give it a minute," Nikki said, wiggling her fingers like she was casting a spell. "Once the music hits, he transforms. Total Clark Kent to Superman situation." She grinned and added, "And you already know Sebastián." Her tone turned playfully conspiratorial. "Daniel, Andrés, and Sebastián. The holy trifecta. Best salseros in the company. Possibly in all of SoCal."

Gia raised her eyebrows and fanned herself. "So I've already danced with two-thirds of San Diego's sacred salsa trinity? Man, did I drop into the right class that day!"

"Careful. That's how it starts. Get used to dancing at that level, and before you know it, you're rearranging your life around social nights and salsa festivals."

"I have a feeling I'm on my way there already," Gia replied. "Okay, what about the followers?"

Nikki nodded toward the group gathered at a giant cooler. "The redhead is Amber. She's Andrés' partner. On stage? Untouchable. Off stage? She's kind of like...an over-caffeinated hype woman who never learned volume control. Loud encouragement, constant opinions, zero filter, but somehow, we all kind of love her for it."

Gia watched as Amber burst out laughing at something Andrés said, then turned and started scolding someone for using the wrong cooler.

"That is such an odd description, yet completely fitting."

Next to Amber, a barefoot blonde swayed to a reggaeton beat, her long hair lifting in the breeze.

"That's Luna," Nikki said. "Kind of a coastal fairy goddess. You know, all the vibes."

"She comes to a lot of the weekday classes," Gia noted. "She never wears shoes."

"And still more elegant than the rest of us in our heels." Nikki laughed. "She teaches the ladies' styling classes. Her cha-cha-cha class is basically witchcraft.

Nikki pointed out the semi-pro dancers, the women's performance team, and a handful of up-and-coming students. At least ten more people showed up while she got the scoop from her cousin. Friendly warmth radiated through the group of longtime friends and newcomers like her, all blending easily.

A sharp whistle cut through the laughter, followed by Camila jogging barefoot across the sand, dragon braid swinging and a volleyball tucked under one arm.

"Alright, people!" she called out, grinning like she was about to start a flash mob. "Net's open."

"Oh no," Nikki muttered, sinking lower into her chair.

Gia glanced at her, amused. "What? It's just volleyball. We used to spend entire summers hustling the guys on Jones Beach. Don't tell me you've lost your edge."

Nikki slid on her sunglasses as if they were protective gear.

"That's what Camila wants you to think. Friendly little game. Right up until the war cries start."

"Let's make it interesting," Camila said. "High stakes. No mercy."

"Winner picks tonight's dance spot?" Andrés grinned at Camila.

Daniel, who had been quiet until now, adjusted his glasses and piped up. "The losers..." He let the suspense build for a beat. "Must publicly declare their partner the superior athlete, sing their praises loud enough for the beach to hear, and swear eternal loyalty to their unmatched greatness."

"Surrender speech!" someone yelled.

"Salute of shame!" another shouted back.

Apparently, outrageous consequences were a regular part of losing around here.

"Let's do this!" Sebastián called, jogging up from the water with his surfboard. As he peeled off his rash guard, time seemed to shift into slow motion. Sunlight caught the droplets rolling down his chest, highlighting every sculpted line of muscle. Salt-water trickled past abs so defined they looked Photoshopped. His board shorts hung just low enough to qualify as a public service announcement.

Gia tore her gaze away as if she'd been caught shoplifting. She turned to Nikki, wide-eyed.

Nikki arched her brows, shimmied her shoulders, and silently mouthed: "Quick, quick, slooooow," drawing out the last word.

Gia laughed and pulled her long waves into a high ponytail. She made her way onto the volleyball court with Nikki. To her surprise, Sebastián squared himself directly across from her on the opposing team. He met her gaze playfully through the net.

"We dance well together. Let's see how we do against each other."

"Challenge accepted," she replied matter-of-factly.

"You don't want to mess with the DeLuca girls!" Nikki shouted at Sebastián from behind Gia. "We have killer instincts and Olympic level trash talk."

Andrés joined Gia and Nikki, still in his fire department t-shirt, eyes half-lidded from the overnight shift. "It's about time the Solanos got humbled on the sand, but you're going to need all the help you can get!" He pointed dramatically at Daniel. "Yo, genius! We need brains and biceps. Let's go."

Camila cupped her hands around her mouth. "Someone film this. I want proof when they start blaming the net!"

"Let's do this!" Luna chimed in.

Once the teams were set, the game was on. Sebastián, Camila, Amber, Luna, and Xander, one of the semi-pro dancers, took one side of the court, playing up the swagger. Across from them, Gia, Nikki, Andrés, Daniel, and Ricky, another semi-pro member, lined up together.

Sebastián narrowed his eyes. Andrés cracked his knuckles. Camila adjusted her braid like she meant business. Nikki stretched her neck from side to side as if loosening up for a prize fight. Gia wasn't sure when her own competitive streak kicked in. Maybe when Sebastián landed a spike two feet from her, turned to the spectators and gave an exaggerated bow.

"Wow," she said emphatically, walking back to her position. "You want a medal or just the applause?"

He grinned. "I'll take both."

One minute, they were laughing. Next, Sebastián was spiking like he was in the finals, and Gia was diving like a woman possessed. Trash talk and jokes flew faster than the ball.

The next volley was a blur of feet pounding, sand flying, and laughter mixing with shouts. Gia dove, arms outstretched, and somehow blocked Sebastián's spike. The ball thudded to the ground on his side. Everyone cheered in response and surprise, including Sebastián's team.

Sebastián blinked, stunned for half a second. "Lucky shot, twinkle toes."

Gia stood, brushing sand off her thighs. "Don't be salty just because your feet are better trained than your hands."

The crew lost it. Nikki bent over, wheezing with laughter, while Andrés hollered, "Ohhh *shit!*" like she'd roasted Sebastián on TV in front of a studio audience. Even Camila was cackling, shaking her head like she couldn't believe what she'd witnessed. No one got the last word with Sebastián, especially not during anything remotely competitive.

Sebastián pointed at her. "I *like* this side of you."

That's when things exploded into a full-on battle. Gia and Sebastián locked eyes across the net, every volley a dare. He sent rockets screaming toward her side. She dove, arms outstretched, sand spraying as she popped the ball back up. She answered his spike with a perfectly placed shot, grinning when he had to lunge like a man saving his life.

"East Coast grit!" Nikki shouted.

"West Coast flair!" Camila shot back.

The sidelines became a chorus of cheers, groans, and dramatic commentary while Gia and Sebastián threw themselves at the ball with reckless determination. Each point ended in laughter or exaggerated moans of agony.

Camila cheered for both teams, which earned her twice the teasing from everyone. Nikki, Amber, Andrés, and Daniel provided nonstop play-by-play, tossing out sarcastic jabs and dramatic sound effects as Gia and Sebastián literally threw themselves into the game.

"Somebody call SportsCenter!" Andrés yelled.

"Ten out of ten for drama," Amber added. "Negative three for aim."

Then, finally, the perfect setup. The ball soared high, arcing toward Gia like a gift wrapped in golden sunlight.

She leaped, muscles flexing, timing her strike perfectly.

Sebastián was already there. Lightning fast, he sealed the net, his hands pressing over as her hit met the block and dropped straight down on her side.

Game. Over.

"Yesssssssss!" Camila cheered, throwing her arms up in victory. She looked at the rest of her team. "Hands up like a winner, people!"

Xander walked off the court, cracked open a kombucha, and

raised it toward Ricky. "Pay up, bro. That's what you get for betting against the Solanos."

Camila laughed as Sebastián threw an arm around her neck and planted a triumphant kiss on her forehead. "Ca-mee-laaa, another year of total domination!"

Nikki dropped onto the sand with a dramatic groan, covering her face. "I'm gonna cry."

Amber cupped her hands to her mouth as a megaphone. "Alright, suckers! Let's hear your speeches."

Andrés, ever the showman, took a knee. "Fine. I'll go first." He cleared his throat and placed a solemn hand over his heart.

"Amber is an unstoppable force. A legend. A warrior of the sand." He struggled to maintain a straight face. "I am but a humble challenger in her presence."

Amber smirked from behind her kombucha. "Keep going."

He cleared his throat and deepened his voice. "From this day forward, I vow to honor her superior skills, bow before her greatness, and—" He cut himself off with a shake of his head. "This is ridiculous."

Amber crossed her arms, eyes sparkling. "Say it, Andrés."

With an exaggerated sigh, he bowed. "And pledge my eternal allegiance to La Reina de Salsa, ruler of the dance floor and beach volleyball."

Cheers, whistles, and cries of "Long live the queen!" filled the air.

Camila nudged Daniel with her hip. "Your turn, Danny boy. This was your idea, after all!"

He sighed, adjusted his glasses as if he were about to read the fine print, then stood tall. His tone was flat, and his delivery was deadpan.

"Camila is a strategic mastermind. A sandstorm of athletic prowess. I was... unworthy of sharing a court with her today."

Camila wiped a fake tear. "I love when you get emotional."

Daniel blinked slowly. "From this day forward, I shall speak of her greatness to all who will listen and also those who won't."

Nikki yelled, "Give him a mic!"

"She's like Christmas in September, magical with a warm breeze," he added, bowing stiffly like a footman in a Bridgerton episode delivering a scandalous invitation.

"Dude. Where do you get this stuff?" Andrés teased him.

"You're the Christmas gift," Camila said, extending her hand like Queen Charlotte at a Bridgerton ball. Daniel kissed it with mock grandeur, and they both burst out laughing.

Sebastián walked over to Gia, looking far too smug.

"And what were you saying? Something about my hands? Care to revise your statement for accuracy?" He couldn't contain the giant, radiant smile taking over his face.

Gia laughed, squeezing her eyes tight.

"Your hands," she began, "are just as skilled as your feet." She looked up at him through her eyelashes. "Perhaps even more so?"

The group howled with laughter. "Wouldn't we like to know!" yelled Amber.

"What comes next?" Gia asked the others.

"I vow to honor your superior skills!" They chanted in reply, barely able to contain themselves.

Gia didn't hide the sincerity of her smile. "I vow to honor your superior skills. And... if I'm being strategic or honest, I'd rather be your partner than play against you."

His smirk softened into warmth.

"I like the sound of that. Pareja."

After the last speeches and subsequent teasing, Gia cooled off by the water's edge. Sebastián appeared next to her. He smiled when she noticed him.

"Do you miss the Atlantic Ocean?"

"Sometimes, but if I get close enough to block out the boardwalk and palm trees, it looks like the same ocean I grew up with. Thankfully." She pushed her hair away from her eyes. "I've always gone to the beach to clear my head. Still do."

"Same. After a match, after training. Something about the ocean makes everything else seem small."

She tilted her head, curious and cautious, unsure if it was a sensitive topic. "Even soccer?"

"Especially soccer. I used to come down here every day after my injury."

"Do you mind if I ask what happened? I heard it was pretty bad."

He let out a slow breath. "Whatever you heard, it was worse."

"I'm sorry. I shouldn't have asked. You don't have to talk about it."

"No, it's okay. Most people are afraid to even mention it, let alone ask me about it. I don't get to talk about it much."

He didn't look at her as he spoke. "I heard it snap. Right on the turf, in front of thirty thousand people. At first, I thought I could walk it off, that it was just another hit, but when I tried to stand..." He shook his head. "I couldn't even move."

Gia's heart squeezed.

"Everything faded. I remember staring at the lights, hearing my dad singing in the kitchen. Seeing my mom dancing with Camila. It was weird, all the flashbacks. I knew something was wrong. The doctors didn't even need to tell me it was over. I knew."

The memory was still vivid in his eyes. "I spent months trying to rehab it. Surgery. Physical therapy. Ice baths. Electro stim. Cortisone. Denial. The works. I would've done anything to play again. I thought if I wasn't on that field, I didn't exist."

Gia didn't speak. She just reached out, gently resting her fingers on his forearm.

"When they suggested dance therapy, I laughed in their faces. Recommending salsa felt like a joke considering my family, but something in me...I don't know, needed to move. To not be angry all the time. Salsa didn't just help rehab my knee. It saved me from disappearing."

Gia's eyes stung. "I had no idea."

"No one does," he said. "They see a guy spinning women

on the dance floor. They don't see the months I spent wondering if I'd ever matter again, or be able to move without pain."

She leaned in, her hand now resting over his. "I see it. I see you."

For a moment, neither of them moved. His gaze held hers, and the sound of the waves filled the silence between them. The intimacy made her chest ache.

His shoulders rose and fell with a quiet breath, like saying it aloud had released something.

Only then did he add, softer, "Now I'm trying to figure out who I am without it." He smiled, but it didn't reach his eyes. "Still working on that."

"I get it."

He studied her for a moment. "You were a trained dancer. That's years of discipline and commitment. Not easy to give up."

"Did Camila tell you that?"

He shook his head. "I can tell by the way you move."

Heat rushed to her cheeks, an unsettling mix of being seen and exposed. "I haven't danced in a long time."

"Doesn't mean it ever left you," he said, stepping closer. His voice was lower now, nearly lost beneath the crash of the waves. "It's still there. I see it when you step on the floor."

Her heart stuttered, and the salty air between them suddenly felt charged. She wanted to look away or make a joke to ease the tension. Instead, she kept his gaze, letting desire and nerves tangle under her skin.

"Why did you stop dancing?"

Gia hesitated, the question hanging between them. The truth was simple and complicated all at once. She didn't talk about it, but Sebastián had been so vulnerable. The least she could do was meet him there.

"I started dancing when I was five. Jazz, modern, ballet, tap. By middle school, I was training five, six days a week. I was never the best technically, but I had presence. My teachers used to say I danced like I meant it."

Sebastián nodded slowly, his eyes smiling, like he was picturing her as a little girl tearing up the floor in jazz shoes.

She laughed softly, almost bitterly. "In my junior year, one of them recommended I audition for a regional company. It wasn't Juilliard or anything, but it was real. It was a shot."

His brows lifted slightly, impressed, but he didn't speak. He only listened.

"I started preparing for auditions and I started getting...feedback. Not about my technique or my style. It was all about my body. They said I was too curvy or too distracting, that I didn't have a dancer's body. I started second-guessing everything. My costumes. The choreo. Every teacher. I stopped trusting myself."

"During my last audition, one choreographer stopped the music right in the middle of the performance to tell me I didn't 'fit the silhouette' he was looking for. Oh my God, what I would have given to have the floor swallow me whole in that moment."

Sebastián nodded slightly, not to rush her, but to say, *I'm here. Keep going.*

"After that, every time I danced, I imagined the song cutting out. A few weeks later, my dad lost his job, and I told myself I couldn't justify chasing such an unstable career."

She took a breath, eyes still down. "But if I'm being completely honest... I didn't just walk away. I ran. Because what if I showed up and wasn't good enough? This way, I could keep telling myself I might have made it. It's easier to live with the maybe than the no."

She looked out at the water, a bitter smile ghosting her lips.

His green eyes were filled with recognition and anger, maybe, on her behalf, but also empathy, like he saw her differently now. Or more clearly.

A cold ocean wave rolled over their feet, breaking the moment. Gia let out a startled yelp, stepping back, but Sebastián grabbed her hand, not ready to give up the connection. He kept her hand in his as the frigid water surged over their ankles again.

"I get it," he said. "Not just the dancing. The way you buried the part of you that felt too risky to keep."

His thumb brushed gently against the back of her hand. "Everyone talks about responsibility and stability like it's noble, but no one tells you how hard it is to live without the version of yourself you gave up."

He searched her face, as if he didn't want her to miss what he was about to say.

"I've been on a field with thousands of people chanting my name, and I've also been in a quiet room trying to remember who I was without the applause. I respect the hell out of you. For being honest about what you lost and for coming back to it anyway. That takes courage."

Gia looked away for a second, steadying herself. She hadn't expected this from the confident, wildly successful Sebastián Solano. A month ago, she'd decided he was a man you danced with, flirted with, maybe even had a little harmless fun with if you were feeling brash, not the kind you cared for or let in. Yet here he was, looking at her like she was the only person on the beach, sharing pieces of himself no one else seemed to see, and quietly inviting her to do the same. The part of her that was still tender after everything that happened with Miles felt exposed all over again, but this time it felt like healing.

Keep it light, she reminded herself. Gia opened her mouth to thank him for the sweet words, but the ocean had other plans. A rogue wave slammed into them like a liquid iceberg, extinguishing the moment and every warm, fluttery thought she'd been having. She shrieked. Sebastián cursed and shook the salty Pacific water from his arms. Water streamed down her face as Gia broke into laughter and swept her soaked hair out of her eyes.

"Alright, alright," he said to the ocean as he backed up toward the shore. "I surrender."

Gia followed Sebastián out of the water to join their friends, who were singing and passing around beers.

The ocean had stolen the moment but not the truth of it. Something had shifted between them, not lost in the waves, just waiting to come back with the tide.

Chapter Seven

By the time Gia hit the final count, her calves were on fire and her tank top stuck to her back, but there was no second-guessing. Not anymore. The drills that once scrambled her brain were finally settling into her legs.

Her days were spent behind a laptop, ghostwriting the stories of executives and business leaders. Evenings belonged to the studio or to social dancing at a local club. On weekends, she ran along the beach with her cousin before heading to training team rehearsal. She loved the routine. The discipline. The way choreography slowly stitched itself back into her muscles. After six weeks of practicing with Ritmo Latino, salsa was starting to live inside her body.

"One more from the top," Camila called out, clapping twice to get the group's attention. "Make it count."

They danced it again, sharper this time, everyone pushing to meet Camila's expectations.

"That's a wrap for today, team. Great job, dancers."

The dancers gave each other a round of applause before dropping into stretching positions and reaching for water bottles. Gia wiped her forehead with the hem of her shirt, her lungs still burning from the final sequence. She was getting stronger week after week, but she never stopped feeling like she had something to prove.

"Before anyone heads out, I have an announcement." Camila stood at the front of the studio, clipboard in one hand. Her pen tapped once against her thigh. Normally, she'd be weaving through the crowd by now, trading jokes, giving high-fives, offering feedback to eager new dancers. Not today.

The room stilled.

Gia pushed forward onto the balls of her feet, one leg at a time, trying to relieve the soreness from the last couple of hours.

"Due to a rule change at the Pacific Salsa Fest," Camila said, pacing slowly across the floor, "each studio can only enter one dancer for each director for the pro-am division."

Murmurs broke out instantly. Gia heard whispers on both sides of her.

"Wait, I thought we just signed up for pro-am. Are you saying we need to audition?"

"Really? Only one partner each?"

"What happened to each director dancing with, like, unlimited students?"

"Who is the male director this year since..."

Camila held up a hand. The studio fell silent.

"To be clear, I'm not happy about this either, but it is what it is. So we're holding internal auditions to determine who gets the amateur spots."

Gia's heart thumped once, hard. She planned to register for the pro-am, but that was before it required an audition against dancers with years of salsa experience.

"We'll choose the students we believe give us the strongest chance of winning," Camila continued, her tone crisp and no-nonsense. "That might mean the cleanest technique, next-level musicality, or it may come down to sabor. We want that special sauce that keeps our eyes on you. So whatever your strength is, lean into it. Bring your best self."

Gia glanced across the floor at Luna and Amber. They stood

shoulder to shoulder, with crossed arms and focused expressions. The air shifted around them like heat rising off the sidewalk.

Camila paused in the center of the room. Her next words landed like a gauntlet.

"The studio's reputation is on the line, which means my reputation is on the line. I want a clean sweep in every category we enter, in every competition, all year. No second place. If you want to compete in the pro-am this year, expect to spend all your free time in the studio this summer."

A few dancers glanced at each other, eyes wide.

"Before anyone tells me that's a wildly arrogant goal, let me say, I know that. But we have the talent. This is the year we can do it. We just have to be strategic about it. It's going to be intense and crazy fun."

"Damn," one guy muttered, half under his breath.

"Clean sweep?" whispered another. "Has anyone ever actually done that? I mean, competitions aren't exactly objective."

Camila looked around, eyes locking on each dancer, Gia included. She wasn't playing. Gia caught Sebastián scanning the room too. When his gaze brushed past her and lingered for half a second longer, that usual heat swept up her neck.

"The audition is this upcoming Saturday. It will be in two parts," Camila continued. "In the morning, we'll run shines. Same combo you learned today, so you've got a week to practice. Consider that a perk of being on the training team. New people will learn it that day. After that, we'll make cuts. The top three leaders and followers will stay to learn one minute of partnered choreography. We'll break for lunch, then hold the final auditions as couples. The finalists will dance with a pro for the final round."

She paused to let the weight of the news land before continuing.

"This audition is about seeing how you handle connection, musicality, and pressure. Not just choreography."

Gia's stomach tightened. She hadn't auditioned since college, and that was a disaster she still avoided thinking about. This could be her way back. If she made it through, it wouldn't be because

Camila handed her anything. It would mean she earned her spot. She needed to do this to prove she wasn't the girl who gave up on herself, who didn't, as Miles put it, "disappear out of her own life."

"If you want in, write your name on the list before you leave. No pressure to sign up, but if you do, show up to win. And clear your schedule. This isn't casual. In a few months, you'll be a completely new dancer. One who changes a room the second you step into it. Guaranteed."

Camila walked over and dropped the clipboard with the signup sheet on the edge of the stereo.

Gia stood up slowly. Her feet ached. Her back was soaked. Her heart was on the brink of imploding, and still her legs moved toward the signup sheet before reason could convince her otherwise.

She signed her name. The scratch of the pen seemed deafening despite the salsa music playing in the background. For a second, it felt like everyone in the room must have heard it, but no one even looked her way.

The clipboard filled up fast. One by one, dancers stepped forward to scribble their names. Some had bold confidence, while others signed with more of a quiet determination. A few hovered by the stereo, glancing at the list and each other, sizing up the competition before finally committing.

The rest packed up their gear and trickled out, some already speculating about who would snag the amateur spot and which lead would dance the pro part. Gia moved slowly, waiting for most of the room to empty so she could speak to Camila privately.

"Hey Camila, can I talk to you about the pro-am for a sec?" Gia's throat went dry, and she swallowed, trying to gain composure before she asked what was sure to rock the confidence she'd been working to build over the last six weeks.

"You want to audition." Camila smiled.

"I want to audition," Gia's voice dropped a little as she continued. "But I'm still not totally sure how it works."

"Here's the deal. The Pacific Salsa Fest is on Labor Day weekend in Los Angeles. It's a big event with workshops all day and social dancing at night. Most events have competitions in tons of categories—couples, teams, dance styles and so on. This one is different in that it only has pro-ams. So, a professional teacher, for this competition that means the company director, is paired with a student. Usually, lots of students sign up, and each director performs multiple times. Since there were *tons* of entrants last year, the event committee changed the rules this year as an experiment. Now, every company director can enter with one amateur only. It's bragging rights, sure, but it's also about showing what kind of talent we develop here."

"So, it's like *Dancing with the Stars*?"

"Yeah. Except no soap stars are doing a foxtrot. The amateurs are real dancers–just not professional ones. Some have less experience, and some have years. There are categories, so if someone like you made it, you'd compete against other students with less than a year of salsa training. If someone like Vanessa made it, she'd compete in an advanced division since she has more than three years of training. All divisions are high-level and high-pressure since everyone is partnered with a company director."

She let the words settle before adding in a deliberate tone, "There's no faster way to grow than one-on-one training with a pro."

Gia's eyes perked up at the idea of that.

"I see...Who is the pro leader? Ritmo Latino doesn't have a male director, does it?"

"I'm still working on that. Most likely Andrés. Possibly Sebastián."

The thought of dancing with either of them sent a flutter of adrenaline through Gia's chest. Her heart skipped, but she anchored herself. There was something more important she needed to know, something that had been simmering since the moment Camila mentioned auditions.

"Can I ask you something? Like... really ask?"

Camila tilted her head, her expression easing. She knew what was coming.

"How do you think I've been doing these last six weeks?" Gia met her gaze fully now. "Do I have a shot? Not just to get through the audition, but to get the spot. I don't have as much experience as a lot of the other dancers. You won't hurt my feelings if it's a no. I'd just...really appreciate your honest feedback."

Camila looked at her friend and saw hopefulness in her eyes. It was less about ambition and more about longing. She took her time in responding.

"You're hungry for this. You take direction well, show up consistently, and put in the work. You have muscle memory from your previous training. That is a *major,* major advantage. Do not underestimate that. So yes, I think you've got something real." Camila stepped closer, lowering her voice to make sure they were having a private conversation. "But you dance like you're afraid to take up space. Like you're hoping no one notices you or how much you care."

Gia's chest tightened, but she kept herself composed. She was grateful for the honesty. It was something she could work with.

"Salsa isn't shy. It doesn't whisper. It shouts. It sings. It grooves."

Gia's throat went dry. She wanted to argue that she wasn't shy, that she was trying, but she knew Camila was right.

"You've got this heat underneath everything you do, but you keep it on a low simmer. That thing people want to watch? You're hiding it. I don't need you to be perfect. I need you to be seen. Own it. I saw it that night at Casa Sevilla, and I see it here sometimes. Embrace it. Let everyone see how much you love dance."

Gia's breath caught. She nodded slowly.

"Listen. As the company director, I want to see you *unleash.* You've got work to do. As your friend?" She smiled. "Same thing. I can't wait to see you light the place on fire. You have enough technique and style. Once you let go, you'll be unstoppable. That's the part I'm waiting for."

She pulled Gia into a quick, fierce hug. "I've got practice. Call me later if you want to talk."

Gia stood still, the echo of Camila's words hanging in the air like the last note of a song that hadn't quite resolved.

Unleash.

She might not have the technique of the other dancers who had been training nonstop or the advantages of growing up with Latin music, but she had something they didn't–the ache of regret, and the rare, incredible chance to try again.

She didn't feel ready, but she was done waiting to be.

Chapter Eight

Gia was awake before her alarm clock buzzed. Her body was still, but her mind sprinted through choreography, interview questions, and how long she could keep her composure with a millionaire client before panic set in about tomorrow's audition. Double life. That's what this was. Today, both parts demanded center stage.

By 8:00 a.m., she was in Carlsbad, standing outside a sleek glass building emblazoned with the name Maddox Biotech. The lobby was cool and modern, all pale wood and steel with succulents arranged on clean white shelves. The receptionist waved her through with a practiced smile, and moments later she was ushered into a glass-walled conference room on the twelfth floor.

Through the glass, Gia spotted Eli weaving his way down the hall, and for a second she lost track of her thoughts. Even though she'd done her homework and seen plenty of press photos of him, they hadn't quite captured him. He walked tall, shoulders back, stride unhurried, with confidence that didn't need announcing. He wore tailored pants and a button-down shirt, his shoes polished enough to catch the overhead lights.

He nodded at people as he passed, offering a smile here, a greeting there. A receptionist straightened in her chair. Even the maintenance guy leaning on a mop stood taller when Eli tossed him a casual, "Hey, man."

Watching him approach, Gia knew he could walk into a room full of strangers and leave everyone thinking they'd just met their favorite person.

Her stomach flipped when his eyes lifted, catching hers through the glass. He smiled like he'd already decided she was in on whatever unspoken joke he was carrying with him.

"Gia, right?" he said, extending his hand to her as he walked through the door. "Eli Maddox. Thanks for coming in. You want coffee? Water? Green juice?"

"No, thank you," she said, sliding into the seat across from him and opening her notebook. "This won't take long today. Mostly, I'd like to learn what your goals are with this book and what you'd like to cover. After, I'll shape an arc and figure out what questions I need to ask to best tell your story."

He smiled and tilted his head. "I've never met a ghostwriter," he said. "What's your story? How did you get into this work?"

Gia blinked, surprised by the question.

He laughed softly. "Come on. If you're going to tell my story, I should at least know who's doing the telling. Fair, right?"

She managed a small laugh. "Most clients don't really ask."

"Well, I'm not most clients," he said, settling back. "If I know a little about you, I'll feel less ridiculous going on and on about myself. I do much better with conversations, you know? So, tell me. Why ghostwriting?"

She hesitated, then said, "Honestly, it goes back to dance."

His brows lifted. "Really? Go on."

"I wanted to be a dancer for as long as I can remember. It felt like this bright, glamorous dream, but the older I got, the more I understood the reality of auditions and rejection. It felt like putting my heart and body on the line again and again, with no safety net." She paused, choosing her words carefully. "I reached a point where I couldn't handle the idea of constantly proving my worth on a stage."

"So you traded one kind of storytelling for another."

"Exactly," she replied. "Ghostwriting lets me be creative without being the one exposed. My clients bring the vulnerability, and I help shape it. I'm still telling stories, just from behind the scenes."

"Do you ever miss being out front?" he asked. "Not as a dancer necessarily, but as the one telling your own story."

The question hit closer than she expected. "Lately, more than I want to admit. I think I chose safety for a long time. I'm starting to realize that came with a cost too."

Eli's smile softened. "I get that. Thank you for being real with me." He squared his shoulders almost like he was bracing himself. "Okay, that level of honesty deserves full access. I owe you now. Ask me anything. I'm an open book."

For the next hour and a half, Eli talked her through his childhood in Carlsbad, his decision to leave Stanford before finishing his PhD, and the spark that led him to launch Maddox Biotech in his parents' garage. He had a rare ability to make even the dry, technical parts sound compelling.

But what struck her more than anything was the way he kept turning the interview into a conversation.

"How do you like living in San Diego so far?"

"Do you think you'll stay?"

"Where do you take dance lessons as an adult? My wife wants to take salsa classes, but I'm dragging my feet, literally."

Each question was delivered lightly but with genuine interest. She found herself smiling more than usual and sharing more than she meant to. In-person meetings were so much more fulfilling than Zoom. By the time they wrapped, she had pages of notes and nearly an hour of recorded audio to work with. Plus, she felt like they were old friends.

"Thanks for making this easy," he said, walking her out. "I'm usually nervous about blabbing about myself."

"Thanks for making it fun," she replied before she could stop herself.

She'd met a dozen executives with polished smiles and well-rehearsed pitches, but Eli spoke to her like a regular person. Like maybe he wasn't only trying to be known but trying to know her too. She wasn't used to that.

She wondered what it would be like to stay in this world during the day. To talk through stories and then to lose herself at night, where stories were told through bodies and movement. For the first time in years, she wasn't invisible in either place.

What a difference it made to get out of the house.

At home that evening, she changed into black leggings and a purple Ritmo Latino cropped tank, let her hair down, and shoved her bedroom furniture against the wall. The mirrored closet doors turned her room into a makeshift studio. Gia planned to drill the audition choreography on repeat until she crashed from exhaustion, as she'd done every day this week.

She connected her speaker, queued up her salsa playlist, and let the slowest song fill the air. She started with a few warm-up shines. "Two, three. Six, seven," she counted to herself, practicing the mambo timing into her bones.

She took it easy at first, letting her weight sink into her hips, rolling her shoulders through each movement. Then she switched to mid-tempo, her breath quickening, her bare feet skimming the wood floor.

Finally, she put on her ballroom heels and repeated the movements over and over until it became muscle memory, now with the modified posture. The long, graceful lines of her early training surfaced again, layered with the bent knees and contrabody motion she had learned more recently. She could see how, in time, it might all blend together into a style that was uniquely hers.

When Nikki's voice cut through her thoughts, Gia startled. No one had seen her like this in a long time. Focused. In pursuit. *Wanting* something.

"Damn, cuz," Nikki said from the doorway, arms crossed, a smile on her face. "You rehearsing for a world championship in here or what?"

Gia laughed, catching her breath. "You scared me."

Nikki strolled in and leaned against the wall. "You're looking good. Cleaner than yesterday but still holding back on the turns. Commit to it."

Gia nodded, wiping sweat from her forehead with the back of her hand. "I have the choreo down, and I think the technique looks good finally. I was about to work on the performance aspect."

"I'll dance it with you," Nikki said, walking toward the mirror to stand at Gia's side.

They went through it together, Nikki calling out counts and clapping her hands to the beat. At the end of the song, she gave Gia's shoulder a playful nudge. "Feels like our high school dance team days, yeah?"

"Definitely. It's kinda nice to have a reason to dance at this age. Seems like people don't have time for passions when they start *careers*."

"I'm not sure that's true. I still have dance in my life. The Ritmo team does too, and they all have day jobs..."

"Are you not so subtly insinuating it's just me, then?"

"Nope. I'm saying, you can find ways to do what you love when you let yourself."

"I'm doing it now, aren't I?" Gia said in defense. Tomorrow wasn't just an audition. It was her shot at proving she could still burn with passion, that she hadn't traded all her fire for stability.

"Hell yeah, you are. Let's run it one more time, full out."

After a few more rounds, they collapsed on the floor, both sweaty and grinning, their water bottles clinking together in a lazy toast. "I'm going to shower off, and then I'll make dinner." Nikki eyed Gia. "Something tells me you've been working and dancing all day and haven't eaten."

"Coffee counts." Gia let her head fall back against the mirror for a rest.

Nikki popped her head into Gia's bedroom just as Gia was toweling off from a shower and winding down for the night.

"Put on some real clothes," Nikki said, her tone leaving no room for argument. "We're going out."

Gia blinked. "Out? I still need to—"

"You need to let loose. You've been in here killing yourself for the last five days, and it's showing. You've got the technique down, but no one wants to watch a robot audition for pro-am. You need a little, what does Camila call it? *Sabor.*"

Gia stared at her cousin unconvinced, but Nikki was unfazed. "We're going to Belly Up. B-Side Players are there tonight. Local band and soooooo good. It won't be a late night, promise. You'll be in bed before midnight. They play salsa, cumbia, samba, reggae. You'll thank me later."

An hour later, they were pulling up to Belly Up Tavern, a small, local music venue located right in the middle of Solana Beach's Cedros design district. It was nearly 10 p.m., so the furniture and art shops were closed for the night, but Gia peeked in every window as they walked by. San Diego had so many pockets to discover.

The Belly Up entrance transported Gia and Nikki from a quiet coastal street to a full-blown surf-town fiesta. The air was cool, salty, and tinged with the smell of spilled beer. Overhead, a massive, open-mouthed paper mache shark hung over the crowd, grinning like it had seen decades of wild nights.

Along the back wall, concert posters climbed to the ceiling, proof that this little room had hosted countless musical giants over the years. Tonight, six hundred bodies packed the house.

The B-Side Players stretched across the small stage, congas thumping, brass gleaming, guitars riffing, and keys dancing beneath quick fingers. Their frontman grinned, lowered his trumpet, and let his voice drive a brassy cumbia that shook the walls and pulled the crowd under his spell.

The audience was filled with longtime B-Side Players fans, locals who knew Belly Up like a second home, and out-of-towners who stumbled in by chance and stayed for the magic.

On the dance floor, couples moved with a loose, natural rhythm. Some had perfect Cuban motion, others swayed with two left feet, but no one seemed to care. Everyone was grooving, laughing, or singing along.

Before Gia could protest, Nikki pulled her into the center of the floor. "Forget the studio salsa. Just feel it!"

When the tempo picked up again, a stranger tapped Nikki on the shoulder and asked for a dance.

Gia barely had time to catch her breath before another man leaned in her direction, his smile easy, his hand outstretched.

"Salsa?"

"Always." She took his hand.

Gia recognized the song. It was a cover of "Todo Tiene Su Final" by Hector Lavoe. This version swerved in and out of salsa to reggae, to cumbia and back again, forcing Gia and her partner to freestyle along with the changes. It was easy to do since she was becoming good at following. More importantly, it was *wildly fun*.

As the band transitioned into an original salsa track "Michaela," her partner drew her into closed position. When the brass section burst back in, the trombone and saxophone chased each other through the groove, and her partner opened the space for Gia to shine. Her feet skimmed the floor in the cascade of shines she'd drilled for the audition all week, now spilling effortlessly into the social dance.

On that sticky hardwood, with a stranger who could really lead and a live band pouring fire into the night, she felt powerful. She was in the music. Sebastián was right. It was easy to get hooked on salsa.

Her smile faded into a thought: Sebastián. The audition. Tomorrow. In front of him. In front of all of them. Oh, hell. She needed to get home and sleep.

She spotted Nikki in the crowd and wove her way through the dancers. "So yummy, right?" Nikki beamed as Gia reached her.

"So, so, so yummy," Gia said, catching her breath. "But I've gotta call it. You good to head out?"

Nikki checked her phone. "Almost midnight." She looked up

with a grin that said, told you so. "Guess that's what happens when you stop dancing for the mirror. Time disappears."

Gia smiled her agreement. "Let's hope I can do the same tomorrow." She slipped an arm around Nikki's shoulder. "Come on. Let's get out of here before I talk myself into one more song."

They moved through the crowd together, hearts light, cheeks flushed, and ready for what came next.

Chapter Nine

When Sebastián stepped into his favorite cafe, he was greeted by the sharp hiss of steamed milk mingled with the rich, familiar scent of espresso and cinnamon. Gloria was behind the counter, already reaching for the blender. "You're early today."

"I figured I'd beat the audition crowd."

Not wanting to hold up the line, he moved aside and drifted toward the window. He watched the world moving on outside, cars gliding past, palms dancing in the breeze, as people rushed off to wherever they were going. Behind him, the bell over the door chimed, announcing a new customer.

He didn't turn around at first. Just heard the soft shuffle of sandals on tile and the quiet sound of a woman with an East Coast accent reading the menu under her breath.

Then he smelled her. Patchouli with a hint of cotton candy. Warm and delicious.

He glanced over his shoulder and saw her. Gia's hair was loose today, velvety dark waves catching the morning light. She wore black leggings and a matching crop top. Nothing fancy, but she carried herself with her usual elegance.

She hadn't seen him yet.

For a second, he just watched her. He knew he shouldn't. Camila would raise an eyebrow. Andrés would crack a joke. Yet here he was, clocking every detail from the slight bounce in her step to the way she bit her lip as she considered her options.

Her gaze lifted to find his.

"Gia," he said, surprised at the softness in his voice. He cleared his throat.

"Hi, Sebastián." She stepped closer, nodding toward the chalkboard menu. "Is it truly the best cafecito in town?"

"Well. Do you want a caffeine boost or something to cool off?"

She hesitated long enough for him to notice her eyes flicker briefly and land on his mouth. His pulse ticked up in response. Noticing was one thing. *Looking* was another.

She blinked, seeming to shake herself out of whatever moment had just passed. "Yes. I need something to cool off. Cool. Definitely. Yeah."

"Then go for the passion fruit smoothie. Best in town."

Behind the bar, Gloria smiled. She'd seen this dance before. "Coming right up, honey," she said to Gia. "I've got your usual here, Sebastián," she said, handing him his smoothie.

He nodded. "Thanks, Gloria."

"Regular customer?" Gia asked.

"Probably the most frequent customer." He sipped his drink and watched her over the rim. "You're heading in for the audition?"

"Yeah." She tugged a strand of hair behind her ear. "Needed a walk to clear my head. And caffeine. Or sugar, I guess."

Her voice had a musical quality. She talked with her hands, as if they danced right along with her words.

"How are you feeling about it?" he asked.

She let out a short, self-deprecating laugh. "I feel good about the shines. The last rehearsal helped. I've been practicing the footwork every day since we learned it. For the partner work... I'm not exactly nervous. More like...um, well, terrified."

That surprised him. She'd been keeping up in practice.

"I've danced on big stages. Used to pick up choreo no problem, but I never had to rely on a partner. I know how to trust myself. Letting someone else lead is... a whole different thing."

"I think you'll do fine."

She gave him a skeptical look. "Easy for you to say. You already know what you're doing."

He tilted his head. "So do you."

She blinked.

"You understand your body. That's half the battle."

The blender roared to life, then stopped. Gloria handed her the smoothie.

"Thank you," she said, although it wasn't clear if she was talking to the barista or Sebastián.

Gia's phone lit up on the counter, breaking what may have turned into an awkward silence. Sebastián glimpsed the background wallpaper on the phone and tried to return the conversation to the lightheartedness it had started with.

"Is that... *Dirty Dancing*?"

"Motivational poster of my life."

He laughed. "Wait. Is that where the watermelon line comes from?"

She gasped, hand flying to her chest. "You've never seen *Dirty Dancing*?"

"I've caught parts of it. Not the whole thing."

Her eyes narrowed in disbelief. "It's got everything. Passion. Rebellion. Choreography in a lake."

He held up both hands. "Guess I have homework tonight."

"You're tall, broody, and dance like a dream... You're basically three smirks away from being Johnny Castle."

"I don't know if that's a compliment or a warning."

"You'll have to watch it and find out."

He couldn't remember the last time chatting with a woman had been this natural. Most women viewed him as a prize, a photo opportunity, or a fantasy. He used to love it, but lately, all it did was remind him how much he wanted someone who actually saw him. Gia looked at him like a person with flaws, questions, and a terrible track record of movie-watching. It was the most human conversation he'd had in forever. He didn't want it to end.

"You're serious about this, aren't you?" he asked.

"About *Dirty Dancing*? Dead serious."

He laughed. "I meant the pro-am. Some people are after the experience, the costume, the applause. A bucket list item. I don't think that's you. I think you want to win."

"You could say that."

"Good, because it's going to be intense. Training is like a part-time job. Every performance builds your rep, or chips away at it."

"Wow, could you make it sound more fun?"

"Trust me, that was the fun version. My sister's on the warpath this season. No room for sugarcoating." They were quiet for a bit and sipped their smoothies.

"You ever had passion fruit off the vine?" he asked.

She shook her head. "Nope."

He lifted his smoothie. "If you think this is good, you'd lose your mind over the real thing. Nothing compares."

"You talking fruit or something else?"

"Fruit." He let the moment stretch. "For now."

She laughed, and he leaned back just a little, letting his voice drop. "I grew up with a vine in the backyard. In Colombia, we pick them fresh. Crack them open. Eat them with a spoon. Sweet and messy as hell. Ten times more flavor than this."

She lifted her smoothie. "And here I thought this was the best in town."

"It is," he said. "But there's nothing like the real thing."

"Now I'm curious. Where can I get fresh passion fruit around here?"

"Well, you still need to try a few basic ones first. Can't appreciate the good stuff without a few mediocre smoothies."

"Seriously?" She stared him in the eyes and shook her head like she didn't know what he was talking about. Sebastián knew he was talking in silly metaphors and probably sounded ridiculous, but he was enjoying himself. He rarely lingered this long in small talk, but it was easy with her.

"I should get to the studio. See you at the audition. I'm rooting for you."

"Oh, right. The audition. Yep. See you then." Her shoulders stiffened, and the calm in her eyes snapped to alert.

Sebastián placed a gentle hand on her shoulder, then added, "Hey, don't stress. I've seen you in class. You've got this."

She nodded, but her posture remained tense.

"Listen, when Camila throws in the improv at the end, don't overthink it."

Her eyes widened. "Improv?"

"Last five minutes. She'll pair people up, give you a concept or a mood, and see what you do with it."

"I didn't realize..." she said, then exhaled hard through her nose. "Okay. Shit."

He chuckled. "I thought you liked performing."

"I do," she blurted. "When I have choreography. A map. A plan. Improv is like showing up for an exam without knowing the subject. I thought this whole thing was like *Dancing with the Stars*. You rehearse a number and then perform it."

"It is like that, but at its heart, salsa is a social dance." He studied her for a beat. "You've been out to the clubs, right? It's like that. Camila wants to see the lead and follow. You know, timing, musicality, creativity, and connection to the music. That says a lot about the chemistry between partners, even if they are dancing a routine."

She didn't respond.

"Listen. Just... don't try to get it right. There is no right. There's just connection. Tune in to the music and your partner. Let it surprise you."

"You've seen me dance. I overthink. I over-prepare. That's where I get my confidence. I mean, I've literally been practicing the audition shines for five days straight. I don't do surprises."

"Well, maybe today's a good day to start."

"I'll try. Thanks for the heads-up." She smiled, and this time it reached all the way to her eyes.

He nodded, resisting the urge to say anything else. Instead, he gave her one last smile and said, "You've got this."

Then he turned and stepped into the sunlight, knowing damn well he'd do whatever he could to help her get that spot.

The mirrored walls of Ritmo Latino amplified the nerves and excitement of twenty-six bodies shuffling around in anticipation for the audition to begin. Afternoon sun poured through the tall windows, casting stripes of gold across the scuffed wood floor. Music played low in the background, only loud enough to keep everyone's feet moving as they waited.

Camila stood at the front of the room in black dance joggers and a fitted Ritmo Latino tee knotted at her back. Her positive energy filled the room. She greeted each dancer as they entered. "Thanks for being here," she said again and again, each time a little different. A touch to the shoulder. A pointed nod. She wanted them relaxed but ready. Encouraged, not coddled.

"Welcome, dancers!" she called, clapping her hands once to get everyone's attention. "I know auditions can be nerve-wracking, but I want you to remember this is about connection and chemistry. Performance, not perfection. I want your fire. We will do everything possible to ensure you have the best audition experience possible. Let's warm up first."

Gia joined the others spread out across the studio floor, glancing briefly at the crowd around her. Five leads had shown up, all familiar faces from the training team. She only recognized a couple of the fourteen other followers. They represented a full spectrum from technical, elegant, showy, to shy. One girl in purple leggings and a crisscross sports bra was already marking through a shine pattern on her own, her face tense with focus. Another, tall and cool in a black unitard, took her space directly in front of the mirror, watching the room in its reflection with barely disguised confidence. Vanessa was in the center, ready to go, with her slick bun, dark red lipstick and studded heels.

"Alright dancers. Luna will lead you through the shines. They are short and spicy. Just four sets of eight-counts. That means you'll pick it up fast so we can spend the time making it *explode.* We want to know what you can do once the choreo is on autopilot."

Luna glided forward, barefoot and radiant as usual. Where Camila sparked, Luna shimmered like moonlight on water. Her strawberry blonde hair was woven into a loose braid that swayed down to her tailbone. Gold hoops flashed at her ears, catching the light each time she spun, like stars orbiting her.

"Five, six, seven, eight," she called. The dancers followed under Luna's fluid lead, a striking contrast to Camila's sharp, fire-cracker style.

The shines were simple by design, leaving plenty of room for each dancer to add their own flair and personality.

They performed the choreography in four staggered lines—five in a row, each line rotating to the back after each pass. Pros were sprinkled throughout the room. Amber watched from the front, sizzling and loud, throwing out cheers and encouragement with every step. Andrés called out corrections and improvements, sometimes dictating the choreography and emphasizing beats in the music. Sebastián couldn't stay still, marking the footwork on the side and grinning when the dancers matched his energy.

Each round built more pressure. One follower added a body roll that wasn't in the choreo, but it worked. Camila raised an eyebrow and scribbled a note. Another threw in a hair whip and caught Amber's delighted laugh.

"Okay, red tank top! I see you!" Amber called out.

"Control your footwork," Daniel said, calm but firm, to one lead. "Watch your spacing. You got this."

Sebastián didn't say much, yet Gia felt his attention, steady as a spotlight, making her feel both seen and supported. The pros weren't there to intimidate. They were there to lift everyone higher, to push each dancer toward the best version of themselves.

From the moment the shine work began, Gia didn't hold back. As the choreography repeated through each rotation, her body slipped into that sacred rhythm dancers crave: when muscle memory takes over, and the mind lets go. After five days of drilling on repeat, she could play inside the movement. She stretched the beat, added an accent inside the pause, and embellished her performance with flavor, just like she had when she danced to B-Side Players the night before.

Somewhere in that flow, she felt a spark that hadn't touched her in years. Gia closed her eyes for a breath. She imagined her heart reaching out to her soul, the two uniting after years apart. Of course, they would dance.

She opened her eyes and ran the sequence again, only this time, she *burned* through it. All-consuming fire.

On the next turn, she was front and center. Sebastián positioned himself to stand directly in front of her, arms loose at his sides now, eyes locked on hers.

He smiled. Raised his brows in quiet invitation. Then he nodded subtly as if to say *show me who you are.*

That was all it took.

The music began. She *unleashed.*

Camila's voice rang out: "There it is! Gia, give me more! I want all your magic now!"

Gia danced like a fuse had been lit. Instead of dancing the choreography, she devoured it, doused it in gasoline, and reconstructed it from the ashes like a phoenix. Her smile was untamed and radiant, the look of a woman who had finally stopped asking for permission.

Sebastián's eyes never left hers. He could see the fire breaking loose inside her. Every step said *this is what it feels like to be alive.* She was daring him to feel it too.

When her head whip snapped the music to a close, something shifted in him too. Pride, yes, but also a jolt of recognition. She wasn't just keeping up anymore. She was calling him into the fire with her.

A whistle came from Amber, loud and gleeful. Andrés leaned toward Camila, saying something Gia couldn't hear. Camila didn't respond right away. Her gaze was locked on Gia with the unflinching attention of someone watching a breakthrough. Sebastián simply smiled, as if knowing exactly what this moment meant to her.

Camila scribbled a note, then looked up and clapped. "That's how it's done."

Gia walked to the back row, heart pounding, skin flushed and tingling.

If this was as far as she got in the audition, it would be enough. She proved to herself that she was still inside her body. Her dancer self wasn't gone. She had been waiting. Now she was free.

Camila turned the music down with a swipe on her phone and let the room breathe. Most of the dancers were glistening now, chests rising and falling, still half-holding onto the rush of performance.

"All right," Camila said. "We're going to take five. Grab water, towel off, stay loose. We'll call out the top three for callbacks in a few minutes."

Gia moved off the dance floor, pulse still thumping in her ears. She had no idea how it had looked from the outside, but from the inside, it had felt *right*. She'd given all of herself with no filter. She'd find out if that was enough within the next few minutes.

At the front of the room, the six judges huddled close.

"Let's start with the leads, since the top three were clear," Camila said.

Daniel responded, "Adam, Johnny, Hector. Top three."

"Anyone disagree?" Camila asked. Everyone shook their heads. "Okay, that is settled. What about followers?"

Amber spoke first. "Gia's a yes for me. That performance had the wow factor. She needs to polish her technique, but that happens in rehearsals. She's already got the stuff that can't be taught. Top choice."

"Agreed," Andrés said. "All the stage presence. Let's see how the partnering goes."

Sebastián kept his eyes on Gia as he chimed in. "She's classically trained. That's a major advantage. She can probably handle the pressure of what we're doing this summer. With under a year of salsa training, she'd land in the beginner category, which, strategically, might be a smart move for the studio."

Camila gave her brother an appreciative smile, pleased that he was invested in the audition and offering sound advice. She shifted her clipboard. "Okay. Now, what about the other two?"

"Vanessa," Amber said. "She's sharp. A little...aggressive, but on the bright side, she's all fire. Plus, she's used to dancing in front of an audience from her time with Mambo Sol."

"She wants the spot," Sebastián said. "She shows up fully committed at every step. Obviously talented, knows salsa, and lives for competition. She'd fit into the advanced category, so we'd be up against all strong dancers and pros."

"All true. Vanessa is in." Camila asked. "Third?"

Andrés flipped through his notes. "I'd say Maritza. Solid fundamentals. Her shines were smart, not flashy, and her technique was clean."

"She blends too much," Amber said.

"We can pull more from her," Camila replied. "I've seen her improve faster than anyone else on the team this year. She's consistent. Teachable. Great attitude."

Sebastián shrugged. "She'd be safe."

Camila smirked. "Sometimes that's all you need with the right partner."

"All right, I'm good with those three," Amber said.

"Luna? Daniel? This sound right to you?" Camila asked.

Luna nodded, and Daniel gave the thumbs up. "Let's see how they partner." Sebastián added.

Camila turned back to the room, the energy shifting as she stepped forward again. The dancers quieted, water bottles paused mid-sip, eyes tracking her.

"Thank you all for bringing your energy today," she said.

"This wasn't an easy decision. Honestly, I wish we could take everyone who wants to compete in pro-am because you've all got what it takes. I hope to see all of you back on this floor, whether at socials or in class. Hopefully next year, we'll be able to register as many dancers as we want. But for now, we've got to choose a top three to move forward." Camila looked down at her clipboard and then back up at the group. "Our top three leads are Adam, Johnny, and Hector."

"And our follows..."

A pause.

Fifteen held breaths.

"Vanessa."

Vanessa stepped forward the instant her name was called, chin lifted in triumph, shoulders sharp with confidence, her smile making clear she fully expected this outcome.

"Mari."

The girl from the training team blinked, surprised. Her hands flew to her mouth as she stepped forward.

"And Gia."

Gia barely heard her own name. For a moment, her body didn't move. Then her feet carried her forward, heart pounding harder than it had on the floor. Maritza was still blinking in surprise, her hands clasped tight in front of her chest. She gave Gia a soft, nervous smile. Vanessa didn't smile. She didn't look left or right. Her eyes stayed on Camila, her spine stretched long and high like she was balancing a crown. She was the only one who hadn't broken a sweat. Her hair was still perfect.

Andrés addressed the leads, giving them a pep talk that faded into background noise.

Camila's heels clicked against the floor as she approached the trio of followers. She looked at them one by one. "Congratulations. The three of you stood out for different reasons. Technique. Precision. Performance. Now I want to see how you partner. Grab lunch. Let's start again at 1 p.m."

Gia stepped out into the noon sunlight, grateful for the break between rounds. She knew it was best to grab a quick bite, but her stomach wasn't ready for anything heavy. She ducked into a juice spot a block down and ordered a small acai bowl and a sparkling water. She sat outside on a bench and texted Nikki.

Made it through!!!!

Her phone rang immediately. Gia laughed and answered.

Nikki's face filled the screen, eyes wide and excited. "Hell yeah, you made it through! *Tell me everything.*"

Gia pushed her sunglasses up onto her head. "I want it so bad I can taste it."

Nikki grinned. "You're glowing. That dance high is real."

"It's *so good* to dance again. Even with the pressure. Especially with it."

"Then lean into that. Tap into all those years of training. You've got something the other two don't."

"Thanks. But Vanessa and Maritza are strong. They're pure salseras. This scene is second nature to them. For me, it's all still new."

"But you've got crossover power. Your lines, your musicality, your storytelling. That sets you apart. Turn up the stage presence. That is your lane today."

"Good advice." Gia looked down at her melting acai bowl. "I ran into Sebastián earlier. He said there's an improv section of the audition."

"Makes sense."

"I'm low-key freaking out about that. I practiced the shines for days to get confident. Now I'm going to make something up on the fly? If I had known that was coming, I would have made something up five days ago and made it fit whatever music they picked!"

"That's not how social dancing works, babe. They want to see the lead and follow, and creativity. Besides, you had no problem freestyling last night to B-side."

"Yeah, but this is an *audition*. It's supposed to look polished. Last night was just, I don't know, *going* with it."

"Nope. It's supposed to have flavor. Seriously. You'll get all the polish once you get the spot and start training. Today you go with stage presence."

"Okay. That's actually really helpful."

"Which pro is competing?" Nikki's voice was tinged with gossip-like curiosity.

"Andrés is dancing in the audition, so probably him."

"Oh, you lucky thing," Nikki teased, before getting back to business. "Okay, Andrés is all about energy. Big charisma. If you're dancing with him, you've got to match that or you'll fade into the background. Think bold."

"Good call. I'll do that." Gia nodded in agreement.

"Good luck. Call me when it's over. Now go get it!" She blew Gia a kiss and ended the call.

Gia walked back to the studio, head high and shoulders back. She'd proved she was still a dancer. Now she had to prove she could dance without the safety net of choreography.

Back at the studio, the crew was warming up for round two. Amber and Andrés stood at the front, flanked by Camila and Sebastián. Daniel and Luna sat on the side, observing. Amber stepped forward, clapped once, and threw Camila a teasing grin as she mimicked her signature instructor voice. "Partner work is next. The choreography is simple. Just ten eight-counts. Clean, sharp, easy to follow. Perform like the floor belongs to you."

Andrés chimed in. "After those ten eight-counts, you'll have four eight-counts to improvise. That's where we'll see how you connect with the music and your partner."

Gia's stomach dipped hard.

Even with Sebastián's heads-up, the word improvise landed like a splash of cold water. If he hadn't warned her, she might've bolted straight out the door. Thankfully she'd had just enough time to wrap her mind around it and tell herself she wouldn't die.

Gia took a deep breath. Her heart still raced, but her feet stayed planted.

When she looked up, Sebastián was watching her. He gave her a deep nod and a quiet smile. She nodded back. Gia wasn't quite calm, but she was ready enough.

Camila paired the finalists together to learn and practice the choreography. Johnny, a wiry lead with endless energy and a puffed ponytail of curls, grinned at Gia and offered a fist bump as their partnership began. "Hey! I've been dying to be in Camila's orbit all year," he said. "This is going to be so good."

"I get that. Let's show them what we've got." To her surprise, she eased into dancing with Johnny in no time. The choreography clicked, and within twenty minutes, they were polished enough to add musicality and style.

Finally, it was time to perform.

Camila would be competing in the pro-am but she sat front and center as the main judge for the audition. One by one, each finalist lead danced with Amber, while the rest of the group watched and clapped along. Johnny brought the house down. His style was crisp yet playful, full of charisma. His facial expressions made Amber laugh mid-spin, and he hit every beat like he'd been dancing with her for years.

Then came the followers. Each would dance with Andrés, while the others sat with the judges.

Maritza stepped up first. She drew in a shaky breath before the music started, and though her feet traced each bit of the choreography with precision, the slight catch before each spin betrayed her nerves. Still, when she extended her arms, the elegance of her lines earned a murmur of appreciation from Camila.

Vanessa took her place with the confidence that said she'd done this a hundred times before. The first beat hit, and her body snapped into motion. She spun without a wobble, her facial expressions daring anyone to doubt her. The ease in her posture made it seem she could've pulled off the routine in stilettos on a tightrope.

Lastly, it was Gia's turn.

She stepped onto the studio floor, spine tall, one leg grounded, the other extended with the elegance of a ballerina in heels. Andrés took her hands and gave her a quick wink as the music began.

Gia moved with more honesty than polish. Her passion spoke louder than her mistakes, every step was charged with feeling, even the uneven ones.

By the time the song swelled, Gia's presence filled the room, unapologetic and impossible to ignore. Then came the break in the routine. The last choreographed step. The end of the map. She stood on the edge, knowing the next move had to be hers alone.

She froze, panic flickering like a strobe under her skin. The silence between notes stretched, cruel and endless. Four eight-counts felt like an eternity she didn't know how to fill.

Her mind went blank. A void. Nothing. Then the old voice cut in, sharp and merciless: *You're not a dancer. They're about to see it. This is why you quit. This is why you ran.*

Her lungs seized, sweat beading cold at the back of her neck, until Andrés reached for her, steady and assured.

Sebastián's words echoed in her mind. She let go of the idea of getting it right. Instead she let herself feel the lead and trust the timing. She focused on the beat of the clave and suddenly, her instincts kicked in like a second pulse.

She was dancing, and *she* didn't have to make up steps as she went. They made it up together.

By the time the music faded, she was breathless, flushed, and electric.

The performance wasn't perfect, but it was enough. She'd stepped into the spotlight, and this time, she hadn't disappeared. Even if she didn't win the spot, she won against herself.

Camila led the pros into the corner of the studio to discuss the final decision.

"Let's get Johnny out of the way first," she said. "He's the clear leader."

"Unanimous," Amber nodded. "He's musical, fast on the uptake, confident without being cocky. Maybe a little too excited, but that totally works here."

Andrés added, "He reads his partner and adjusts. I didn't have to explain anything twice."

Sebastián gave a curt nod. "Agreed. I'd help train him over the next few months."

Camila smiled at him, appreciating another signal that her brother was on board. "Done. Now the real question. Gia or Vanessa?"

They all paused.

Amber crossed her arms. "Vanessa's technique is undeniable. All around, she's the strongest dancer we saw today. Every step is flawless, her body movement is gorgeous, and she sells it the whole way."

"She's also used to pressure," Andrés said. "She's performed tons and knows how to compete."

"Yeah... but Vanessa is a lot," Amber added. "She plays by her own rules, which is fine, unless you want someone who actually works with a team. But hey, it's a partnership, not a full team event, so maybe her shitty attitude won't matter as much."

"Take it easy. Vanessa's attitude comes from fear," Camila said quietly. "She's been here the longest. Every new dancer looks like a threat. If she stops fighting, she disappears. People think she's bitchy, but that's just her armor. Underneath, she's terrified."

Sebastián was silent, his eyes scanning the room, watching Gia laugh quietly with Johnny near the mirrors.

Camila noticed. "Say it."

He uncrossed his arms. "Gia has something that can't be taught."

"Stage presence," Amber said, knowing exactly what he meant.

"More than that," Andrés added. "She gives her partner room to breathe, but still brings the heat. I don't think she even sees her own potential yet."

"Can she handle the pressure? This is our one shot with a follower in pro-am this year," Amber asked. "Gia's new to salsa and partnering. Not to mention, she hasn't danced in years."

Sebastián responded first. "I think that's exactly why she can. She's not performing for applause. The other girls dance for Camila's approval. Gia dances like she is chasing something in herself. Watching her feels like we're intruding on a private moment."

"Okay, Mr. Poet." Amber raised an eyebrow at him. "Let's go over the advantages of each. Vanessa?"

"She's a killer," Andrés replied. "What we saw today is what we'll get on stage two months from now."

"And Gia?" Camila asked, adding notes on her clipboard already filled with scribbles.

"She's still unfolding. Which means she has somewhere to grow. Sky's the limit." Andrés paused. "So we're choosing between a known entity and an evolution."

Camila tapped the end of her pen against her clipboard. "Between a dancer we can count on to be fabulous and one who is unproven but might give us something unforgettable."

She pulled a packet out of her folder. "Let's try to think of this strategically. There are four student levels in the salsa division. Novice: under a year of training. Beginner: two years or less. Intermediate: up to three years. Advanced: anything over three years."

She glanced up. "Vanessa is advanced. Gia qualifies as a novice."

"Which means they're not even in the same category," Daniel said. "It's not about who's better, but who is more likely to win in their division?"

"The beginner level comes with less pressure," Luna added. "Considering Gia's previous training in other styles, she'd have a major advantage."

"Let's look at this another way," Amber said, turning to

Andrés. "Do you want to partner with a beginner or someone with experience?"

The advanced category was his default mode, and Vanessa could surely keep up.

Luna cut in. "Wait. Before you answer that. What are the limitations for each level?"

Camila scanned the rulebook. "Novice: Single, double or triple turns only. No extended spin sequences. One foot on the ground at all times. No splits. Essentially, that means no crazy tricks."

She flipped the page. "Advanced: All turn patterns allowed. Floorwork and tricks are permitted, but can't exceed fifty percent of the routine. No aerial stunts."

"So basically," Luna said, "complex spin patterns and tricks win the day in the advanced category."

"Definitely more fun," Andrés said, grinning.

"But in Novice, it's sabor and chemistry," Luna countered. "That might actually benefit us."

Amber added. "For the record, chemistry and musicality aren't easier than tricks. They're just harder to measure. We should think of each division as a different game." She shot a look at Camila. "Two contenders. Two totally different strengths. How will each one do against the competition in their category?"

Andrés nodded. "Exactly. Tricks? Vanessa will crush them. But so will every advanced couple. In novice, it's the intangibles—style, flavor, connection. That's where Gia's got the edge." He stood up. "Okay, I have an idea. If we want to know who can follow and perform when it counts, we should throw them a curveball to add pressure. Sebastián should get in there and dance with them as a tiebreaker."

Sebastián lifted a brow skeptically. "Oh, yeah?"

"Switching leads will push them harder. They'll have to think fast, follow, not rely on the connection they're used to with me. No one can fake that." Andrés's grin widened. "And let's be real, man. You have a way of shaking people up."

Camila laughed. "He's not wrong. You good with dancing a tiebreaker round, Sebas?"

He gave a nod. "If it helps make the right call, I'm in."

"I want to thank all three of you," she said, voice strong but warm. "You showed up, and today you each brought something real. Each of you deserves to be there, and if it weren't for this one pro, one student rule, you would be. Hopefully, next year we can all go together."

She glanced at Mari, who stood tall despite the flush in her cheeks.

"Mari," Camila said gently, "you've come so far, and we're so proud of you. We've narrowed the decision to Vanessa and Gia."

Vanessa looked surprised that she wasn't the clear winner. Gia was dumbfounded that she had made it to another round.

Camila opened her arms. Mari walked into the hug without hesitation and sunk into Camila.

"You're on the edge of a breakthrough," Camila whispered, just loud enough for the others to hear. "Keep going."

Mari nodded with her lips pressed hard together as the rest of the pro dancers applauded her. Then she quietly gathered her things and slipped out of the studio with grace.

As Mari stepped off the floor, Gia's chest tightened with a pang of empathy. She knew that sting that comes when you pour everything out and still don't land where you hoped.

Camila turned back to the group. "That leaves us with a tie," she said, looking between Vanessa and Gia. "Two dancers, both talented, both capable, and with very different strengths."

She set the clipboard down. "So we want to do one more run of the choreo and improv section. This time with Sebastián as your lead."

Vanessa lit up, eyes sparkling like she'd been waiting for this moment all day. Gia, however, felt her pulse slam against her ribs. She had danced with Sebastián before, but never like this. Not with every eye in the room locked on them and only them. Not with Camila scribbling notes. Definitely not with her heart trying to claw its way out of her chest.

Did this mean he might be dancing the pro's part? While the thought of spending hours of one-on-one time with him gave her all the feels, adding a student/teacher relationship to her growing desire sent a dozen red flags through her brain.

Please don't melt down, she told herself.

Vanessa went first, and Gia had a moment to mentally prepare. Or at least try to.

When the music kicked in, Vanessa hit everything so clean it seemed rehearsed for TV. She matched Sebastián's flawless technique and enhanced it with her femininity.

When they transitioned into improv, Vanessa amped up the flash. She tossed in triple spins and added styling that showed off her experience. Technically perfect.

When the music ended, she smiled, breathing hard but satisfied. Light applause followed. Andrés gave a soft nod. Camila scribbled a note. Sebastián simply stepped back and offered Vanessa a polite "lovely" before turning away.

Camila called out, "Gia, are you ready?"

Gia was gone, pacing in the lobby, fixing her hair, undoing her hair, fixing her hair again and trying to summon a self-pep talk that actually worked.

If you leave, you'll always wonder what would've happened if you'd stayed.

Her legs were heavy as stone. She'd braced herself for footwork and partnerwork, but the improvised lead-and-follow had already drained her. Now she had to face one more round, go head-to-head with Vanessa, who'd been sending death stares since day one, and dance with Sebastián, all while pretending she wasn't slowly unraveling every time she touched him.

She heard the music change, followed by a muffled cheer. Then Camila's voice was calling her.

You didn't get this far to sit backstage in your own life again.

Gia gave up on smoothing her hair and let it hang loose. She walked back into the main studio.

"Gia, you're up. You ready?" Camila asked.

Gia smiled and nodded. Autopilot.

All she heard was her heels clicking softly on the hardwood as she went to meet Sebastián. Her spine was tall and her breath slow. She carried the weight of every gaze in the room, especially his.

Sebastián extended his hand.

"You good?" he asked, voice low so only she could hear.

"I think so."

With a firm touch, he pulled her into the starting closed position. He looked her in the eyes, nodded along to an imaginary beat, and subtly rocked back and forth with her, establishing a connection.

The music started. It was the same song and choreography as with Andrés, but it felt different with Sebastián.

He gave her just enough space to be herself within it.

She made one tiny misstep in the second eight-count. She was half a beat behind, but she recovered quickly, catching up before most would notice. When she glanced up, Sebastián's mouth curved ever so slightly. Encouragement. Not judgment.

Then came the last counts of the choreo. She breathed through it and performed the steps that were on autopilot by this time. The improvised lead/follow section loomed closer.

That's when it happened.

The music faltered. One speaker popped. The other dimmed. The volume collapsed into an eerie hush.

Someone cursed and darted toward the speaker. Gia froze inside. A flash of memory seared through her. The cold sting of her last audition years ago, the judge's hand silencing the music mid-spin, her body floundering in silence until shame swallowed her whole.

Sebastián didn't stop.

The clave was inaudible through the speakers yet alive in his body. It was in the press of his hand, the shift of his weight, the cadence of their shared breath. His chest rumbled against hers: "Quick, quick, slow...quick, quick, slow." He vocalized the percussion like he did in class, leading her through the pattern. Then louder and more playful, "Doom doom dak. Ti-ka, ti-ka Ta!"

Her panic cracked, and she let out a nervous laugh. She let him carry her, let the rhythm pass through him into her. No over-thinking. No stopping. Just his voice as the drum, moving them through the dance.

Ironically, the speakers started working again on the last note of the song.

Their final pose was improvised but a natural extension of the choreography. Her thigh lifted high against his hip with one arm slung around his neck like she'd never let go. His hand splayed across the small of her back, holding her in a dip. Her head tilted backwards slightly, lips parted, eyes locked with his. It wasn't clear if they'd just finished a dance or foreplay. The heat between them blurred the line.

The room stayed quiet for a second too long.

Then Luna whispered, "Damn."

Amber grinned. "Well, I'm off to take a cold shower." Andrés laughed out loud and clapped.

Sebastián's fingers lingered on her before he pulled her up and stepped back.

"Looks like I was right," he said, and this time his voice wasn't unreadable at all. It was warm. Impressed. She sensed a bit of pride that they hadn't given up when the music did.

Gia's eyes stayed glued to Sebastián as she mouthed the words *thank you* to him.

Camila cleared her throat. "I think that settles it."

Andrés nodded, still smiling. "That was connection...and damn hot."

Amber chimed in, "That might have been the best chemistry I've ever seen, and there wasn't even any music."

Camila looked at Sebastián.

He didn't say a word. He gave just one small nod and a big smile.

Camila turned back to the clipboard and circled a name. "Gia."

Vanessa stood off to the side, arms crossed tightly over her chest. Her grin, the one she'd worn like a permanent fixture all morning, had vanished. She didn't say anything right away, but as Gia walked toward the bench to get her things, Vanessa shifted into her path.

"Impressive recovery. Of course, if the music hadn't cut, we might have actually seen how well you keep up."

Gia blinked. "Are you serious right now?"

Vanessa's razor-thin smile returned. "Glitch like that? Excellent diversion. But hey, points for powering through. Even if it wasn't exactly on time."

"You're insinuating that I *planned* that?"

Vanessa's gaze flicked to Camila, who was watching them.

"No," she murmured. "Of course you didn't, but we both know you can't keep up unless it's choreographed, and that little *mishap* was perfect timing."

Then she turned and walked away, heels snapping like punctuation on polished wood.

In all her worry about toxic teachers and trusting partners, Gia had forgotten about the other danger: dancers who'd do anything to protect their place.

If she wanted to stay in this game, she was going to have to toughen up, and fast.

Once the audition was over and everyone filed out, Camila slid up beside Sebastián, flashing him a perfect smile. "Hey, got a minute before you leave?"

"Cami..." Sebastián laughed and shook his head no.

She held up a hand. "You don't even know what I'm going to say."

"I can tell by your voice. You're up to something."

"Hear me out before you make excuses."

He sighed, rubbing the back of his neck and waiting for the pitch.

"That was quite a performance with Gia. What do you think about officially representing Ritmo Latino as co-director for a few months and competing in the pro-am?"

He didn't see that coming, and it must have shown on his face because his sister kept going.

"Before you start with the usual," she said, imitating Sebastián's deep voice. "I'll help train, but I won't compete. I'm a soccer star. Blah, blah, blah. Here's the thing, Sebas. It would be a taste of getting back in the ring again. Not soccer, I know, but competing. You miss it."

"Cami, I'm still trying to get my head on straight. I play with a bunch of guys who are as crazy as I am. Dancing with students? You don't want my baggage around beginners..."

"Look, it's not the same scale as your soccer career, but Gia isn't a beginner."

"I hear you. And yeah, she's got a lot of potential. I'm committed to helping you train her. But compete in it? I compete on the field, not the stage."

"We've been working together for almost two years. You train all my pro-level dancers. This could be really good for you."

"I already said I'd fill in for Andrés or Daniel for a one-off. This is totally different. It's developing a beginner for months."

Camila's eyes sparkled. "No. It's developing a beautiful, classi-cally trained contemporary dancer," she corrected. "She's picking up salsa fast. You've seen her. You felt it."

He had felt it, and in inconvenient places. Still, he shook his head. "Modern and Latin are not the same thing."

"They're not. But what is the same? Discipline. Body awareness. Musicality. Athleticism. Talent. Sabor. She's got *all* of that. All she needs is the right partner for salsa. From what I saw today..."

"I thought Andrés was going to be your temporary co-director and do the pro-am this year?"

"He said he'd do it if he's the only choice but it's tough with the fire season. He needs a break more than he's letting on."

"Daniel, then."

"Nope. He needs to focus 100% on me and our performance. He has big shoes to fill, and I need him on point, a straight and narrow point. Pointed at me. He can do it next year."

"Camila. Seriously?"

"You're the one I trust the *most*," Camila said, stepping closer, eyes locked on his. "You're the best we've got, Sebas—and you love a challenge. Daniel and Andrés can't make it happen this season, so you're literally it. Otherwise, we don't send any followers to the pro-am this season."

The idea of Gia fighting her demons, winning the spot, and then not being able to compete made him almost as sick as the thought of losing soccer forever.

"Gia's new to salsa, yes, but she's the one who could take this all the way in the less-than-a-year division. A classically trained dancer in a social dance competition."

Sebastián arched a brow and said nothing. She read the doubt in his silence and softened her voice a notch. "Please. I need *your help*, Sebas."

Sebastián exhaled, shaking his head, but Camila pressed on.

"Think about it. A contemporary dancer fine-tuning salsa every damn day. An athlete who happens to be the best social lead in SoCal and drilled technique harder than anyone for the last two years." She gave him a confident look. "That's not good. That's unbeatable."

Camila inhaled, modulating her tone to sound inspiring.

"Listen. What you two bring from your previous experience... it's fresh. Unexpected. They're used to seeing polished routines, but not the skill that comes from *years* of training. I've seen the chemistry when you dance together. Plus, you're Sebastián Solano. You could win on that alone."

Camila nudged him, her voice quieter and laced with vulnerability. "I'm competing, but let's be honest, it's always stronger when the pro is the lead, not the follower, following a student. You get it. How important winning is."

She didn't have to say it outright. Sebastián understood what it meant to her. Camila built her company from the ground up, and she had big plans for the next year.

Sebastián breathed slowly, stretching out his knee to ease the tightness that never went away. There was one thing Camila wasn't saying. Emilio Cruz would be at the L.A. pro-am. Her former partner. Her former everything. Sebastián remembered the fallout and Emilio's cruel accusation: You wouldn't have built any of this without me. Camila never forgave him, not for that or for setting up shop in her backyard. This year, every title mattered. Beating Emilio most of all.

Sebastián knew his sister well enough to recognize this pitch for what it was: strategy. Convincing him to compete was just one more way of leaving nothing to chance. He had to admit it was a good one.

"Help me do this, Sebas. I want the sweep. Every category we enter this year."

She held his gaze steady. "Gia is our best shot. She's got genuine talent, and with her background, she'll bring something different to the floor. An original style they won't see coming. All she needs is a killer teacher."

Then Camila played the card he couldn't ignore.

"Come on. You miss the rush. You do. Don't tell me you're not itching to compete. Inside the arena. Not on the sidelines. To win."

The words hit Sebastián like a gut punch. The ache lingered

from the injury, constantly reminding him he may never experience that thrill again.

Sebastián gave her the side-eye. "You know I am. You've also seen how I get when I'm training."

"A little obsessive," Camila replied without missing a beat. "Yeah. I'm counting on it."

He crossed his arms, leaning against the barre. "You sure you want to pair me with a beginner? I'm still working things out with my knee. That's not exactly the energy you like around your dancers. Social dancing and teaching are one thing, but competing..."

"She's not new to competing. Only to salsa. There's a difference." She gave him a pointed look. "Technically, you're new to Ritmo Latino, too. This would be your first competition without a team of guys backing you up. Competing as a pair is a whole different animal."

"Camila, I get it. I do. But I've barely gotten my head on straight since the injury, and I have a knee that might give out any day."

"The novice division means no stunts or tricks. Easy on the knees. I would never ask you to risk that."

He gave a small nod of acknowledgement, his jaw tight. He appreciated his sister looking out for him, but the facts still stung. The idea that the novice category might be better for his injury wasn't something he was ready to accept. He never preferred easy. He wanted to be *worthy*. He shook his head, refusing to tumble down that rabbit hole.

"I don't even know if I can lock in the way I used to. That's not really what I need a...partner to see." His voice softened on the word partner, then hardened again. "I also don't need the soccer world turning me into some pathetic 'where are they now' story."

"Sebas. Come on, you're not being fair to yourself."

"Fair? None of this is fair. I'm still mad. At the way it all ended. At this damn knee. At the fact that I didn't get to choose when it was over."

He dropped his gaze. "Rehearsals, classes, socials—that's easy, I love that part." His voice roughened as the heat crept in. "But training? That's where it hits. It's where the limits show up. Every drill reminds me of what I lost, what I can't push past anymore. It pisses me off every fucking time. Just talking about it..." he exhaled sharply through his nose. "I don't know if I can rein that in for—"

"A talented, beautiful woman who has something to prove, just like you?"

"Camila. You're missing the point." His tone was a warning.

"Sebas, I get it. You're a public figure, and you have a reputation to keep. But you're still a competitor. That part of you didn't just vanish, and you're allowed to do things you enjoy."

She reached up and tilted his chin towards her until their eyes met, letting him see the truth in hers.

"This isn't the arena you're used to. The lights are smaller. The stakes are different. Don't underestimate the social scene though. It'll challenge you in ways the field never did. Athleticism that's creative and sexy. If you give it a try, you might actually fall in love."

He didn't say a word, but the tight movement in his throat showed he was trying to choke something back.

She softened even more. "Why would the world judge you for dancing? Everyone knows who our parents are. We've been dancing since we're kids. Who would criticize you for helping your sister's company?"

"Have you ever read the shit they say about players online?"

Camila was undeterred. "I'm confident she can handle it, and I'm even more confident you can."

Sebastián tipped his head back. His eyes flicked toward the mirror, catching his reflection. He saw the smoldering fire in his face, begging to return in full force. Was he really about to do this?

"Come on. This helps both of us," she said, dragging out the words like a bribe.

When he didn't respond, Camila tilted her head with that familiar don't-make-me-beg look.

"Okay, fine. Pretty please?" She said, laying it on thick. "With a cherry on top? You get your win, I get mine."

Sebastián cracked a smile despite himself.

"Say yes already. Please."

He blew out a breath. "Fine."

Camila beamed. "You're the best! I knew you'd say yes!"

"I didn't even know it until five seconds ago."

"That's why I'm the best."

He chuckled, shaking his head. "You love winning."

"Damn right I do, and so do you, *co-director*." She did a little victory dance, holding her arms up in a V-shape and swinging her hips from side to side. "Don't be late for practice. Sunday, 10 a.m."

As she walked away, Sebastián exhaled, eyes shut, pulling his focus inward. Post-injury, he was still learning how to live differently, but his ego was too big to aim small. Dance lit up his competitive fire. Gia lit up his desire. Was he ready to let her witness the mess of his identity crisis? No. He wanted her to see only the best of him.

Chapter Ten

It was finally happening. Gia arrived early at Ritmo Latino's private studio, her ballroom heels clutched in one hand, the weight of her hopes in the other. The smaller room was quiet, with no thumping bass and no crowd. It was only mirrored walls and a polished wood floor, gleaming like a blank slate.

This was her second chance. After years of watching dance instead of living it, she refused to waste the opportunity to dance again.

She slipped into her new ballroom shoes—suede soles, copper satin, with rhinestones that caught the light. Three-inch heels. They were half an inch taller than her practice pair, but the difference felt seismic. In her past life, she'd danced barefoot to maximize the connection with the floor. Salsa heels tipped her forward, forcing the balls of her feet to take command. Elegant in theory. Awkward in reality. She bent her knees deeper and drew her shoulders back to better ground her center of gravity.

She started warming up, stretching her legs, shifting through the footwork she learned yesterday in the training team session, and getting her body used to the feel in these new shoes.

The door swung open. Gia turned, already smiling...and froze.

Sebastián Solano strode in like he owned the room, dressed in a fitted sleeveless shirt and joggers that clung to every sharp angle of his body. His dark hair was damp, and he wore running shoes.

Gia's stomach flipped. *No way.*

Sebastián dropped his bag onto a chair and pulled out a fresh t-shirt before approaching her.

"Hi, Gia. Camila made some last-minute changes, and I'm going to be your partner for the pro-am." His voice was warm with a hint of excitement.

"Wait. You're... my what?"

He quirked a brow, like she'd asked if the sun planned on rising tomorrow. "You make it sound like that's a bad thing," he said with a friendly laugh. When she stared at him in response, he followed up with a more sober, "Okay. This isn't going how I expected. You actually seem really uncomfortable about it."

Understatement of the year.

She'd spent days convincing herself she could handle their connection leading somewhere, even if it was short-lived. But this? Him as her coach? His hands on her *as a job*? That changed everything. He wouldn't just catch her missteps; he'd witness her grappling with the raw, messy work of falling back in love with dance, the awkward stumbles of reconnecting with her body, and the blur of desire she hadn't figured out yet. Was it salsa, Sebastián, or the thrill of connecting with different partners after years in a committed relationship? No, she wanted him to see her at her best, not at her most vulnerable.

Plus, being her coach meant his job now was to watch her, correct her, tell her what to do, how to move, how to look. Not hot. Not at all.

She swallowed hard, forcing a smile. "I thought I was dancing with Andrés. Why didn't you mention it in the cafe yesterday or at the audition?"

Sebastián grabbed the hem of his damp muscle tee and peeled it off in one fluid motion, revealing a body that looked like it had been carved out of marble: sculpted arms, ripped abs, and that V-cut disappearing beneath the waistband of his low-slung pants. *Damn.* Gia forgot how to breathe for a second.

He didn't seem to notice. He pulled on a fresh short sleeved t-shirt, the fabric stretching over muscle as he rolled his head back and forth to loosen up.

"I actually wasn't planning on it. Camila asked me after the audition. Andrés doesn't have the bandwidth with fire season. Daniel is on Camila duty," he joked. "Would it have changed your mind?"

Yes. No. Maybe. She finally managed, "No. It wouldn't." It would have given her a chance to compose herself, though. To prepare.

"Then what's up?" he asked, his tone lighter than his expression. "You look like I just told you I eat puppies for breakfast."

Gia forced a small laugh, hoping it sounded convincing. "Nothing. I... didn't expect it, that's all."

He could see past her words and straight into the knots she was trying to hide.

"You don't like it," he said. Gia thought she sensed a hint of disappointment in his tone.

She straightened, defensive without meaning to be. "No, it's not that. I just..." Her voice faltered, and she hated how fragile it sounded. She lifted her chin. "I just wasn't expecting it. I told you I don't do well with surprises. Remember? Seriously, that's all."

For a minute, he didn't say anything. "If you don't want me to coach you, say so. It doesn't have to be me. You don't owe me anything, Gia. Not in the studio or anywhere else."

"No," she said finally. "I'm ready. Let's do it."

"Alright." His green eyes met hers, unwavering. "It's going to be good. Promise." He scrolled through his phone, tapped a song, and sent it to the sound system. Jimmy Bosch's "Otra Oportunidad" filled the space. Thank God it was slow, she thought. Her heart was already racing fast enough.

Sebastián stepped closer and held out his hand. "Let's figure out where we should start."

Gia placed her hand in his. Like last time, her entire body stirred with awareness when they connected.

Sebastián led her through a simple pattern. Basic steps. Right turn. Basic steps. Left turn. Basic again. Cross-body lead. Another basic. A single turn.

Then, a shift in momentum, the slightest increase in pressure from his hand as he set her up for another turn. A double.

Gia barely had time to process before she was spinning, her feet carrying her through the motion as if they'd always known how. Her body responded before her mind caught up, surrendering to the exchange.

"Beautiful," he said, his hand pressing at her back, adjusting her posture. "Again."

She followed. Every shift of his weight dictated the next step, and every small pressure point signaled what was coming. He repeated the same pattern but raised the stakes, abandoning the steady clave to follow the wild improvisation of the trumpet solo. His lead shifted, sharper now, more daring. With the flick of a wrist, a little more tension in the setup and a surge of momentum, he launched her into a quick triple turn.

He let out a soft *hmm*.

She narrowed her eyes. "Are you testing me?"

"Yes, and you've got it. Barely, but almost there." The words could have stung, but they didn't because his tone was anything but judgmental. It was warm and encouraging, like his smile and his hands. It was a challenge. An invitation to do it again. To do it better. He believed in her and gave her the information she needed to work with.

Heat flared in her chest, but not from embarrassment. From determination.

"Again," she said, squaring her shoulders.

This time, she was ready. They kept going, again and again.

Sebastián spoke little, and didn't offer more praise than necessary. She noted the way his grip adjusted and the way he led her through space, signaling that he trusted her to follow.

The more they moved, the more she melted into their effortless, natural sync. It was like breathing together to a beautiful soundtrack.

She swallowed, trying to ignore how her skin burned under

his touch, how even the most minor adjustments he made at her hip or bare shoulder sent sparks along her spine.

It's just dance, she reminded herself.

Finally, Sebastián pulled them to a stop. He stepped back, rolling out his shoulders, unfazed. She had to catch her breath.

He studied her for a second, eyes sharp and assessing. "You've got obvious potential," he said.

Gia lifted her chin. "But?"

His gaze held hers. "I need more than potential."

"Okay... what do you need?"

"Commitment."

All her warning bells rang in unison.

It's different this time. He's not only my teacher. He's my dance partner. We're a team in this.

After two hours, her tank top clung to her back and her ponytail to her neck. Her arms hung heavy at her sides, and the thought of another turn made her stomach twist. Sebastián had barely broken a sweat.

Gia had pictured late-night practices filled with laughter and music. She'd imagined Andrés offering light, friendly corrections and her progress unfolding in joyful bursts. Instead, her lungs burned and her feet ached. As she stood in Ritmo Latino's private studio, staring at Sebastián Solano, she realized this was going to be nothing like she expected. He was so charming at the cafe yesterday and when he helped with the training team's practices. In competition mode, Sebastián was a different person. On the upside, very few people ever got this close to a legitimate athlete, much less trained under one. This was a chance most dancers would kill for. Which meant that if she blew it, she'd have no excuses.

She swallowed, pressing her palms into her thighs. "So, you said you want commitment. What are you thinking? Should we add another practice each week?"

"I'm thinking more like three times a week once we get closer to the competition. Minimum. Social dancing a couple of nights a week. We only have a few months to train together. We need to make it look like we've been partners forever."

Her brows lifted. "It sounds like this isn't about training. It's about proving something."

"Isn't it?" Sebastián answered, his voice laced with hope.

Gia reached for the part of herself where dance wasn't an activity but an identity. Competition had once been her pulse, practice the rhythm of her life. All she had to do was shake loose the cobwebs and step in, heart first.

"I'm in. Let's go again."

He stepped forward, guiding them back into the dance for one more hour of rehearsal.

As much as Sebastián's lead made her feel safe, it also asked everything of her: attention, trust, and a willingness to keep up. She refused to shrink under it. When he gave her space to shine, she took it, adding her style and flavor. This balance of power, surrender, control, and release intoxicated her.

She cautioned herself that every woman felt that way in Sebastián's arms. A lengthy queue awaited their dance with him. She reminded herself she was in rebound territory, fresh from a long-term relationship breakup.

But the way he moved. The way she felt in his arms. It was almost impossible to resist.

As they wrapped up the last pattern, Sebastián held her gaze, eyebrows raised with a flicker of playfulness. His look said it all: We might just pull this off.

She let out a breath she hadn't realized she was holding, her chest rising against his.

"Again on Tuesday?"

Gia nodded. "Yeah. Tuesday works."

He let her go slowly, drawing out the shift from the charged closeness of the dance floor back into the ordinary world. Gia pressed a hand against her racing heart, steadying herself. She was here to train, to prove she still had a spark. Not to lose herself in salsa dancing with Sebastián Solano.

Gia sank into the back seat of her Lyft, sweat cooling on her skin. She stared at her reflection in the window, at the flush still in her cheeks, her lips parted, her eyes heavy-lidded. She could still feel him: his hands on her hips, his voice low in her ear, his gravity impossible to resist. Gia told herself it was just the dancing, but the look he'd given her before she left said he knew it was just a matter of time until their dance became something else.

Chapter Eleven

When Gia arrived at Baila del Rey, she stepped into a wave of music and motion, air kisses, loud greetings, and the whoosh of bodies dancing. On stage, Costa Candela, the city's only all-female salsa powerhouse, kicked into a cha-cha so irresistible it pulled partners onto the floor like a tide. Tonight felt like the entire city had shown up for one reason: to celebrate Camila Solano on her birthday.

If the crowd was electric, Camila was the lightning.

She was impossible to miss, standing near the bar, chatting with the bartender, and sipping a cocktail. Camila's black catsuit hugged every curve. Her red heels were skyscrapers, perfectly matched to the bold, fiery swipe of cherry-red lipstick. Her dark hair was pulled into her signature dragon braid, blunt bangs framing eyes that sparkled with mischief and fire. Watching her made Gia want to take up more space.

Gia headed straight to Camila for a celebratory hug and kiss. "Happiest birthday to you!"

"Thank you, love! So glad you are here. We're going to have a fabulous night." Then she took a step back as if to get the full picture of Gia. "Girl. I don't think I've ever seen you wear anything besides black! You look gorgeous."

The sun-kissed, effortless style of San Diego was starting to claim Gia. Her ocean blue dress was short, flirty, and cinched at the waist before flaring into a skirt that shimmered with every step. The fabric caught the light, floating around her thighs whenever she moved, like it was designed for spins.

She wore her hair long and loose, her dark waves spilling down her back. The sharp East Coast urgency she once carried had melted into an easier, breezier, and sun-warmed energy. Tonight she was pure SoCal.

Gia kicked off her street shoes and slipped into her sparkly salsa heels, determined to break them in before the pro-am. The upcoming performance lived rent-free in the back of her mind twenty-four seven.

It was mid-July now, and Gia's focused practice had transformed her from a hesitant newcomer to a dancer who could hold her own. Between training with her teammates, one-on-one rehearsals with Sebastián, and night after night of social dancing, her confidence and timing were on point. What she lacked in technical skill, she made up for in musicality, presence, and unmistakable joy on the floor. Her ability to follow had improved dramatically, and her connection with partners felt intuitive. Immersing herself so completely in the scene hadn't made her an overnight sensation, but it had helped her progress faster than she ever thought possible. Not to mention, she was having the time of her life.

She scanned the crowd for potential partners until her eyes landed on Sebastián. He wore head-to-toe navy. His linen slacks whispered luxury with every step. His open-collared, button-down silk shirt caught the light with the faintest sheen, sleeves pushed up just enough to reveal tanned forearms and a leather-strapped vintage watch. His dark hair swept back in waves that looked more wind-tossed than styled. Gia thought maybe he had wandered out of a GQ spread and into the party by accident.

The music quieted down suddenly, and the lead singer's voice called through the speakers. "And now, the reason you're all here tonight. Give it up for our birthday girl! Come on up here, Camila!"

A roar of cheers filled the club as Camila stepped into the center of the room.

"You know what to do!" the singer shouted.

A flurry of movement followed as a handful of leads rushed onto the floor. The rest of the crowd backed up, creating a giant circle for a stage.

"We've got two very special guests with us tonight. Please welcome Antonio and Rosa Solano!" Camila and Sebastián's parents joined Costa Candela on stage, their father on the drums, and their mother on the microphone. They performed "Cali Pachanguero" as a birthday tribute and family anthem. Camila's eyes shimmered, and she stood motionless for the first time that night.

The song's lively rhythm set the perfect mood for partner stealing.

Daniel started the dance, his hand already reaching for hers before anyone else even had a chance. He led her into a copa, brought her back in for a triple turn, then slipped smoothly into shadow position. Their bodies moved in sync, the connection built on practice and trust rather than passion, though the untrained eye could never tell the difference.

When Daniel spun Camila out, Andrés took her into a cross-body lead, claiming his spot as her new partner. Where Daniel was polished, Andrés was carefree and full of swagger. He shook his shoulders at the crowd, daring them not to cheer. Andrés' salsa was athletic and electric. He led Camila through windmill turns and clever dips that made her laugh the entire time. He sang to Camila as he pulled her into a series of rapid overhead wraps and pretzel variations.

Next, Sebastián cut in. When his hand found Camila's, the energy shifted again because Sebastián could be elegant *and* play-ful. He led her through a sit spin, complicated patterns, and light-ning-fast Salsa Caleña, a distinctive Colombian style of salsa that had the crowd cheering. Then, with a grin, he pulled her in and flashed a look that said, *Guess what's coming next?* He held the moment just long enough to build anticipation, then dipped her on the beat, perfectly timed to the entire crowd shouting, "Cali!" along with the song.

Camila's laughter spilled out, bright and unfiltered, like she was seven again, spinning around the living room with her older brother. In all that playfulness, their footwork never missed.

Standing at the edge of the circle, Gia realized she wasn't yet fluent in the language of salsa, but she wanted to be. *Was this how salsa was everywhere?* She didn't know yet, but she planned to keep dancing until she found out.

Just as the next partner positioned himself to take a turn leading Camila, a challenger appeared and beat him to it. Tatiana was a professional dancer and studio director in Los Angeles. She blocked the eager young man waiting for his dance with Camila, flashing him a smile as she scooped Camila in her graceful arms. Catcalls surged through the crowd.

Camila melted into Tatiana as if they'd been partners for years. Then, with a sly shift, Camila claimed the lead, and Tatiana slipped into the follower's role without missing a beat. They passed control back and forth in a flirtatious game, seamless enough to look effortless but rare in salsa, where roles are usually fixed. It was the kind of mastery only top dancers pulled off, more common in West Coast Swing than here. Gasps gave way to cheers as the pair teased each other through every daring exchange. The heat was in their flawless execution, where each step was a tease and every turn a dare. The inherent sex appeal of two gorgeous, talented dancers didn't hurt either.

Gia added "learn how to lead one day" to her mental bucket list.

Mid-song, Antonio Solano saluted the Costa Candela drummer before descending the stairs toward the dancers. He slipped between the two women, took one in each hand, and spun them both at once, cutting into the dance floor with a flair no one else could match. Then he kissed Tatiana's hand and offered a quick bow. She blew him a kiss, melting back into the crowd as Antonio turned to his daughter, inviting her into his arms with quiet reverence.

Camila finished the song in her father's embrace, every step graceful and rich with unspoken history. Onstage, Sebastián took his mother's hand and danced beside her as she sang. The Solanos danced for family, for music, and for everything that had carried them here tonight.

The song closed with a final blast of brass, and the whole club erupted in applause. Gia's eyes stung with unexpected tears.

Antonio, Rosa and Costa Candela started another song, and Camila left the dance floor to get some water. That's when Gia saw Camila's face go cold.

Following her gaze, Gia spotted a man leaning against the bar. He was tall and lean, all sharp angles and slick black hair, knife-cut cheekbones, and startlingly blue eyes, bright enough to catch even from across the room.

The moment Camila's gaze met his, his posture faltered and his hands dropped to his sides. He grounded his weight as if bracing for impact. Whatever he came for, Gia bet it wouldn't be a casual hello.

Camila froze. Just for a breath. Then she lifted her chin, tossed her braid back with practiced elegance, and walked to the other end of the bar, far from him.

That had to be Emilio.

Gia didn't know what Emilio had done, but Camila's avoidance spoke louder than words.

Something between them was far from over.

Sebastián was leaning against the DJ booth when he saw Emilio.

His whole body tensed, and heat flashed beneath his skin. He hadn't seen that bastard in months. Now here he was, leaning against the bar as if he were welcome here.

Sebastián pushed off the booth and cut through the crowd, eyes locked on his target. No way was this guy ruining another one of Camila's nights. Especially not on her birthday.

Emilio saw him coming and stood his ground.

"You lost?"

"Come on, Sebas. I just wanted to show up and say happy birthday to Camila. I've never missed her birthday."

"This isn't the night to just show up out of nowhere, man."

"You know, we're all part of the same community. We're bound to run into each other sometimes."

Sebastián remained silent.

"After everything we've been through, don't you think it's time we all moved on?"

"Emilio, there's a time and a place for this, and Camila's birthday ain't it."

After an agonizing moment that seemed to stretch forever, Emilio drained his drink and set the glass down. His voice dropped, more tired than defiant. "I miss this, you know. All of it. This was my family too. Just because Camila and I aren't partners anymore doesn't mean all that history goes away."

Sebastián's jaw locked. "Should've thought of that before you blew it all up."

"You think I don't know I ruined it?" Emilio looked down, swallowed hard as if to get his composure. "Look, I only wanted to say hello on her birthday. To see everyone."

"I'll let her know."

Emilio paused, watching Camila as she laughed with her friends, radiant and untouchable. Longing or regret flickered on his face, but it vanished before it settled. "For what it's worth, I still see you as a brother. I always will." He straightened his shoulders and left without another word, pride holding his silence all the way out the door.

When Sebastián turned back toward the dance floor, Tú con Él by Rauw Alejandro was spilling through the speakers. He saw Gia being pulled into a dance and immediately recognized the lead. Marco was an up-and-coming dancer on the semi-pro team with Mambo Sol. Marco understood musicality on a visceral level and always made his partner shine. According to Amber and Luna, he was also a "walking distraction."

Sebastián folded his arms across his chest and watched as

Marco led Gia into an inside turn. As she completed the rotation, Marco caught her right hand behind her back in a smooth, practiced motion, closing her into a hammerlock, her arm gently pinned behind her, while he moved closer into her space. Marco unwrapped the hammerlock by leading Gia into a traveling left turn. The skirt of her dress flared wide, flashing her beautifully toned legs and drawing eyes from every corner of the floor. Her hair lifted with every spin, swirling around her like a frame. And her lips. They were deep fuchsia tonight, her smile so vivid it outshone the lights, impossible to miss, even from a distance.

She smiled as her feet traced a quick, playful pattern that looked more like flirtation than footwork. He laughed and responded with shoulder shimmies and smooth body rolls. There was plenty of space between them, but each step dared the other to come closer.

Marco guided Gia's left hand up and over his head into what seemed to be the start of a drop-catch, but instead, Gia let her hand run straight down the back of his neck, skimming his shoulder before sliding along the length of his arm. It looked like a caress disguised as styling. Was it? Or was Gia simply experimenting to find her own style? By the time her hand reached its place in a closed position, Marco had all the encouragement he needed to make a move. He locked eyes with her and smiled in a way that made it clear this wasn't about the dance. He wanted her.

Something shifted inside of Sebastián. *When did this start?*

Of course, he *noticed* her early on. Everyone did. It's hard to miss a beautiful dancer when she first arrives in class. He was invested in her progress and ability to hold her own on the floor. Yes. That's all this was.

When the music melted into the slow, buttery bachata, "Fallarte Nunca" by Ralphy Dreamz, Marco didn't let her go. Gia followed him into the next dance, even closer this time.

Sebastián felt it as a sharp, unexpected punch to the ribs. He tasted it in his mouth. Its flavor was remarkably similar to jealousy, not something he was familiar with.

In soccer and salsa, Sebastián always got his way. He was still adjusting to settling for second best in his career. In salsa? In his personal life? No room for that.

Could he silence what he felt? Or get rid of Marco?

Before he could reason his way through his thoughts, Sebastián was moving.

His eyes stayed locked on Gia and Marco as he closed the distance between them.

When Marco caught her waist in a slow turn, she melted into his hands. She danced as if she were the music. Every subtle shift in weight landed perfectly on the beat, her body interpreting every phrase naturally. Sebastián spent weeks drawing that out of her, encouraging her to feel the rhythm, trust her body, breathe into the pauses. He remembered the moment she finally stopped counting in her head, the night she let go and gave in to the music with him. Now here she was, giving that version of herself to someone else. Not just letting Marco lead her, but matching him, adding her own flavor, daring him to keep up. It was gorgeous.

It stung.

By the time Marco dipped Gia back, her hair spilling toward the floor, Sebastián arrived.

She came up with a breathless laugh, still lost in the moment until she realized that Sebastián was all but standing over them.

Sebastián flashed his million-dollar smile, tilting his head just enough to suggest an apology without meaning it. He was about to bend the rules.

"Mind if I cut in and dance with my partner?" Sebastián asked too casually, as if he hadn't crossed the entire club to get there and shatter their moment.

Marco raised his brows, surprised. "Didn't realize we had assigned partners tonight." Besides birthday dances, cutting in wasn't part of the usual dance etiquette. Not at a social, not mid-song and not by Sebastián Solano. Around them, the ripple of attention was instant. Dancers slowed their steps, eyes drifting toward the trio in the middle of the floor. Conversations paused. Everyone was watching.

Sebastián smiled, but didn't move.

Marco wasn't stupid. He understood what was happening.

"Um. Of course," he said, letting go of Gia's hand with a bittersweet smile. "I'll steal you back later."

Gia had no chance to respond, because Sebastián was already in Marco's place. She looked at Sebastián sideways, half amused, half confused. "That was... a little extra."

Sebastián shrugged, leading her into motion. "Didn't like the way he was leading you."

She raised an eyebrow. "Right. That's what this is about?" Her eyes lit up with amusement. She wasn't letting him off the hook. "Marco's a *great* lead," she added.

Sebastián didn't bother with words at first. He pulled her close into his arms until the crowd dissolved into nothing. His eyes and embrace said it all: *You want a great lead? Then dance with me.*

"Okay, coach." Her voice was light and teasing, but her pulse betrayed her. "Show me what you think I've been missing tonight."

"Not your coach. *Partner.* There's a difference."

"Sebastián..."

"I'm the man you should've been dancing with all along."

He felt the surprised hitch of her breath against his chest and the way her fingers gripped his shoulder, as if she'd expected the heat between them to explode eventually, just not here in the middle of a packed dance floor where anyone and everyone could see.

He didn't care who was watching. Let them.

The studio rules didn't apply here. With Gia wrapped in his arms and a slow bachata threading through the speakers, Sebastián forgot himself. His hands slid across the curve of her back, gathering her closer until nothing, not even air or music, could slip between them.

Her body softened into his, then trembled at the same time, as if caught between surrender and self-preservation. He felt her hesitation and her hunger in equal measure, a push and pull that only stoked his own fire. Every sway, every shift of her hips against his told him this wasn't about practice anymore. It was about them colliding with a force neither of them could control any longer. He shifted them into a proper closed position, one hand at her back, the other cradling her hand. With Gia, every step was closer and slower, as though he couldn't quite breathe unless he felt her body align perfectly with his. They'd danced together countless times in rehearsal and class, but the way he held her tonight was sensual and possessive.

The press of bodies around them left barely enough room to move, so they slipped into small, synchronized steps, her right thigh between his, and his between hers, moving side to side and deeper into each other.

The intimacy lived in the details. In the way she mirrored him and the languid roll of her hips that sent a slow burn crawling beneath his skin. When she turned, her whole body brushed against his, coconut and heat clinging to him as her hair grazed his cheek. His fingers skimmed her ribs before settling her flush against him, chest to chest, hip to hip.

Nothing about the dance was showy. It wasn't for the crowd, no matter how many people were watching. It was theirs alone.

Her eyes lifted to his, and everything else faded. Then she sighed. Soft, breathy, and barely audible. The sound of it, quiet in his ear, made him imagine what it would be like to make her moan, unrestrained, without the music or the crowd to hide behind.

Her gaze held his with something she hadn't let him see before. Desire.

When he slid his hands lower on her back, she surprised him by guiding his hands even lower, placing his fingers at the soft curve of her hips. And then, tracing her hands up his arms, across his shoulders, and settling around his neck, drawing him even closer. A silent invitation.

His control cracked under the weight of that look in her eyes. He reminded himself he should wait and let her dance with others to get the rush of the scene out of her system before he made his intentions clear, but every hour they spent together in rehearsal only tangled him deeper in her. This moment was the breaking point. Hunger rose inside him. Coach. Partner. Upcoming competition. None of it mattered to desire. Maybe she didn't need more time with other partners to recognize that their connection was different. With Marco, she'd been fiery, flirtatious, lighthearted, but with him, she let go in a way that felt unguarded, real. He clung to that, needing it to count for something.

Her fingers flexed at his shoulder, her hips pressed into his, every subtle movement telling him she wanted this too.

He kept his face just above hers, near enough to kiss if he only leaned a fraction closer. The restraint it took not to was testing him.

The music ended, but Sebastián wasn't ready to let Gia go.

Finally, Gia pulled away. Sebastián exhaled, trying to shake whatever had just happened.

Gia reached for his hand. "Let's get some air."

She led him past the bar and through a side door that opened onto a small outdoor terrace strung with dim lights overlooking the nighttime ocean. A handful of people were out there, but they kept to themselves, wrapped up in their own moments.

The salty night air was cool against his skin, but it did nothing to clear his head.

Gia leaned against the railing, her hair catching the moonlight. She looked amused, curious and beautiful. "So. What was that about?"

Sebastián leaned next to her, mirroring her posture. "What was what about?"

She rolled her eyes. "Don't do that, Solano."

He forced a laugh. "I didn't like the way Marco was leading you."

"Uh-huh." She gave him a sugary-sweet look. "Because Marco

is... what? A terrible dancer? Or because he was dancing with *me*?"

He wasn't used to being called out. He glanced away, pretending to check his watch. "Didn't realize I needed permission to ask my partner for a dance."

"Sebastián. I'd think you were jealous if I didn't know better." She spoke with the same trash-talking tone they had played with during volleyball weeks ago. He realized this was Gia giving him an out, an opportunity to rein it in before they crossed a line. He stretched his neck right, then left, searching for words that would make this less risky than it felt. Then he gave up and went with honesty instead.

He stopped his stretching to look her in the eyes. "I couldn't stand watching someone else dance with you like that."

Gia's teasing smile faded. "And everything after?"

"That was me saying everything I've been biting back in rehearsals. If you didn't know how badly I want you, you do now."

His hands found her wrists, circling them as he pulled her closer.

She was so close. Warm, soft, and his, if only for this breathless moment. He knew he should step back, keep the line between them clear, but every part of him screamed to break it. To stop pretending.

Her eyes fluttered shut as she tilted her face up.

And then the space between them disappeared.

His lips brushed hers tentatively at first before pressing into a firmer, surer kiss. Her breath hitched softly against him, and that was all it took for his control to snap. He kissed her deeper, one hand sliding up her neck, the other anchoring her at the small of her back, fingers splaying over warm skin, like they were slow dancing.

Gia's hands gripped his shirt as though she needed something to hold on to. The kiss was sweet and urgent at once, all the weeks of unspoken tension spilling into this single, delicious moment.

He didn't even notice when her back pressed against the railing, or when his thumb traced the curve of her jaw.

When he finally pulled back, it was only far enough to rest his forehead against hers. Her lips were still parted, her breath tangled with his. He couldn't remember the last time anything had felt this right. He was hers. Maybe he had been from the very first dance.

"Nothing could have prepared me for that," he whispered.

Her quiet laugh trembled between them. He smiled at that, leaning in for another kiss when a warm, familiar voice cut through the moment.

"Sebas, mi amor!"

The words felt like a bucket of cold water. His mother's presence was always delightful, but right now horribly misplaced.

They broke apart, straightening like guilty teenagers as Rosa and Antonio Solano appeared at the terrace door, smiling and oblivious.

Sebastián's father clapped a hand on his shoulder. "We're heading out, mijo. Wanted to say goodbye before we left."

Rosa's warm gaze slid to Gia, her smile bright and inviting. "You must be Gia."

Still catching her breath, Gia nodded quickly. "Yes. Hello. It's so nice to meet you both."

Rosa beamed. "We've heard so much about you! Camila says you're the one who's going to help them take the pro-am title this year."

"Well, I've got the best...partner," Gia offered a polite smile, then added, "Speaking of dance, I should get home. I've got training team practice tomorrow."

"Well, I hope we get to see you again soon," Rosa said.

"Hopefully, you'll be seeing a lot more of Gia." Sebastián returned to his cool, casual composure. "Come on. I'll walk you all out."

They strolled together to the parking lot. Before he could catch Gia's eye again, his parents swept in, filling the space with conversation. Rosa asked about Gia's writing, Antonio launched into a story about the orchestra, and every chance for Sebastián to circle back to what really mattered slipped further away. By the time Gia's ride pulled up, the moment had dissolved into polite laughter and easy chatter.

Sebastián smiled, said his goodbyes, and held the door as Gia climbed into the car. He'd have to wait longer than he wanted to tell her how he felt. When he did, it couldn't be over text. It couldn't be casual. Face to face. Alone. With nothing and no one to interrupt, just in case she let him show her–with his hands, his mouth, his body–exactly what he felt.

Chapter Twelve

The last notes of music faded as Camila clapped her hands, dismissing the training team.

"All right, ladies, enjoy the rest of your day. Fellas, don't go far. We start again in ten."

As the followers left, a fresh wave of leads arrived, including familiar faces from the advanced teams along with newcomers Gia didn't recognize. Everyone looked a little too eager for just another workshop.

Gia lingered at the mirror's edge, curious, watching the room fill. She caught sight of Sebastián strolling in last. As usual, he was hard to miss, dressed like he were headed to a social in a fitted black button-down, rolled sleeves, dark jeans, and dress shoes. Hair styled and gorgeous. Not a hint of rehearsal attire.

Gia raised an eyebrow at Camila. "What's this?"

Camila smiled, wiping sweat from her brow. "How to Make Every Woman Want You." She gave Gia a mischievous smile. "This workshop is for the guys only. I usually run it solo, but I've learned they listen a hell of a lot better when my brother's the one saying it."

"Smart." Gia laughed though her stomach sank. She was falling for the guy who ran a class called "How to Make Every Woman Want You."

Camila caught Gia's expression and shook her head. "The name gets them in the door. What it's really about is respect. Boundaries. Too many guys think leading is a license to get handsy—or worse. This keeps the scene safer and better."

Shame prickled at the back of Gia's neck.

Camila smirked, scanning the studio. "Honestly, I could call it How Not to Lose Partners and Alienate Women, and it'd be more accurate, but that doesn't sell out as fast."

She tipped her chin toward Sebastián, who stood across the studio casually chatting with a group of younger guys, their eyes wide and eager.

Camila's voice dropped to a murmur. "He doesn't know it, but I use him as bait. They show up hoping for a magic trick from a celebrity athlete. Joke's on them. The real insight is just basic human decency."

Gia smiled as she observed Sebastián laugh at something one of the guys said. As if he could sense her stare, he glanced over, caught her watching him, and held her gaze. His eyes sparkled, like they shared a secret.

Heat crept into her cheeks as she waved back in acknowledgment.

Camila slung her towel onto the bench and nudged Gia with her elbow. "Let's go. I step out for the first ten minutes so they can get their macho nonsense out of the way."

"Aww, can't we stay and watch?" Gia teased in a tone that sounded more like begging.

"Nope. Gentlemen only."

From the hallway, Gia lingered by the glass window, trying to listen as Sebastián started the workshop.

He stood with his hands loose at his sides and addressed the room. "So," he began, "you want to be the guy women are lining up to dance with."

A few of the younger leads nodded, some wearing the cocky grin of men who thought this might be a shortcut to charm or at least hearing the conquests of a star athlete.

Sebastián smiled. "Here's the real secret. Make her feel safe.

Make her feel seen. Protect her space. It's about putting all your attention on her."

Gia tilted her head, her chest warming at the words. That sounded like the man she danced with last night.

The room was quiet, as if the class was asking, "That's it?"

"I'm serious, guys. Every time you dance with a woman, she's trusting you. With her body. Her balance. Her time. If you lead like she's just another follower, she'll sense that. And if you lead like your goal is *anything* but connection on the dance floor, you'll be the guy they warn each other about in the restroom."

That got a few uneasy shuffles. A couple of the guys looked confused.

"Oh, you haven't heard about the bathroom chatter? The ladies call it a 'creep sheet,' and you're shit out of luck if your name lands on it because it's near impossible to get off."

Gia watched through the glass window and saw that no one made a move to dance. It was a room full of men talking and listening.

Behind the desk, Camila, nose in her laptop, didn't even glance up. "See?" she whispered to Gia. "Told you. They listen to him."

She snapped her computer shut. "I'm gonna head in and make sure those fellas really get it. I'll see you later." Camila slipped quietly to the front of the room, and all the men immediately quieted down.

"Hello, gentlemen. Welcome to How to Make Every Woman Want You...on the dance floor. I'm here to help demonstrate. Sebas, please continue."

"Alright," Sebastián said, clapping his hands once. "Let's talk about the seven deadly sins of salsa."

He motioned to Daniel to step forward. "Daniel here is going to show you what *not* to do with Camila. Hopefully he survives it."

Daniel smiled nervously and moved to the front of the room beside his partner.

Sebastián began, "One: Don't touch her face or head." Daniel attempted a hand-to-head move, trying to lead Camila into bending down so he could lift his foot over her head in a windmill kick. Camila smacked his hand away playfully before he could even get her to crouch down. Sebastián provided the commentary, "Don't be the guy who thinks grabbing her head for a dip or anything else is a good idea. Instant salsa fail."

Camila added, "Double fail if you try to be sexy doing it. It's never hot."

Gia smiled through the window. She'd seen that exact maneuver too many times in salsa clubs. Some guy trying to be slick and ending up on her list of guys to avoid.

"Sin number two: Keep your head above the belt line." Daniel attempted a move where he stood in front of Camila, his back towards her, holding her hands outstretched to the sides. He dipped himself backwards, using her arms for balance and support as he lowered himself into a backbend. At the bottom of the dip, he had a clear view up her imaginary skirt. Sebastián raised a brow. "We're not here to play limbo, fellas. If she's in a dress, you've just ruined her night. Don't do it. Also, not smart to assume she can carry your weight. Aside from earning a spot on the creep sheet, you might end up flat on your ass."

A few of the leads winced. One guy in the back muttered, "I saw a dude try that once."

Sebastián shot him a grin. "Did he survive the song?"

Camila helped Daniel up to standing, and he gave her a crooked smile. He was here to demonstrate, but performing moves he'd never actually do made him uncomfortable, even if it was for a good cause.

"Who else has seen something on the social dance floor that we should put on the sins list?"

A tall dancer in the back said, "Hands off the goods. Her chest, her ass, or anything that could even slightly be considered an erogenous zone. Off-limits. I've seen girls get really uncomfortable. I've seen a few guys get slapped too."

"Both warranted," Daniel added.

"Before you say, *but it's sensual bachata!*" Camila used a

rough-guy voice. "*Some women like it!* No, they like consent. If you haven't danced with her before, assume nothing."

Daniel lifted his hands in mock surrender. "Nope. I'm not showing this."

"That's because you pay attention," Camila replied. "And that's the sexiest. That's why you're *my* partner."

Daniel scratched the back of his neck, eyes flicking to the guys before settling on Camila again. He caught the silent acknowledgments that he'd just scored the kind of compliment every guy in the room wanted.

"Four: Chill with the body rolls." Sebastián sighed, shaking his head. "You know the ones I mean. When a guy looks like he's auditioning for an R-rated music video? Don't."

Uncomfortable laughter rippled across the group.

Daniel took Camila into a closed frame and exaggerated a body roll, dragging it out theatrically as Camila stood still, unimpressed. The mismatch made him look ridiculous, and a few guys snickered.

Sebastián let the moment hang, then added dryly, "See? Without her buy-in, you just look like an idiot."

Camila softened the edge with a small smile. "Listen. I love sensuality. I teach sensuality. But it's about timing and chemistry. Not pelvic...I don't even know. Pelvic ambition."

Daniel straightened, rubbing the back of his neck again, his jaw tight and a faint flush creeping across his face while a few guys chuckled.

"What else should we add?" Sebastián asked.

"How about surprise dips?" another dancer replied.

"Absolutely. If there's no prep or no signal, it's a trust fall with zero trust," Sebastion went on.

Daniel pulled Camila into a closed position, prepped her for a dip, and supported her securely through it. Camila took the time to lean into it. She closed her eyes and stretched backwards with abandon into a deep arch. Her crop top moved along with her, letting her perfectly toned abs peek out beneath. Time slowed. She lifted back out of the dip one vertebra at a time, like a stretched-out body wave from the hips, through the torso, and finally to her head. When she balanced upright, she opened her eyes, locking them into Daniel's. When she broke the connection with Daniel and turned toward the room, the seduction stopped abruptly, and it was back to business.

"Damn. That was hot," someone muttered under their breath.

"Exactly. That's how you do it. One well-led dip is sexy as hell," Camila said. "Three in a row feels like whiplash. She's dodging you for the rest of the night. Along with her friends."

"Six: Rough leading." Sebastián's expression sobered. "This one's serious. I've seen teammates injured because of forced turns. Don't be that guy."

Daniel added, "I think this one speaks for itself. If your lead looks like a wrestling match? You're doing it wrong."

Gia scrunched up her nose. She had the experience of fighting through a song to keep her body intact. It was the fastest way to ruin the magic of dance.

"Seven is the worst sin of all: ignoring the no." His voice dropped to a low, deliberate tone. "If she stiffens up, avoids eye contact, pulls away? That's a no. Even if she's smiling. Even if you think the move was perfect. You stop."

Camila added, "Always remember, consent is sexy. Seriously. I promise you that."

She looked around the room. No one said a word.

It was a shame these kinds of workshops had to exist, but Gia understood why they did. It didn't take much imagination to guess what had gone wrong in the scene to make these conversations necessary. There was a fine line between the passion of partner dancing and the moment it tipped into something inappropriate. She appreciated how Ritmo Latino handled it, keeping the heat where it belonged: mutual, respectful, and absolutely delicious.

It turned her on that Sebastián was one of the people leading that charge.

"If you make her feel like the star of the floor, she'll remember you for all the right reasons. And if you don't?" A shrug. "She'll remember that too."

Daniel looked at the crowd of guys and tilted his head toward Sebastián as he said, "Funny how the guy who makes it all about *her* has the reputation for being the best dancer himself."

Sebastián simply shrugged and replied, "What can I say? I love women. Giving them what they want has always worked out for me."

Gia froze.

It was nothing—just a throwaway line to impress a crowd full of dudes. Her stomach tightened anyway.

"Okay, Romeo. For the inside scoop on Sebastián's love life, please stay after class." Camila clapped once. "For now, gentlemen. Partner up. I will show you exactly what to do to get that perfect connection. You're going to learn to lead well and follow. Because if you don't know how it feels to follow, you won't understand what it takes to lead well."

As the students paired off, Sebastián turned to offer a hand to one of the newer guys. That grounded, approachable energy was sexy as hell, and clearly not reserved just for her. He gave it to everyone. She may have gone down a rabbit hole thinking about this, but Camila walked over, tapped on the glass and smiled. "Gentleman only, babe. We'll see you later."

She put her hands in a heart shape and mouthed the words *sorry, not sorry* before she slipped quietly away from the glass.

His voice lingered in her mind, replaying his words. No matter how hard she tried, she couldn't decide what scared her more—that he was running game and making her feel like the only woman in the world or that he meant every word he said.

Gia hadn't planned on stopping by Ritmo Latino again that same evening, but her feet had a mind of their own. She told herself she was picking up the jacket she'd left there earlier that day, but deep down, she hoped he might still be there too.

Inside, the studio lights glowed at half-power, casting a soft haze over the polished floor. Camila and Daniel were mid-rehearsal, gliding around the room in a tight, closed frame. They were preparing for the San Francisco Salsa Open in March, where they planned to qualify for the World Salsa Championship. Though months away, they were already pushing themselves to perfect every detail. Their partnership was new, and they were working to develop the right chemistry. Watching their choreography unfold so early in the process gave Gia goosebumps.

Sebastián stood with his arms folded, watching intently. He noticed Gia peeking her head into the room and walked over.

"Gia, hi." Then came the smile, like her being there had shifted his entire day. "Didn't think I'd get to see you again today."

"I was just..." she gestured vaguely. "Grabbing my jacket."

As soon as the words left her mouth, she cringed. *Seriously? Did I just say that?*

Sebastián raised an eyebrow. "You mean... you carried a watermelon?"

Her eyes widened. "Oh my God, I was literally thinking that in my head!" She laughed. "Wait. Sebastián, did you actually watch *Dirty Dancing*?"

He gave a casual shrug, but the grin tugging at his mouth gave him away. "I do my homework."

Before she could recover, Camila's voice called across the studio. "Perfect timing. We're stuck on this section and need your fresh eyes."

Gia turned toward her, but not before catching Sebastián's lingering smile. He was already walking to the sound system, calling over his shoulder, "Alright, you two, take your mark. Let's run it from the top."

Gia joined him in the corner to get a better view, settling into the only chair. Sebastián planted himself in front of Gia, standing over her, shoulders squared and arms braced at his sides, channeling Johnny Castle's brooding stance from the last scene of

Dirty Dancing. He held the pose for a moment, but the hint of mischief in his eyes betrayed him before he could open his mouth.

"Don't even say it," Gia warned, shaking her head and holding up a hand with a half-smile.

"Nobody puts Gia in the—"

"—In therapy if you finish that sentence!"

His laugh broke free, rich and genuine. She couldn't help laughing with him.

"Whenever you're ready, people!" Camila sang across the room.

Sebastián leaned in slightly. "Damn. I was gonna toss out that 'God wouldn't have given you maracas' line when they started, but Camila might kill me."

Gia looked at him, happily stunned. This goofy side was a different dimension of the charmer she saw in rehearsal and the heartthrob that smoldered in nightclubs. Reciting lines from *Dirty Dancing* was unexpected and oddly intimate. He was attentive and layered, and even a little dorky in the best way. Somehow, that made him more irresistible. *How many layers of Sebastián Solano were there to discover?*

He winked at her and pressed play.

The music filled the space, and Camila and Daniel lit up the floor. Every beat was sharp, fluid and full of chemistry. By the time they hit the final dip, Gia had goosebumps.

"Well?" Camila asked, breathless, stepping out of Daniel's arms. "Be brutal."

Gia stood up. "It's gorgeous. Honestly. But..."

Camila arched a brow. "But?"

"There are moments you could lean into the heat a little more. Sometimes you break the spell when you face the audience instead of each other. It pulls the tension outward instead of keeping it between you. If you lock eyes, it'll land harder. It'll feel like we're intruding on something private."

Daniel's brows rose, and he gave a slow nod. "That's a good note. Makes sense."

Camila grinned. "See? I knew you'd be helpful. Daniel, let's run it again without music. Gia, stick around, would you? I want you to watch the difference. And give more notes."

While Camila and Daniel rehearsed, Sebastián turned to Gia with a glint in his eye.

"I have something for you."

He went to the lobby and reached into the mini-fridge. He returned with a small purple fruit and a spoon, placing them in her hand. His fingers lingered against hers.

"I was going to wait until tomorrow, but since you're here..."

She glanced down. "Passion fruit?"

"*Fresh* passion fruit," he said, voice low, like the words themselves were meant to tempt her. "Straight off the vine from my parents' backyard. You told me you'd never had the real thing."

She turned it carefully, as if he'd handed her a jewel. "You even brought a spoon."

"I come prepared. "

Mid-dip, Camila caught sight of them and grinned. "Never tried one? Oh, you're in for a treat."

Sebastián took the fruit back, cracked it open with practiced ease, and returned it to her. His gaze never left her as she scooped out the pulp and lifted it to her lips.

The flavor was sweet, tart, alive. "Okay... yeah. This ruins smoothies forever."

"Yep. The real thing's always better."

Gia's gaze dropped to the fruit, then rose to meet his. "I'm a believer. Thank you for this."

He nodded. "Anytime."

Camila and Daniel exchanged silent smiles.

Gia parked herself on the edge of the dance floor, against the mirror, spooning out another bite while Camila and Daniel reviewed the next sequence. Sebastián walked over with his own passion fruit and spoon and sat beside her, close enough to touch.

They watched Camila and Daniel rehearse, nodding here and there, pointing out details and offering ideas.

Camila turned to Sebastián, hands on her hips. "We still haven't locked in the song. I'm starting to second-guess using a

Celia song. Don't get me wrong, she's iconic, but maybe a little expected?"

Daniel rubbed his temples. "Yeah. Her songs are always in the mix."

Sebastián leaned forward, elbows on his knees. "You need something fresh. Not mainstream radio, but not the classics every-one's heard a thousand times."

Camila tilted her head, thinking. "Tee up something unex-pected and let's experiment."

He queued up a song, and within seconds, they were debating counts, arguing over musical breaks, and reimagining entrances, exits, and tempo changes.

Gia sat back and watched the whole thing unfold. They were designing a moment that would steal the spotlight.

She scooped out the last bite of passion fruit and glanced around the room. There were fewer than twenty-four hours before she got to experience this same creative push-pull with Sebastián for their own performance. The thought sent a little spark low in her belly, and she shifted her legs just enough to ease the tension building between them.

Chapter Thirteen

Gia had no idea how she was supposed to act when she walked into Ritmo Latino. Not after their kiss two nights ago. They hadn't been alone since—only exchanged glances and stolen moments in crowded rooms.

Now here they were, just the two of them, finally back in the small studio, where their chemistry seemed to bounce off the mirrored walls, colliding and amplifying by the second. Should she break the tension? Joke about it? Ask him how he was doing? She stood there frozen, unsure of the right move.

Sebastián studied her with a slow sweep of his gaze, and something in him faltered. Her awkwardness seemed to slide right into him.

"Is this awkward?" he asked, voice a little too careful.

"Um, kinda?"

He let out a short breath and a laugh. "I don't want this to be awkward." He clapped his hands once, the way Camila did when signaling a transition class. "Give me a minute."

Sebastián crossed to the studio door, leaned into the hallway, and called out, "Andrés! Amber! Can I borrow you for a few?"

A moment later, Andrés and Amber stepped inside. Their shirts were clinging and their cheeks were flushed, hair damp at the temples. Amber fanned herself with her hand while Andrés swiped his forearm across his brow, both of them grinning like they'd just nailed a tough sequence.

"What's up, boss?" Andrés asked, catching his breath.

"You need a break? We need a warm-up. Mix and move? No choreography. You up for it?"

Amber perked up immediately. "Oh, I like this already."

Gia's whole body seemed to exhale. She didn't know what "mix and move" was, but she understood what Sebastián was up to and appreciated his thoughtfulness. He played an up-tempo salsa cover of "Would I Lie," and the sounds of Cubaneros filled the room. It sounded like a party.

The four dancers took their places on the dance floor. The rules were simple: anyone could cut in on the other couple whenever they wanted.

Andrés started with Amber. Sebastián, with Gia. His lead was light and playful, letting her know that what happened off the floor wouldn't interfere with what they were building on it.

Andrés cut in first. Instead of taking Gia's hand, he went straight for Sebastián.

Gia and Amber barely had time to process what happened while Sebastián let out a full-bodied laugh, shaking his head but rolling with it.

"Oh, we're doing this, huh?" Sebastián mused, accepting Andrés' lead, already bracing for chaos.

"Relax, bro," Andrés said, spinning him with surprising finesse. "This is the partnership destiny intended."

Amber catcalled at the guys. "About time! We've all been waiting for this bromance to blossom." She turned to Gia with a grin. "Don't let them steal the spotlight. That belongs to us."

Gia spun into Amber's lead and nearly stumbled. The connection was all wrong, the timing a half-beat late. Amber grinned anyway, chin high, as if confidence could cover the gaps. "Just make it look good."

Sebastián smirked over Andrés' shoulder. "Careful, Andrés, if we outshine them, they might quit salsa altogether."

"Please," Amber shot back. "If that day ever comes, I'll eat my dance heels."

"Bold words," Sebastián replied. "Especially when you're leading like you're steering a shopping cart with a busted wheel."

That earned a howl from Amber and a snort from Gia.

In retaliation, Andrés broke into an exaggerated body roll. Sebastián matched him instantly, both of them committing so hard that the ladies doubled over laughing.

"Ladies?" Andrés said between rolls. "This is pure artistry. Try to keep up."

"Artistry?" Amber scoffed. "Pretty sure I just lost brain cells watching that."

Then Sebastián scooped up Gia, Andrés swept up Amber, and suddenly they were dancing as if they were at a family party.

Sebastián met Gia's eyes, his expression soft and easy.

"We're past the awkward part now, right?" he asked.

She smiled, breathless. "Absolutely."

By the time the song ended, all four of them were doubled over, gasping for air and shaking their heads at the ridiculousness of it all. Andrés and Amber returned to their rehearsal space, closing the door behind them to drown out their music.

"Alright," Sebastián said once he was alone with Gia. "We spent weeks on the basics. Drilled technique. Built...connection." His voice caught slightly on the last word. He glanced at Gia, then rubbed a hand over his jaw as if he were considering whether he was going to stay on the dance topic or not. "We've got all that down. Time for the next step."

Gia lifted a brow. "Oh? And what's that?"

His eyes sparkled. He was excited.

"Picking the song. Starting the choreography for our piece."

Gia straightened, more alert.

"I've been thinking about this for weeks. Working with Cami and Daniel last night gave me an idea."

This was it. The moment everything would shift from training to building something real. She had been so focused on getting through rehearsals, keeping up with Sebastián, proving herself worthy of being his partner, that she hadn't let herself think this far ahead.

"What are you thinking?"

Sebastián's smile widened, and he walked over to the sound system, scrolling through his playlist.

"We could go with something flashy and explosive that plays to the crowd. A classic salsa song that the audience loves and expects. Something from Fania All Stars or Grupo Niche. All the things we talked about yesterday with Cami."

Gia crossed her arms and cocked her head. "But we're not going that route either."

Sebastián glanced at her over his shoulder. "Nope," he said with a touch of adventure in his voice.

He pressed play, and the first few notes drifted through the speakers. She immediately picked out the congas, cajón, and the crisp tick of the clave. A rich rumba intro built slowly, pulsing for nearly a minute before the beat dropped into a full-bodied wave of earthy salsa. In the final third, the tempo shifted again, slipping into a groovy cha-cha-cha before cutting out in a sharp, unexpected finish.

As the salsa section hit, Gia felt the warm guitar line and stand-up bass beneath bursts of brass. She closed her eyes, already picturing how their bodies could carve shapes into the music. There would be sweeping partnerwork and a crisp break before perfect shines that hit every beat with precision.

"It's 'Donde Se Fueron.' Ozomatli. What do you think?" Sebastián played it again. Gia listened closer this time, now that she was familiar with the overarching structure of the song.

She was lost in the possibilities, imagining the textures of the movement, when the music slid into the cha-cha-cha, which seemed to slow time and stretch out the song's sexiness. Her eyes snapped open, and her mind raced ahead, plotting how they could play with that pace and make it theirs.

It was a bold, creative choice. She searched for the right word, something that captured the soulful heat of it, the way it slipped under your skin and made your body ache to match its rhythm.

Delicious, she thought. Not how most would describe a pro-am performance. She turned to Sebastián, her voice certain. "This is what we'll compete with."

"This is what we'll win with."

His words lingered between them, heavy with promise.

"What made you pick this song?"

"I want us to create something unforgettable—not just a performance you watch, but one you feel. You have that effect on people. I want a song that captures it."

She wasn't sure how to respond because she felt the same way about him.

"Let me show you what I'm thinking." Sebastián started the track over and turned the volume up, letting the soulful melody fill the space.

His hands lingered on her hips as he eased her back against the mirror at the edge of the floor, pinning her in place as his captive audience. She had nowhere to look but at him. He toed off his shoes, crossed the room, and dimmed the lights to a hushed glow. Then, barefoot, he claimed the center.

With one smooth motion, Sebastián tugged off his shirt and tossed it aside. Every flex, every ripple of muscle caught the low light. He was impressive at rest, but when his body began to move to the music, he was something else entirely.

Gia held her breath, transfixed. Part of her wanted to admire him like art, a masterpiece in motion. The other part burned to close the distance, to touch, to feel the heat rolling off him for herself.

It started with a solo. Sebastián performed guaguancó, a rumba style defined by sharp body isolations aligned with the percussion. His chest expanded and retracted in pulses, like a heartbeat echoing the clave. His torso moved in smooth, undulating waves, disconnected from the rest of his frame, while his shoulders rolled with a fluid rhythm, sometimes languid and sinuous, other times quick and accented.

Sebastián's control was total. Every sharp line and quiet pause hinted at a force held in check. He was a storm restrained but ready to unleash.

That one minute and twenty seconds of percussion was an offering. With every slow, deliberate pulse of his body, he made her a promise of movement of another kind. The kind that happens in the dark. The kind that would leave them both breathless. Heat spread low in her belly as she watched him dance for her. All she could think was God help me, I want to feel that body on mine, moving like that.

When the beat dropped and the salsa rushed in, Sebastián extended his hand to her. His eyes shone brightly.

"You ready to make this ours?"

"So ready."

Conversation had carried them as far as it could. Now, only the dance could say what they needed to. She slid her palm into his and let him pull her into a closed position that locked out the rest of the world. The dance they would choreograph together began.

The next two hours were a blur of movement and experimentation. They tested ideas, played with footwork, and found pockets of the music where their bodies fit together seamlessly. Every lift, spin, and dip demanded trust and connection.

The heat crept in steadily, sweat glistening along Sebastián's neck and chest, dampening the edges of Gia's sports bra as they worked harder and closer.

When Sebastián finally said, "Let's run it through from the top," Gia was breathless but wired.

They started side by side, body isolations and rumba motion in sync with the percussive opening. His earlier solo was mirrored, elevated, and even more beautiful with Gia's strong and feminine touch.

When the beat dropped, Sebastián gave Gia a cross-body lead into a seamless, sweeping combination across the floor. He slid his hand down the curve of her spine, pressing firmly enough to remind her who was leading. Gia responded just on time, as if to point out to him he was leading only because she was letting him.

Her chest brushed against his again as he swept her into a deep, fluid dip, first lowering her to his right, flowing through a weightless arc, bringing her up to his left.

At the peak, he held her there, suspended for a pause too long. It was a decision, not a mistake.

When the sexy cha-cha section came in, she made a choice. She took the lead by drawing out the steps until they melted into the sway of a slow dance.

Her hands skimmed over his neck first, then his shoulders. She slid down his chest and lower, down every single abdominal muscle, flexed and hard. Her touch was soft and unhurried. It was a silent request set to a beautiful song.

She arched slightly, shifting closer, pressing her weight into him as he took the lead from her, stronger and back on pace with the song. Sebastián's grip was firm and measured. He kept the tension on a razor's edge, guiding her through a series of turns before slowing again to the tempo she had set a moment ago, stretching each step long enough to let it burn.

His hands lifted hers above her head, their fingers laced together, matching the pattern of their legs: his right thigh pressed between hers and her right thigh between his. He traced his palms down the length of her arms, down the sides of her ribcage, stopping as low as he could reach before moving back up, mapping her body like he wanted to memorize every inch.

Then he led her into a slow body roll. Gia instinctively responded to the faintest tilt of his palm pressing against the top of her back, shifting her weight slightly backward so her chest lifted first, as the wave made its way down. She rolled through with him, her stomach grazing his, her hips following, flush against him. That's when she felt the undeniable proof that he was as affected as she was: muscle-bound and hard in all the right places.

Gia's breath grew shallow and uneven. She couldn't take

another second of this excruciating tension. Her body took over her mind, and before she could stop herself, the words slipped out in a breathless whisper.

"You're killing me, Sebastián. Kiss me already."

Her legs were laced between his. With one step, all the space between them disappeared. His hands, no longer a firm dancer's hold but a hungry lover's grip, spread over the sides of her ribs, as if to claim his territory.

When his mouth took hers, she felt weeks of tension break open. It wasn't gentle or careful. It was ravenous, possessive. The kiss confirmed what her body already knew: she was past the point of pretending this was only dance.

Having lost all sense of restraint, Gia melted deeper into him. When she felt like she might lose her footing, Sebastián lifted her up. Her legs wrapped around his waist as he walked to the edge of the floor, pressing her against the cold studio mirror, a stark contrast to the fever burning between them. One arm circled her waist, holding her up seemingly without effort. His other arm braced them against the mirror. His mouth found her neck. When she dared to open her eyes, the reflection on the mirrored wall opposite them hit her so hard she forgot how to breathe. Her body pinned against the glass, legs clinging to the solid band of muscle at his midriff, every ridge of his back taut and glistening with sweat. Steam fogged the mirror in the shape of their bodies tangled together. She barely recognized herself, breathless, consumed by a desire she hadn't felt in years.

The music continued to swell in the background, their breaths mingling with the melody.

The song's abrupt ending hit, and from the other studio, a classic salsa tune spilled through the walls. Andrés and Amber were still rehearsing next door.

Sebastián exhaled sharply, ran a hand through his hair and across Gia's collarbone. His eyes flickered to the mirror and back to her.

"Wanna get out of here?"

She nodded, heart pounding. He didn't say another word.

She grabbed her bag. He grabbed his keys, took her hand, and led her out of the studio into the cool San Diego night.

Gia slid into the passenger seat of Sebastián's convertible. The engine's purr filled the silence, the coastal highway stretching before them. Cardiff was far enough to cool off. Or at least, it should have been. She could still feel his hands mapping her ribcage.

They didn't speak. Words would've broken the tension that pulsed between them, thick and electric, building like the beat of a song that refused to drop.

Sebastián's modern house was tucked into the cliffs of Encinitas, where the ocean stretched endlessly in the distance. When they finally arrived at his place, they stepped into a new world. A world for them alone. Sebastián opened the door and let her step inside first.

His place was minimalistic, yet stylish with hints of warmth. A guitar propped against a shelf, an old fútbol jersey draped over a chair, family photos, the faint scent of the ocean a few blocks away.

She dropped her bag near the entryway, turning to face him. No music. No choreography. Just the reality of the choice they were making.

Sebastián flexed his hands at his sides. "Gia. Tell me to stop," he said, voice low. "Otherwise, I'm not going to."

Sebastián watched her, waiting to make sure she wanted this.

Gia closed the distance and pressed her lips to his.

The kiss started slowly, like the first bars of a salsa romántica danced with the person you'd been craving from across the room. Sebastián kissed like he danced, with total command and no second-guessing. One hand slid to the small of her back, pulling her closer, anchoring her to him. The other traced up her spine.

This was a different dance, and one where she wasn't in a follower's role. Gia claimed as much as she gave. Her hands gripped the back of his neck, fingers threading into his hair, tilting his head just enough to deepen the kiss, to shift the pace.

He let out a half-growl, half-groan that sounded like approval and surrender.

His hands curved over her hips, pulling her tighter against him like he was closing the frame of a sensual bachata dance. His fingers traced a slow, deliberate line down the center of her chest, a whisper-light touch that turned her skin to gooseflesh. At the same time, his mouth followed the curve of her throat, leaving a trail of heat in its wake, soft and teasing, a body roll made of lips and barely-there pressure. She melted into it, head tilting back, her breath catching as she bared her neck to him, offering him more.

He let the tension stretch until it was all-consuming. Until it was painful. Until it was everything.

His hands slid down, gripping the backs of her thighs, lifting her effortlessly, as he had done in the studio. Once again, her legs wrapped around his waist, picking up where they had left off, only this time, he carried her into his bedroom, each step bringing them closer to the inevitable.

The room was flooded with warm amber light. A floor lamp, a linen duvet, the low murmur of waves outside. Sebastián laid Gia down on soft pillows, eyes locked on hers. He took his time peeling off her dance clothes, letting each layer fall aside. When he reached her undergarments, he paused for a heartbeat, eyes tracing her face as if asking without words. She nodded yes, and he removed them with the same unhurried care, savoring the reveal.

He spread her thighs, running his hands up the length of her legs, anchoring her with a grip just tight enough to make her shiver. "The thought of this has been driving me crazy for weeks," he said, lips grazing the sensitive skin of her inner thigh. "I want to learn every way your body says yes."

Her breath caught as his mouth left a slow trail of kisses along the inside of her leg, his hands steadying her hips when they bucked at the first warm swipe of his tongue. Then he was on her, in her, completely absorbed in the way her body reacted beneath him. Gia gasped, her hands grasping for the sheets, fingers gripping hard as his tongue slid slow at first, tasting her. When she whimpered, thighs trembling, he adjusted, pressing deeper, learning the rhythm of her breath and the tension of her muscles.

He read her like he read music. When she arched, he followed the curve of her body, tongue pressing firmer, then backing off enough to avoid the edge. When she softened, hips rolling toward him, he met her there, matching her pace. Every flick of his tongue was a conversation with her body speaking, him listening and answering.

She opened her eyes momentarily to look down at him. The sight of Sebastián there, between her legs, mouth devouring her with that same focus she'd seen on the field, on the dance floor, completely dialed into her, made her dizzy.

When his eyes lifted to hers, she lost all composure, and a wild, primal moan broke loose. He didn't stop watching. His hand clamped around her thigh, and the other slid to her ribcage, pinning her there while he devoured her.

"Sebastián…" Her voice broke on his name, breathless, pleading.

"Don't hold back. I want to hear you." He groaned against her, the vibration making her jolt. The pressure inside her coiled tighter, growing harder to fight. His tongue moved faster, then slower, drawing her in and letting her go, keeping her on the edge until she was begging without words.

Finally, her body arched, hips lifting off the bed, thighs clenching around his head as wave after wave tore through her.

Sebastián didn't stop until she was spent and trembling beneath his mouth. Only then did he ease up, kissing the inside of her thigh, slow and reverent, before crawling back up her body.

She was still catching her breath when he leaned down, his mouth brushing against her ear.

"I'll never get enough of you."

She caught his face between her hands, pulling him into a kiss that was raw and hungry.

"I want the rest of you," she breathed against his lips, legs still trembling from the aftermath of his mouth on her.

She pulled him closer, but Sebastián's hands came to her wrists again, firm but impossibly gentle, holding her still. He pulled back just enough to meet her eyes. "Let's not. Not tonight."

Gia froze, confused, her pulse thundering in her ears. "What... why?"

He pressed his forehead to hers. "I don't want to rush this. Not with you. We have all the time in the world for the rest of it. Let me... let me take care of you tonight. Just you."

Her heart flipped. She swallowed hard. Her throat was tight.

When she stayed quiet, still trying to catch up to the moment, he kissed her temple, then her cheek, then her lips.

"I want you, Gia. I've wanted you since the first time we danced."

He exhaled, his voice barely above a whisper. "I need you to know what's between us...it's not just about dance floor chemistry. This... what I feel for you... it's more than that."

He pulled back enough to meet her eyes.

His hand slid down to her hip. "When this happens, it's because you want me. Because you trust me. No teacher-student thing. No lessons or titles. Nothing else blurring it. I'll wait. I'll earn that. All of it."

Gia looked at him in disbelief. She wanted to say she was already his. She didn't want time or promises. However, she wanted to be an exception, not a "thank you, next." Every nerve in her body screamed for more, but she understood his restraint wasn't rejection. He was proving she mattered. That made the desire burning between them feel not less, but infinitely more. If waiting was the proof, then she could wait too.

So instead, she nodded.

He smiled faintly and brushed his lips over her jaw, and then in that sensitive spot where her neck met her shoulder.

"Good," he said against her skin. "Because I'm going to spend as long as it takes to make sure you never doubt how much I want you."

Her nails dug into his shoulders. "Then don't stop."

He wrapped around her, murmuring in Spanish, his hands gentle but possessive, holding her close as if his body itself was the promise.

When sleep finally claimed her, her last thought was of his words. I'll earn it. All of it.

Gia woke before sunrise. The room was still dark, with the faintest hint of dawn stretching across the horizon beyond Sebastián's bedroom window. The air smelled of salt, sweat, and him.

Sebastián's arm was draped over her waist, his chest a solid wall of heat pressed against her back. For a long moment, she let herself sink into the quiet intimacy of being held and waking up wrapped in someone else. Her body was calm, but her heart wasn't.

What if this version of herself, the woman who danced in glitter and got lost in terrace kisses, existed on borrowed time? She was supposed to go back to New York. How would she survive that if she let herself fall any deeper?

Sebastián was used to being wanted. Desired. Worshipped. She'd told herself she could handle it without attachment, but staring at the door, the panic started to rise in her chest. If she left now, they could still call it a one-night thing. They could say it was simply a moment where the dance got the better of them.

He murmured something in his sleep, shifting but not waking. She peeled herself from him and searched the floor for clothes.

She'd tugged on her shirt when she heard his voice, low and drowsy.

"Don't go."

Her hand froze.

She turned. Sebastián was watching her, still half-asleep, green eyes open and clear.

"Sebastián..."

He shook his head, slow and sleepily. "Come back to bed."

She blinked, caught between emotion and rationality.

"I have work in a couple of hours."

"There's time," he murmured.

A pause stretched between them.

Sebastián sat up straight, the blankets gathered around his waist. "Gia. Not yet."

She walked back to him.

Sebastián smiled and lifted the edge of the blanket in invitation. "Yesssss."

She slid beneath it, into the warmth of him.

It wasn't practical. It wasn't smart. For once, she didn't want all that. She wanted alive.

"Morning, Sebastián," Gloria called from behind the counter. "You're late."

He glanced at the clock on the wall. "Four minutes."

"That's how I know something's up." She slid a pastry to the customer in front of him, giving him a knowing smirk. "You're never late."

"I'm just well-rested."

Lie. Sebastián hadn't slept a full hour. He'd been too busy lying beside Gia, watching her breathe. He spent the night memorizing the curves of her body and the way they fit against his. She'd fallen asleep so peacefully, her hand against his chest like she trusted him to keep her safe. That tiny detail was one of countless things about Gia that made him want to be worthy of her.

He ordered a double espresso and paused when he reached the counter to pick it up.

"Add one of those guava croissants, please," he said on impulse.

Gloria gave him a suspicious look. "Since when do you eat pastries? Something is definitely up."

He shrugged, still smiling.

When he stepped out of the cafe and into the sun, his smile

lingered, along with the image of Gia tangled in his sheets, moaning his name.

It would've been easy last night. Too easy. He'd seen it in her eyes when she pulled him closer, felt it in the way her body fit against his. Every nerve in him had screamed to take what she was offering. It was right there, and damn, he wanted her. Badly. But not like that. Not yet. Not when she was trusting him bit by bit. He needed to know she saw him. Not the soccer player nor the local celebrity everyone gossiped about. And definitely not as her coach.

If he rushed the sex, it would blur everything they were becoming. She deserved more, and if he was honest with himself, so did he.

He'd never admitted it before, but he wanted to fall. Not only into bed, but into love. Everything in his gut said Gia could be it. He just needed to let the feelings grow stronger before desire drowned out everything else. Now that he'd had a taste, he didn't know how he'd hold himself back if she opened up to him again. If he gave in to his desire too fast, he risked losing the very thing he craved: the chance for this to be real before it became about sex.

By the time he stepped onto the soccer field, he was grateful for the distraction.

He blew the whistle and watched the San Diego Soccer Club kids set up for drills, their bright jerseys bobbing across the turf. Under a cloudless sky, sunlight poured down, the ocean breeze cutting the heat to perfect, golden Southern California warmth. The field smelled of fresh-cut grass. Laughter rang out, mixed with the rhythmic thud of soccer balls against net.

Everything felt quiet in his head. The usual mental static of pressure, expectations, and what-ifs was gone. He wasn't thinking about the future or the past.

"Coach Solano," one of the youngest players called out, squinting at him. "You're smiling. Should we be worried?"

"What? I smile all the time."

"Yeah, when we win. Or when we nutmeg someone in a game. Not at practice."

Laughter rippled through the boys.

Sebastián chuckled and tossed a ball toward them. "Okay, fellas. Just for that, I'm jumping in. Let's go."

The team groaned in mock horror, though their bright smiles betrayed them.

"Oh, come on," he called, jogging onto the field. "I'll race all of you. Every lap I beat you? That's an extra lap for you."

The groans turned to chaos. Half bolted forward, launching into a sprint. The kids shouted protests through their grins. Sebastián laughed in response, already picking up speed. Practice was for training, but sometimes you had to play for the love of it. Today, everything felt different.

For the first time in his life, he didn't just want the win. He wanted it all.

When Gia got back home, her cousin had already left for work. There was a note waiting on the kitchen table, scrawled on a pink Post-it in Nikki's unmistakable, loopy handwriting.

"Yeah," she said to herself with a little laugh. "Might need a whole bottle of wine for that conversation."

Her body was alive this morning, buzzing with restless energy. She couldn't remember ever feeling this way about a man. Not even with Miles in the beginning.

There was just enough time to squeeze in a run, knock out some editing work, and meet with Eli Maddox in the afternoon.

When she laced up her sneakers and stepped outside, the morning sun was already soft and golden over Mission Bay. The water glittered like someone had scattered a million tiny diamonds across its surface.

Gia popped in her earbuds, looking for a playlist that matched her mood. She wanted something bright and full of drums and brass. She played the B-Side Players on shuffle and started to run.

Her ponytail swung behind her as her feet fell into rhythm on the sidewalk. Everything just clicked. Her breath came easy. Her legs were light. Even the usual chatter in her head had gone quiet, replaced by one blissfully ridiculous thought: He wants to earn me.

Then another thought, more primal, took over: Damn. I. Want. That. Man.

The smile that spread across her face was unstoppable. Even when a passing cyclist shot her a funny look, she didn't bother to hide it.

Once home, she showered quickly, humming to herself as she rinsed sweat, salt, and Sebastián from her skin, and set up her laptop at the kitchen table. Eli Maddox's manuscript was waiting in her inbox, another round of revisions to tackle.

Normally, she read her clients' drafts with a cool, editorial eye. Detached. Efficient. She was skilled at pushing them toward emotion when their stories sounded like white papers and just as good at trimming when they rambled. Get to the point, she'd remind them. Don't make people wait for the punchline.

Today, staring at Eli's lofty paragraphs, her own rules blurred. She lingered, reread. Instead of cutting, she typed a note in the margin: *What if you held back here? Sometimes restraint makes the reader lean in. Drawing it out builds suspense. Makes them want it more. Let's try that?*

Chapter Fourteen

In the final weeks before a competition, most dancers performed in nightclubs and at socials, treating those nights as dress rehearsals. With just two weeks left before the pro-am, Sebastián scheduled a few performances for them so they could practice under real pressure. Tonight there would be two shows, Gia and Sebastián, and another local pro-am team that was competing in the advanced division.

As Sebastián spun Gia across the dance floor, the crowd's roar crashed over her. She loved dancing with Sebastián from the beginning, but performing with him was its own kind of magic. If rehearsal was flirtation and social dancing was foreplay, performing on stage with him was the full-blown, all-consuming love affair. She was in deep.

As the last notes of their first practice performance played, the crowd's cheers confirmed what Gia already knew. Every ounce of chemistry, heat, and connection between them was undeniable.

When they stepped off the dance floor, Nikki barreled toward them. "Girl, you torched that stage!" she shouted, bouncing on her heels. "That was unreal! I can't believe how far you've come in just a few months!" She wrapped Gia in a big hug before turning to Sebastián with a grin. "You weren't bad either, Sebas," she teased, pulling him into a quick squeeze.

"Well, I have an incredible partner, as you know." Sebastián smiled. Gia laughed, breathless and glowing. Her cheeks were still flushed from the adrenaline running through her.

"I came to see you guys kill it on your first show, but I gotta run. We'll catch up at home." Nikki put her hands in the shape of a heart as she walked off, mouthing the words, *love you. Congratulations.*

Gia should've savored the rush a little longer but couldn't resist watching the next couple take the floor. Gia noticed Gabriel's confidence first. He high-fived his way around the audience, hyping them up before escorting his partner to the center of the room. Natalie shimmered under the lights like a sliver of diamonds in human form. Her golden hair matched her dress, or the tiny bit of fabric that served as a sexy costume. She couldn't be over twenty-one. Maybe younger.

Natalie was in her dancing prime, and not only in age. The girl had presence, polish, and poise. Her hips were as fluid as water. Her every step dripped with sensuality. With each open break, her eyes flicked toward the crowd, not to seek approval, but to revel in it. Gasps and murmurs followed her like a second rhythm.

It's fine. Unique style. Different vibe. Despite the pep talk she gave herself, Gia's confidence from a few minutes ago began to fray at the edges.

Gabriel led Natalie into a dazzling spin that started upright before melting into a low, seated position. Her arms floated effortlessly, her body centered, and her skirt flared as she spun in a blur of blond hair and sequins. She performed with the finesse and control that came from daily training. Years of it. Hours upon hours. She never took years away or settled into a full-time desk job.

Gia closed her eyes as her heart sank. She abandoned her dream for reasons that had once seemed logical, but now, watching this dancer light up the floor, felt like a betrayal.

"You good?" Sebastián's voice cut through the fog, warm and grounding.

She snapped out of it, blinking fast. "Yeah."

He followed her gaze to the dance floor. "Hmm." His hand tightened slightly on her lower back. "They look strong."

Sebastián switched into strategy mode. "Let's clean up our transitions at the next rehearsal."

"Good idea." Gia nodded. *It's okay. Keep it together.*

"We need sharper lines for the judges. I'll film our next practice so we can analyze where to add more impact."

"Right," she murmured. "Good plan." She nodded again.

What was I thinking? Uprooting my life like this? Like I could slip back and belong?

Sebastián's gaze shifted, studying her more closely now. "What's going on?"

"Just thinking."

The music changed to a slower, smoother rhythm. A salsa romantica set a new atmosphere in the nightclub.

"Come on," he said.

"What?"

He reached for her hand. "We're done performing. Let's dance."

Sebastián led Gia to the dance floor, where the music curled around them, soft and seductive. Instead of letting Sebastián take her into a salsa frame, Gia rested her cheek against his chest.

"You okay?" Sebastián asked, his breath warm near her temple.

She pulled back slightly, shaking her head. "Not really."

"Tell me."

She looked up at him, voice low. "I feel like a fraud, Sebastián. Like any second, someone's going to figure out I don't belong here. That I'm playing dress-up in someone else's dream."

He held her gaze for a long time, then gently led her off the floor to a quieter corner near the lobby.

"You want to know what I was doing three months before I started dancing with Ritmo Latino?" he asked.

"What?"

"Crying in the dark while icing my knee. Wondering if I'd ever walk right again, let alone dance."

Gia stilled.

Sebastián leaned back against the wall. "I lost everything when I got hurt. My career. My plan. My identity. I thought if I wasn't a soccer player, I was nothing."

"But you're... you," she said in disbelief.

He gave her a half-smile. "Not in my own head. I was broken. Angry. Embarrassed to limp into a dance class because it made me look weak." His eyes softened. "You know what healed me more than anything?"

She didn't answer, but she already knew.

"Letting go of who I was supposed to be," he said. "And moving my body again. Not for a title, but because it felt good."

Gia sat quietly, trying to keep the tears from spilling over.

"You're not faking it, Gia. You're building something. It's okay if it's still under construction."

Her throat tightened, and she wiped away a tear before it fell.

He reached for her hand, linking their fingers. "You're not alone in this. You've got me. Camila. Nikki. The whole crew. Don't carry it by yourself."

"Thank you," she whispered.

"Do you want to dance?"

"Actually, I think I'm ready to go home. I hope you're not disappointed."

"Of course not. Let me just say good night to Camila."

Sebastián's face smacked of surprise when Gia took out her phone to flag a Lyft.

"I can drive you."

She tilted her head and smiled up at him. "I have work in the morning. If you drive me home, I have a feeling I won't get any sleep."

"Well, let me walk you out at least."

Once they slipped outside, away from the crowd and noise, Sebastián slowed the pace to a stop, pulled her close and kissed her deeply, hungrily. Instinctively, she melted into him, her body fitting perfectly against his. Immediately, flashbacks of their first night together flooded her mind. His incredible body, his fingers pressed into her thighs, his eyes looking at her from between her legs...

"You know, my meeting doesn't start until noon. Maybe I don't *need* to rush home."

Sebastián looked at her in surprise. "Gia, are you hitting on me?"

"Oh my God, seriously?"

"Definitely not." He laughed. "Get in," he said with mock bossiness, taking her bag in one hand and pointing to his car with the other.

When they arrived at his place, neither of them bothered to turn on the light.

They kissed the entire way to the bedroom, hands tangled in hair and fabric, shedding clothes piece by piece until her back hit the mattress and his mouth was on her again.

When she tried to pull him on top of her, he caught her wrists gently, shaking his head, his voice low and rough against her ear. "Gia, I want you. You have no idea. But after everything tonight, I don't want it to be like I'm taking advantage."

She let out a breathless laugh. "Then let me take advantage of you."

He didn't smile this time. Just looked at her with that steady, unshakable gaze.

"You really want our first time to be tonight? Right after everything we talked about?"

"We met in the dance world. Emotion and drama are a given. If we wait for perfect timing, we'll both be eighty."

That earned a smile, but he still didn't move.

"We only get one first time," he said, brushing her hair from her face.

"Sebastián." She kissed him hard. He groaned as she ran her mouth down his throat, around his neck and down his chest.

"You realize there's no going back after this."

"I'm a big girl. I know what I want." She reached up, pulling herself to him, closing the distance again, her body aligned against every inch of his. "I want you. Tonight. Now."

Sebastián had been bracing himself for lust, heat, and desire. Her trust and certainty hit something deeper. Something he hadn't let himself hope for. He had to lock his jaw, ball his fists, anything to keep from rushing her, from losing himself in the way she looked at him.

She peeled off her undergarments, baring herself to him completely. The cool air gave her goose bumps, but Sebastián's gaze as she stripped off her bra sent heat through her just as fast.

Gia took her time removing his clothes, wanting to see every inch of him, every carved line, every sculpted muscle honed by years of training, discipline, and competition. She'd seen him shirtless before, admired the broad chest and the hard-cut lines of his abs that had tortured her in rehearsal. Now, with nothing between them, his raw power was almost too much.

Sebastián's jaw clenched. He was hardly holding himself together. His chest rose and fell, each breath sharper and heavier. The restraint in his body was coiled tight as a loaded spring.

The first time only happened once, and neither wanted to waste a second of it. So they moved slowly, greedy for every gasp, every shiver, stretching each touch like it could suspend time itself.

She dragged her palms down his torso, soaking in the texture of his skin, hungry to absorb all of his power. When she came to the sharp cut of his lower abs, she slowed, following the deep V-shaped groove that led downward, beckoning her touch.

Her fingertips drifted lower, exploring the way his muscles tensed beneath her, until finally she reached him. Every thick, heavy, hot inch of him was straining with desire.

She couldn't take another second. When she pressed him onto his back and straddled him, there was no stopping either of them.

She positioned herself above him, teasing him with the slowest descent, the promise of full connection drawing a sharp inhale from his lips.

"God," he rasped, his hands gripping her hips like she was something he couldn't bear to let go of, "look at you…"

She took him in. A moan escaped her as he filled her, making her arch as white-hot pleasure flooded through her veins.

Sebastián groaned, his grip on her tightening, fingers digging into her skin like he was holding on for dear life. For a moment, they didn't move.

"You feel…" The thought dissolved on his tongue, replaced by a groan as he sank further into her.

The rhythm found them easily, their bodies slipping into counterpoint: one pushing, the other pulling, a perfect balance of control and surrender. When he rolled his hips against hers, she met him halfway, not just receiving him, but giving back. When she shifted his weight, allowing him to be on top, he pressed deeper into her.

She moaned. Arched. He drove harder. She pushed into him, matching the intensity beat for beat. He ran his hands up her legs, pinning one against his hip, exploring angles and shapes that made her breathless.

Their breath tangled between them—ragged, uneven, gasping. Sebastián rolled his hips into her, each thrust sending a fresh surge of pleasure through her, his grip tightening as he led them both closer to the edge. She felt it coming—the swelling, burning pressure gathering in her core, every muscle tensing in anticipation of the crescendo. Just when she thought she might lose it completely, he changed the rhythm. Slowed. Pulled back. Opened his eyes to find hers. He stretched her desire until it was deep and aching.

She whimpered. The tease was unbearable. She was right there, balanced on the edge, needing more.

His eyes met hers, and he gave her exactly what she needed. One final deep, rolling thrust, and everything inside her unraveled. The climax surged through her, her body clenching around him, pulsing, waves of heat crashing over her.

"Sebastián—" The sound was a breathless, desperate plea. He'd heard stadiums scream his name, whole crowds chanting it into the night, yet nothing had ever hit him like the aching whisper of Gia's voice against his ear.

His hips faltered and his rhythm fell apart as her body clamped down around him. His breath caught as he followed her into release. The sound that tore from his throat was low and broken. It sounded as though something sacred was coming undone.

They stayed there for a long while, limbs tangled, hearts pounding in unison like the last notes of a song neither wanted to end. His forehead rested on hers, her hands curled around his neck as though letting go would undo everything they'd just experienced together.

Eventually, he eased down beside her, pressing a soft kiss to her bare shoulder.

Gia closed her eyes and tried to burn this sensation into her memory. This is what it was to feel alive. To finally take the lead in her own life. *Please don't let this ever end.*

Sebastián drew her closer, his lips brushing her temple. His whisper was rough but certain. "Quédate conmigo, Gia. Siempre."

She opened her eyes, searching his face. "What did you say?"

"Stay with me," he said.

She studied him, then shook her head faintly. "That's not the full translation."

"No, it's not."

The word he left unsaid—always—hung between them, too sacred to be spoken twice just yet.

Chapter Fifteen

Gia adjusted the collar of her blouse, tucking the fabric neatly under her blazer. Her cheeks still held the faintest flush from her night with Sebastián.

She smoothed the crease on her sleeve and gave herself another look in the mirror. Apart from a light sunburn, Gia looked professional, put together, like the woman she'd spent the last ten years becoming. She opened her laptop, sat up straight, and joined the Zoom meeting.

"Morning, Gia." It was Diana, her manager based on the East Coast, in her usual brisk tone. She was already scrolling through a shared document, her reading glasses perched on her nose.

"Good morning," Gia replied, offering a smile.

"You doing okay? You've been a little quiet for the last couple of weeks. All good on your end?"

"Yes, everything is on track."

Diana nodded, lips curving like she accepted the answer, but her steady gaze told Gia she hadn't quite bought it.

"Well, I'll cut to the chase. I have something to run by you. You've done amazing work with the AcuGene and Biolux accounts. Eli Maddox is over the moon with how the manuscript is coming along. You have strong client relationships, kept things moving even when timelines were tight, and, most importantly, the team respects you."

"Diana, thank you." The warmth behind the comment surprised Gia. Praise wasn't exactly Diana's love language.

"I'm opening a director role. This is what you've been working towards. Same team but in a leadership position. You'd help oversee a few of the junior specialists. More client strategy. More ownership."

Gia blinked. "Wow. That's amazing. I wasn't expecting this for a while."

"To be clear, it's a full-time position." Translation: Expect lots of overtime. "Some travel." That was Diana-speak for frequent trips, packed schedules, and no real downtime. "Nothing major. Client visits, maybe a conference or two." Which of course meant monthly flights, keynote speeches, and all the behind-the-scenes hustle to make it look effortless.

Three months ago, Gia would've jumped at this opportunity. That was before San Diego, when long days were the norm and Miles was right there beside her, just as buried in work. They were building demanding careers and parallel lives. The extra hours felt like part of the plan. That wasn't her life anymore.

Her mind still danced with the memory of Sebastián whispering, "Stay with me." It clashed painfully with Diana's voice talking about *ownership* and work travel. Two different futures tugged her in opposite directions.

"Could I have a few days to consider it?"

Diana blinked, just for a beat, then composed herself.

"Of course. I'm offering the role before posting it to the rest of the company or opening it externally because I assumed you'd jump at it. It will start in September, after your part-time stint in San Diego, but I'd need you to sit in on meetings now to get up to speed. To be clear, the job is yours if you want it."

"Thank you," Gia said again, quieter this time.

The call ended with polite goodbyes, and the screen faded to her blank reflection, washed out, small in the top corner of the

Zoom window. She stared at herself for a beat, then closed the laptop.

Gia shut her eyes and stretched her head from side to side to prevent the "tech neck" that she got from stressing out at the computer for too long. This was what she used to want. She spent the last eight years chasing the next thing: a step up, a promotion, a bigger title, a better salary, more security, and everything she thought would make her feel whole.

Now, all she could think about was how many rehearsals she'd have to miss. Gia imagined how late she'd get home on weekdays, her body sore from sitting at a desk all day rather than from dancing all night. She might treat dance like a hobby she squeezed in between deliverables and deadlines, or worse, resort to living vicariously through her movie collections again.

The offer should have thrilled her. Instead, there was that quiet, creeping voice: *You can't have both. You don't get passion without consequences. Every choice has its cost.*

Promotions like this didn't come often. She'd be a fool to pass it up if she wanted to keep her career on track and make vice president one day. A title and a plan. Something tangible and sustainable...two things that dance and dating a heartthrob celebrity didn't really offer.

The trouble with perfect plans is that they're worthless when your heart isn't in them.

Chapter Sixteen

Mambo Sol's high-profile salsa social packed the room wall to wall with San Diego's best dancers, instructors, competitors, and die-hard salseros. It was the perfect venue for Gia and Sebastián's second performance.

Gia had been there five minutes before she felt eyes on her. Not the usual curious glances and "who's she?" looks she'd come to expect standing next to Sebastián Solano. No, these three pairs of eyes were different.

One leaned casually against the wall, with short, chic, golden hair and smoky eyes. Another, a redhead wearing a cherry colored body suit that matched her fiery hair, laughed so loud she could be heard over the music. The third, with long silky chocolate-colored hair that hung down to her waist, sat quietly looking out across the room, following Sebastián's every move. They reminded Gia of Charlie's Angels, if Charlie had picked villains.

Sebastián and Gia had to pass all three on the way to the staging area.

Their eyes slid down Sebastián's body like they already knew every line of it, each one carrying the unmistakable hunger of a woman who had been there before and wanted more. The brunette with curves made for a music video, tilted her head and beckoned Sebastián with one finger.

Sebastián gave a friendly hello and kept walking, oblivious to how she was mentally undressing him. Video Vixen didn't appreciate being blown off. When her eyes landed on Gia, they held the flat annoyance reserved for a speed bump.

The woman stepped forward and caught Gia's forearm for a beat. Then she let go and folded her arms across her chest. Her long, sharp nails tapped a slow rhythm against her skin, each click deliberate.

"You must be the latest?" The woman's voice was casual.

Gia forced a polite smile. "Latest... what, exactly?"

She leaned in, close enough for Gia to catch the scent of her perfume, a heady mix of florals with a hint of darkness. "The latest student star and teacher's pet. He always finds the ones with something to prove. He makes you believe he sees you. I bet you feel like you're the only woman in the world. Like you have so much potential. Right? And you probably do. At least until he gets you in bed. Then it's only a matter of time until the competition is over. Is that a few weeks from now?"

The words landed exactly where they were meant to. "I've seen it a million times. Especially with the new girls. Woman to woman, I'm looking out for you."

Gia held her smile, even as her stomach tightened. "Thanks for the warning, but I don't scare that easily. And for what it's worth, he hasn't made me feel like the only woman in the world. Just the only one in his. Now, if you'll excuse me, I have a performance to get to."

Gia walked on, hoping her stride looked steadier than she felt.

Confusion climbed higher in Gia's chest. She tried to process what she was feeling. It was complex and layered, a bruising mix of embarrassment laced with self-reproach. It made her want to pack up and go home. East Coast home. She felt exposed, like she'd wandered into a game mid-play, where everyone else already knew the rules. Worse than that, she broke her own rules. Never get involved with a man who has sway over your goals. Was everything she experienced with Sebastián real?

Ten minutes later, Gia stood in the bathroom, gripping the edges of the sink.

Breathe. You belong here. You fought too hard to let anyone rattle you. You've got this.

When she looked up and met her reflection, she barely recognized herself. She wore a glittery dress and the stage makeup of a salsera who took risks and took up space. From the outside, she shimmered with confidence. Inside, every heartbeat whispered, *run.*

You're not going to run. Not this time. Don't let their petty bullshit intimidate you.

Twenty minutes later, they took their places to start their performance.

Sebastián knew something was off the second he held Gia's hand.

She smiled at him, but it didn't reach her eyes. Her fingers felt stiff in his grip; her shoulders were tighter than usual.

"Hey," he murmured, low enough for only her to hear. "What's happening?"

She nodded quickly, looking straight ahead at the crowd. "I'm fine. Nerves."

But it wasn't just nerves. He could sense it in the way her body moved with his. Her dancing was precise, beautiful as always, but she never quite let go. From the outside, no one would have known anything was wrong. They nailed the choreography and the performance. She even flashed him a smirk on a particularly intricate move, and for half a second, he let himself believe everything was fine, but when the final note hit and the audience roared their approval, she dropped his hand before the applause faded.

"I need some water," she said, her tone light but a little too quick. "Be right back." As he watched her weave through the crowd and disappear down the hallway, his chest went heavy.

A moment later, a familiar voice called his name. "Sebastián!

There you are." He turned to find Camila's friend, Martin, who also happened to be a scout, grinning at him.

"Hey man. I've been looking for you all night. I just got word that Club Atlético Marbella needs a new assistant coach. They're considering you. Coastal club on the rise in Spain's top division. Not a bad way to return to soccer, right?"

Sebastián felt his pulse spike. The need to prove himself, to matter in the soccer world, lit up his veins.

As Martin talked about the La Liga offer, Sebastián forced a smile, nodding at all the right moments. This was everything he could have hoped for at this point in his career. Everything he needed to be whole again after the injury. And yet, his eyes kept drifting toward the hallway where Gia had disappeared.

She'd never known him as a soccer star. Never cheered his name from the stands or reposted his highlight reels. She'd met him here, in this quiet, unglamorous chapter of his life, coaching kids, dancing on weekends, just trying to figure out who the hell he was without the roar of the crowd. Lately, with Gia, he felt at home in his new reality.

Is this enough? I'm a soccer player. This is La Liga. Working with Camila was never supposed to be permanent.

If he didn't take this opportunity to be great again, would he ever feel like himself again? Worse, would she eventually see him for what he was now and decide it wasn't enough? The thought twisted in his chest as Martin clapped him on the back.

Finally Gia reappeared. "Any chance we can call it an early night?"

"You read my mind." He slipped his fingers through hers, their hands fitting perfectly as usual. They walked out of the venue, leaving the music and the strange weight of their performance behind them.

Gia curled onto the couch beside him, legs tucked under her, head resting lightly on his shoulder. She wore his old T-shirt with the faded Gravity logo. The worn cotton draped in places and stretched in others, just enough to trace the soft lines of her curves before skimming mid-thigh. She looked devastatingly gorgeous like this. Natural and unguarded, with no makeup and loose hair cascading down her back. He loved seeing her wrapped up in something that was his. Heat stirred in his chest, spreading deeper with every breath he took. What leveled him was how unaware she seemed of it all. She simply sat there, barefoot and rumpled, and undoing him with a beauty that asked for nothing, offered everything, and left him aching for all of it.

They'd ordered takeout and settled into what was their first truly peaceful night in weeks. Just her, here, leaning against him like she'd been doing the same thing for years. Sebastián let himself think that maybe this could be the norm.

Her phone chimed on the coffee table. She reached for it absently, unlocking it with a swipe. He didn't pay much attention at first, just kept tracing slow circles over the back of her hand, until her body went stiff.

Her brow furrowed as she opened something. It was a link from her cousin, if he caught the name correctly. Her eyes narrowed and then flickered wide with surprise.

He glanced down.

The Instagram app was open, with a post from @RedCard-Rumors filling the screen.

There were two photos, placed side by side.

On the left: Gia's agency headshot, where she looked neat, polished, and professional.

On the right: the dip from their first performance. Gia's glittering costume caught the light as her body arched backward with abandon, surrendering completely. Eyes closed, cherry red lips parted, she was pure ecstasy in motion with his hand firm against her back, holding her there, claiming her.

Even he had to admit it was provocative. A still shot taken in the middle of their performance looked like much more than a dance.

His gut tightened as he read the caption.

Former soccer star turned salsa dancer? Sebastián Solano was spotted heating up the floor with his student/partner. Sources say she landed the coveted performance spot after a few 'private lessons.' Looks like his type hasn't changed. Thoughts? •• *#CurvesForDays #FromGoalsToGlitter #Spicy*

The heat started in his gut and spread, tightening every muscle on its way through his body. Then came the comments.

> Is he ever single for more than a month? 🙄

> She's about to spill out of her top. Gooooooooal! 🙄

> She better enjoy her fifteen minutes of fame. 😈

> Y'all haters are just jealous you can't sack 'em like Solano. 👊⚽

> If this is his idea of talent, no wonder he's not playing soccer these days.

Each one landed like a blow to the ribs.

"Wow. Is this for real?" Gia's voice sounded fragile.

He ran a hand down his face, shaking his head. "This... isn't..." The words stuck. He swallowed hard. "They do this all the time. It's been worse. I don't even read it anymore."

She nodded faintly, avoiding his eyes as she placed her phone facedown on the cushion. "Hmm."

Her fingers slipped out of his. Suddenly, the warmth of her against him felt impossibly far away.

This was exactly what he'd feared. Gia getting dragged into his mess. He was already in this painful "in between" phase, and this post confirmed that everyone around him knew it and was waiting to see how he would define himself after the injury. The world was watching and measuring.

The familiar weight on his chest grew heavier, like someone had quietly added another stone.

She shifted, untucking her legs from under her and rising to her feet. "I should get some water," she murmured, already halfway to the kitchen.

He nodded. "Yeah. Sure."

She disappeared down the hallway. He stayed frozen on the couch, staring straight ahead, the glow of the comments burned into his mind.

Former soccer star turned salsa dancer?

What the fuck did that even mean? His name was still synonymous with soccer. Hell, he had a La Liga opportunity waiting for him. Salsa had *always* been in his blood. This wasn't his next chapter. Did these people forget about his parents? His sister?

Reading the caption that reduced his situation to a punchline only made the question he'd tried to bury roar back louder. *What am I without soccer? And what kind of man does that make me?* He hated himself at that moment. He hated the way the world saw him. Most of all, he hated the way Gia probably saw him now.

In the kitchen, Gia stood frozen, her reflection in the floor-to-ceiling windows staring back at her. It was the same eyes, same face, same body she'd spent years trying to love. She'd come so far, but right now all she could see were those ugly, cruel Instagram comments.

Her chest rose and fell in shallow breaths. Too many feelings, all colliding. Shame, hurt, anger, and worst of all, doubt.

That night, she'd trusted him. When he'd dipped her, she'd let go completely, certain Sebastián would hold her no matter how far she fell. She'd stretched back, her eyes closed and her heart open.

Seeing those two versions of herself side by side was like slamming a sledgehammer into every bruise she thought had healed. A woman in glitter, too much skin, too much everything, body on display for all the world to criticize and tear apart. How could she let herself think she could dance again without the merciless, judgmental parts that inevitably come with it? Without inviting the same scrutiny that had nearly broken her years ago?

When she looked down at her phone again, there were another forty-seven comments. New ones seemed to appear by the second, each one more cutting than the one before.

> It's giving midlife crisis vibes.

> She looks like she's just happy to be there.
> Bless.

> Dancing with the Stars? So Solano's the celebrity, but this gal ain't a pro.

In the comment, she spotted the hashtag, #SebastiánSolano. She shouldn't have tapped it.

Dozens of images filled her screen.

#SebastiánSolano on the field, arms raised after a goal. #SebastiánSolano at galas, in tailored suits, with some model or actress draped on his arm. #SebastiánSolano at restaurants, grinning across a candlelit table at yet another impossibly perfect woman.

Then the dance clubs. Los Angeles. Miami. Puerto Rico. Colombia. Each photo showed a new partner but always the same smile. She assumed Sebastián enjoyed the benefits that come with being a pro athlete, but wow, it felt different to have the proof in bright, vivid photos with countless comments where the world weighed in.

Her heart sank, leaden and cold. She set the phone down and pressed her palms hard to the counter, as if bracing against the weight of her own foolishness. Was she really just another in a long line of women who'd been dazzled by the way he moved?

And worse, had she actually let herself believe that chasing her passion for dance, laying her body bare, *especially* in the glare of a celebrity's spotlight, would somehow hurt less than the last time she'd made herself vulnerable on stage? She always knew that getting involved with Sebastián would eventually mean heartbreak, but never in her wildest nightmares did she see this coming.

When Gia returned with her glass of water, she kept her eyes lowered. Sebastián readied himself for a talk, but the words he'd rehearsed got tangled in his throat. Instead, they pounded through his head, desperate to be spoken. *I'm sorry you got pulled into my mess. I never meant to let it go this far before I figured myself out. I'm more than soccer, and salsa, and the playboy they make me out to be. Please don't write me off.*

None of it left his lips.

"I'm gonna turn in," Gia announced, still not looking at him.

His chest tightened, but he forced a nod. "Yeah. Of course."

For a heartbeat she lingered, her silence daring him to speak. He opened his mouth, but no sound came. She turned away, her bare feet whispering against the floor until the bedroom door closed with a soft click, leaving him alone with everything he couldn't say.

Sebastián stayed on the couch long after, staring at nothing. He knew he should go to her and ask her to hang in there while he was working himself out. What if she now saw him the way the rest of the world did—washed up and nothing more than some retired player who broke hearts for sport?

Sebastián's ribs seemed to close in around his heart.

When he finally stood hours later, he tiptoed through the dark house and slipped into bed beside her. She was already asleep, turned away from him, curled tightly under the sheets. He lay down on his back, staring at the ceiling, listening to her quiet, uneven breaths. Even though he was inches away from her, she felt so far away.

When he woke, her side of the bed was cold. On the kitchen table was a note.

That was all it said. Just three words and her name. Not the three words he wanted to hear most.

He stared at it for a long moment, the heaviness settling deeper into his chest. She was already gone.

Chapter Seventeen

Gia stared at the rehearsal reminder on her phone, her stomach twisting in knots. She could text Sebastián and tell him something came up. Work emergency. Migraine. Plumbing leak.

Messages began popping up on the screen, forcing her out of her spiral.

CAMILA

Twelve days to go till showtime! I can't wait to see where you guys are at. Let's lock it in!

ANDRÉS

Count on me! I'm coming too. Let's win this thing!!!

The excitement in the messages burned a hole straight through her gut. This performance wasn't only about her and Sebastián. It carried the weight of the company and, importantly, the legacy Camila continued to build. Backing out was never an option. Gia drew a deep breath, squared her shoulders, and grabbed her dance shoes.

Meanwhile, Sebastián sat outside the studio in his car, waiting until the last second to head inside. His phone buzzed in the cupholder.

He promised Camila he would do this for her, way before Gia was even…Gia. Bailing wasn't an option. He shoved the car door open and headed in.

When Sebastián stepped inside, Gia was already stretching, her back to him, her body tense and cold. He dropped his bag against the wall and walked over to meet her. They gave each other a quick air kiss without meeting each other's eyes. The memory of last night hovered between them, unaddressed yet understood by them both. They warmed up, silent and separate.

The door flew open, and Camila burst in with a gust of energy. "Okay, campeones!" she called, tossing her purse on the front desk. "Let's get this thing locked in. Sí o yes?!"

Andrés and Amber trailed behind her, chatting and laughing.

"Damn! Full house tonight!" Andrés said, winking at Gia. "You ready for this?"

Gia forced a tight smile. "Absolutely."

Sebastián heard the tightness in her voice. The tension between them was sharp, like barbed wire strung through the air.

No one else seemed to notice except for Camila. Her assessing eyes flicked between them, but she said nothing. Instead, she clapped her hands together. "Alright, let's run it. I want to see the whole thing, full out."

They rose to take their places. The instant Sebastián's hand closed around Gia's, his stomach knotted hard. Something felt so wrong it churned in his gut. Her frame held perfect elegance, thanks to countless hours of practice. Her technique was on point, each movement clean, precise, unshakable. She danced like a flawless instrument, every beat struck exactly where it belonged. However, the intoxicating fire that made their performance feel alive had vanished. A dangerous heat simmered under the nausea that was climbing in his throat. It was the start of a rage he couldn't push down.

They were simply dance partners. They may as well be strangers. They were no long *Gia and Sebastián* dancing together. The realization drove him fucking furious.

Her touch was foreign. Their chemistry was gone. Without the electric charge between them, the whole routine fell flat. The choreography collapsed under this unexpected weight, and Sebastián took the blame. He always locked feelings away from the field in order to stay sharp and untouchable. Salsa always offered physical and emotional connection without commitment. Now, in a partnership with emotions tangled in everything, he was wildly off balance. He had no playbook for this. What was the strategy? How the hell was he supposed to fix it?

By the time the music ended, Sebastián turned toward her, still holding her hand, searching her face for a crack, a signal, anything that might show him how to reach her again.

The dead silence was finally broken by Camila. "Okay..." She crossed her arms. "Technically? That was solid."

Andrés let out a low whistle. "But that was the coldest shit I've ever seen in my life."

Amber spoke softly, her voice steadying the swirl of confusion in the room. "This routine should sizzle. Normally, you two look like you're seconds from ripping each other's clothes off. Now's the time to lean into that."

"Let's go again." Gia and Sebastián responded simultaneously.

They danced the routine for a second time. Same result. Technically flawless. Emotionally flat.

Camila stepped forward, pressing her fingers to her temples as if fighting off a headache.

"Okay, pause." She turned to Sebastián. "What's happening here?"

Sebastián wiped the sweat from his brow with the back of his hand. "Nothing. We're fine."

Camila's eyes moved to Gia, waiting. Gia wouldn't meet her gaze.

"Alright. Clearly, we're not going to push through whatever this is tonight. Go home. Rest. Meditate. Take a bath. Scream into a pillow. I don't care what you do, but fix it. We'll pick it up again tomorrow."

Gia breathed a quiet thanks when Camila called it an early night. She needed to get out of there immediately. However, Sebastián refused to let her go so easily. He gathered his things in silence and followed her outside, holding his composure until they stood alone. Then he caught her hand, forcing her to stop walking away.

"Gia." His voice came low and clipped. "What the hell just happened in there?"

Gia pulled her hand back, but he didn't let go, as if keeping that physical connection would remind her of their emotional one.

"I don't know." She avoided eye contact.

"Bullshit."

Her spine stiffened. "I'm serious, Sebastián. Let it go."

A muscle ticked in his jaw, his frustration simmering beneath the surface. "I don't let things go when they affect my partner in the middle of a performance." He braced himself for her to tell him to get his shit together, to figure out his life before dragging her through the mud with him.

Gia yanked her hand away. "Well, maybe I'm not the right partner."

Sebastián's breath stilled. "Gia," his voice softer now. "What? Where is this coming from?"

She swallowed hard, looking anywhere but at him. If she looked at him, she might break. Gia crossed her arms, putting a barrier between herself and Sebastián, and everything else.

"Talk to me," he pressed. "Whatever it is, say it."

Gia tightened her hands around her elbows. Her body was stiff, and her voice was flat. "Look, I just think we should keep things simple."

Sebastián's pulse hammered. He couldn't read her or even get past the wall she'd thrown up, and it made his skin crawl.

His eyes flickered in disbelief. "Simple?"

"We have a competition to win. Let's focus on that."

"You're serious right now?"

She didn't answer.

"Are you really gonna stand here and talk to me about competing like none of this means anything to you? Like I don't mean anything to you?"

She stayed silent.

"Jesus. If you're freaked out, just say it. Don't give me this 'let's focus on the competition' crap."

She was obviously freaked out. Her shoulders were rigid as she wound her arms tight around her chest. Tears shimmered in her eyes, but she blinked them back, forcing her face into a flat and unreadable expression. Whatever it was, he wished she would say it so he had a chance in hell of fixing it.

Then she whispered, her voice so quiet he almost missed it: "It's just dance, Sebastián."

He looked like she had slapped him. "That's what this is?"

"Isn't it?"

A long, suffocating silence stretched between them.

He let out a slow breath and ran a hand down his face and throat before pulling his shirt collar from his neck as if it might choke him.

"You think I'm just playing?" There was hurt beneath the anger.

"Seb—"

"No." He cut her off. "Answer the question."

She shook her head, looking away. "I don't know what to think."

"Yeah. You do." The bitterness in his laugh set her off.

"Okay. You want to know what's wrong?" She snapped, voice shaking. "I can't trust this."

Her words were knives. She didn't trust *him*.

Sebastián took a breath, trying to steady his tone. "Gia, whatever you think—"

"I get it," she cut in. "You make dancing feel like more—heat, connection, maybe even love if someone's not careful. But that's the game, isn't it? I'm not the first to fall for it."

"Gia—"

"There are a million photos of it online," she threw back. "You and whoever you're dancing with, all looking like it's something real."

"Gia, wait—"

"And you've got groupies everywhere you go. Stop pretending you don't notice."

He stepped forward. "Let me explain—"

"I'm not interested in being another dance fling!"

He opened his mouth, but nothing came out.

Gia saw shock in his eyes and the hurt she'd meant to protect herself from. Sebastián dragged his hand through his hair. His breath grew increasingly unsteady. He had a temper but kept it under control off the field. Here, it was slipping.

"Since when have I given you a single reason to believe that's what this is?"

She said nothing, just shook her head back and forth, refusing to engage further.

"So that's all it takes? One stupid Instagram post and a few idiots at a club, and you're done? That's enough for you to write me off?"

He wished she'd fight back. Anything would be better than this silence. Her calm made him feel like he was the only one falling apart.

"Unbelievable," he muttered, pacing. "I can't even tell if we're having the same argument."

She crossed her arms, jaw tight. "Maybe we're not because I'm not sure what you're even fighting for right now."

"I'm fighting for my life, Gia. For the part of it that's still mine." His voice cracked under the strain. "You think this is easy for me? That I don't have everything on the line already?"

"On the *line*?"

He raked a hand through his hair, breath coming hard. "I've got a team depending on me, a career hanging by a thread, and I can't even think straight because I'm—" He gestured at her, exasperated. "Because I'm caught up in this. In taking things slow and doing it right. And it still blows up."

"Well, I'm sorry that doing things *right* is such a big deal for you."

He laughed once, sharp and humorless. "What am I even doing here?" He gestured between them. "You get to walk in and feel things for the first time in years, like this is some kind of rebirth. I'm happy for you. Seriously. But for me? This isn't a game. This is the last thing I have left that feels alive."

Her arms dropped to her sides. "That's not fair."

"I know it's not. None of this is." He looked at her then, jaw clenched hard enough to ache. "You think I don't know what people say about me? That I'm just some washed-up playboy athlete who fucks around for sport? I thought you saw past that. I needed you to."

"Sebastián, what am I supposed to think when I have women confronting me about you in nightclubs and then my pictures are smeared all over the internet next to all your other women?"

"Gia, I can't control what other people do. Can't you get that?" He exhaled hard, his voice breaking as he started talking to himself. "Maybe that was just me fooling myself. If this, whatever this is, has just been a nice fantasy, well fuck, I can't live inside something that's only real to me."

Gia's face went still. "A fantasy," she repeated, her voice barely above a whisper. "Right. Every woman's fantasy. Thanks for the clarity, Sebastián."

He froze. "No, that's not—are you not hearing me?"

She took a step back, shaking her head. "Oh, I heard you loud and clear."

"Gia—"

Gia's expression went blank. She turned on her heel, walking away before he had a chance to say another word.

All Sebastián could do was stand there in the silence, staring at the space she'd left behind, and hate himself.

Sebastián didn't know how he ended up on the soccer field. He didn't even remember the drive. One minute he walked out of the studio parking lot, frustration knotted so tight in his stomach it threatened to split him in two. The next, he stood in the same place he'd spent his earlier years grinding, sweating, chasing the dream. The grass seemed to welcome him home, even if this world no longer belonged to him.

Darkness cloaked the stadium, save for a few stray beams stretching shadows on the field. A handful of young players ran drills under the glow of the lights. They chased something only they saw, just like Sebastián used to.

Sebastián stepped out of the car, grabbed the sack of soccer balls he kept in the trunk, and made his way toward the bleachers, his body moving on autopilot. He sat on a bench, elbows on his knees, watching the kids cut across the field like streaks of light. A clean step-over here, a sloppy pass there. His fingers flexed, restless, wanting to jump in and shout corrections. He kept to himself, and let the frustration pool in his chest instead.

How did it all fall apart so quickly?

His hands clenched, then released, over and over. Mistakes with women in his past. Sure, he'd made plenty, but never with her. Never this. So why did she look at him like just another player running the same tired play? As if he was a gamble she couldn't afford to take?

One of the younger guys weaved through cones on the field. He had clean footwork but was too tight. Sebastián watched him miss a pass, stumble, and recover. He knew what was happening in that kid's head. He was overthinking, focused on the last messed-up play instead of on the next opportunity.

Sebastián rubbed the back of his neck, then his knee, the old ache flaring beneath his fingers.

He'd spent two hours replaying every moment he shared with Gia, searching for the thing that broke. He combed through it all, desperate to find what he missed. There was nothing. The tabloids, the noise, the nightlife were all things he couldn't control. All he'd ever tried to do was honor her.

As he watched the kid sprint drills in the darkness, a thought crept in. Maybe he didn't actually do anything. Maybe it was just him. Too much. Too intense. His energy made sense on a soccer field, not on a dance floor. He'd let his guard down with her, shown her more of himself than he bared to anyone. He should have waited until she understood the social dance scene better. He wanted her to feel the same heat he felt with her and know it was theirs alone. It wasn't the surface chemistry that happens between good partners on a crowded dance floor.

The tension in his chest wouldn't break. Her words looped in his head. *I feel like a fraud. I don't want to be a dance fling. I can't trust this.* All he could hear underneath it was one truth: she didn't trust him.

He jumped to his feet. The restless energy demanded release before it consumed him. Sebastián grabbed the soccer ball bag and walked out onto the field. He spilled the balls out, took a few slow steps back, and squared his shoulders toward the goal. His first shot went fast, clean and straight into the net.

He lined up another shot and ripped into it. The ball hissed through the air. The next one came off his foot even harder, the impact stinging through his shoe.

Maybe I really am better off taking the damn job.

He pictured the job offer on his phone, with its looming deadline, and laced into the next shot.

La Liga doesn't care about gossip. Club Atlético Marbella isn't concerned about who I dance with.

The ball slammed into the net. *They care about results.*

That, he knew how to deliver. That, he understood.

His foot connected again, a perfect strike, but there was no satisfaction in it.

What can you do when your teammate doesn't trust you and there's no one on the receiving end of your pass?

The next kick sent the ball sailing high, missing the net completely, slamming into the chain-link fence behind the goal with a metallic rattle. He let out a hard breath, hands on his hips, shoulders rising and falling as he stared down the field like it might have an answer.

He pressed the heel of his hand to his eyes, willing the frustration back down where it belonged. He could stand out here all night breaking himself against the goal, or he could figure out how to get through to her.

He spent the next hour running laps, pushing his body hard and burning the anger out of his system one stride at a time. Each lap made it clearer. Club Atlético Marbella and La Liga were the only way to have his life make sense again.

He stopped to check his watch. The other guys had left the field 30 minutes ago. It was 10 p.m., and he had to be up early tomorrow. He ran his hands around his knee for a minute and then kept running.

Chapter Eighteen

Gia stared at her phone, one heartbeat away from sending it to voicemail. Why tonight, of all nights?

Curiosity got the better of her, and she swiped across the screen. She lifted the phone to her ear as she sank onto her couch, already bracing for impact. "Miles?"

"Gia. I saw the post," he said gently.

"Not you too."

"I wanted to make sure you're okay." His voice was steady and familiar. Even worse, it was comforting. "I know I don't have the right to call you, not after the way I ended things, but when I read those comments, Gia, I couldn't stop thinking about you. It takes courage to put yourself out there again. You don't deserve any of this, not after what you've pushed through to get back on stage."

His voice reached her like a life raft.

"Miles, you can't imagine. The comments...they keep coming."

"Gia, don't read them. People are assholes on the internet. In that photo, the happiness on your face said it all. I couldn't see anything else. You look like yourself again. Like when we first met, before the world shut down, and everything else...just radiant."

"Miles."

"No, I mean it. You have to keep at it. Dance looks amazing on you. "

"Thank you. Dance and..." She caught herself before saying his name. "Dancing makes me feel alive again."

"In the photo, you're in a costume. Are you performing? Competing? And with Sebastián Solano, no less. Gia, that's incredible."

"We've been rehearsing for a pro-am competition. I've been training almost non-stop since I got here. Honestly, it's been life-changing."

"I can tell by the picture." His voice softened. "I'd love to come out and watch you perform. Cheer you on the way I used to at your marathons." A pause, quieter this time. "If having me there would be a good thing."

In that moment, Gia didn't only miss Miles. She missed the version of herself who never asked for more. She pressed a palm to her forehead and stared up at the ceiling. "You said we wouldn't go the distance, Miles. A few months don't change that."

"It does." His voice was calm and certain. "Gia, when we first got together, there was a fire in your eyes. Somewhere along the way, it went out. I thought that meant we weren't right for each other or that you were giving up on us. Now I'm not sure that's true. You needed something that was all yours, outside the apart-ment and outside of us, to bring that spark back. And I needed to grow up enough to recognize the difference."

Gia squeezed her eyes shut. He wasn't wrong.

Miles pushed further, his tone gentle but insistent. "You remember, don't you? Those Sunday brunches at the diner, falling asleep halfway through a movie on the couch, weekend drives with no destination. We were good for each other before Covid shut us in and shut everything else down. That would test anyone."

She could almost smell the scent of hot syrup and coffee at their favorite breakfast spot. She remembered the weight of his arm around her during those lazy movie nights. It might not have been burning passion, but it was warmth and peace of mind.

"Gia, we had a good life."

She let out a dry laugh. "You mean boring. You said you wanted fire, remember? You said I don't *light up* anymore."

She pictured him shaking his head, pacing the way he always did when he was trying to say something that mattered.

"No," he said, more firmly. "Not boring. Grounded. Responsible. You make smart choices, not boring ones. There's a difference."

"What about the fire you're looking for, Miles?"

He gave a small, almost helpless laugh. "For me, you're it, G. You always have been." He went quiet for a few seconds, and she could hear him breathing, like he was working up to words that hurt to say. "But you...you need a fire that burns from the inside. Look at you when you dance. That's you alive. You haven't been there in a long time. Not with me. That's what I wanted for you."

His voice dropped, rough around the edges now. "I didn't leave because I stopped loving you. I left because I thought maybe being with me was dimming you. If salsa is what brought that light back, then... damn, I wish I'd seen it sooner. I would've signed us up for classes years ago." He sighed. "I never wanted to hurt you, G. I want you to be happy. I'm sorry I made you think it meant anything else."

Her stomach twisted. Salsa had lit a fire inside her, and with Sebastián, that flame was impossible to contain, but after the last few days, she found herself second-guessing everything. She wasn't built for the spotlight that came with Sebastián. Maybe the steady, responsible kind of love she'd shared with Miles offered the better choice. It was safe and sustainable. Maybe that was enough.

"When you come home," Miles said. His voice softened. "Let's pick up where we left off. You said you felt safe with me. You said you trusted me with your future, and now you've found something that lights you up. You can dance here. I've been looking into it, and New York has a salsa scene. Live music, nightclubs, even famous teachers. It's a whole world we can discover together."

"Seriously, Miles?" Gia said, her voice tinged with the resentment she'd held back since the beginning of the call. "You're talking like you didn't shatter our future, and we can just jump back in like nothing happened. I thought you were going to *propose*. Instead, you broke up with me over shrimp scampi."

"Gia, I am so sorry. I will spend the rest of my life making that right if you'll let me."

She stayed quiet, emotions crowding her chest.

Gia sank deeper into the couch, gripping the phone. She wanted to let go of the fear clawing at her heart. "Miles..." Her voice cracked. "It's not that simple."

"It can be. Let's call it a break, not a break-up. You needed an adventure. That doesn't mean we aren't right for each other."

"But—"

"This doesn't have to be hard. We already built the foundation. We know how to live together, how to support each other. And hey, I can even take some dance lessons too. You wouldn't be starting with something unknown."

That last part landed hard. She wanted to scream. Wanted to cry. Wanted to crawl into his arms and forget everything that had happened since they split up.

"I want the life we dreamed about," he said. "The house on the North Shore. The Sunday brunch with all our friends. The family. You and me. Together."

She swallowed.

"I can fly out next weekend," he offered. "We'll drive the coast, get brunch, talk. You and me, like old times. I need to see you. Let me show you that the life we wanted is still possible."

He paused. Then, gently, "or tell me you're happier now, and I'll let it go."

Gia opened her mouth. Nothing came out. He let the silence stretch. "I miss you, G. I still love you. That hasn't changed. Think about it. I'll check in with you in a couple of days."

The line clicked dead.

Gia stared at the phone in her hand, her heart thundering in her chest. She hurled it across the room. The sound of it cracking against the wall broke her resolve. She collapsed inward, drawing her knees in close. She rocked forward slightly, a tremor starting low in her chest.

The tears came fast and hot. Not just for Miles, but for the steady, predictable life she'd left behind and the woman who once believed safety was enough.

She hated how comforting her old life still sounded and how easy it would be to say yes.

The conversation with Miles repeated in her head all night and into the next morning. Gia needed to stay busy. She started work before sunrise.

By eight, she had cleared her inbox. By ten, she'd polished two client decks, denied three calendar invites, and mainlined enough cold brew to keep her fingers flying. To a manager, it probably looked like ambition. In reality, it was about survival.

Her phone chirped. She didn't check it. She knew it wasn't Sebastián. It was too soon to be Miles again. She dove deeper into her emails, typing fast enough to outrun the thoughts clawing at the edge of her mind.

When a bottle of green juice materialized beside her keyboard, she startled. Nikki stood there like a warm hug ready to scoop her up.

"I would have brought you a latte, but you've had enough caffeine to power a small village."

Gia laughed and shut her laptop. "Thank you. How are you? Did you just get back in? How was the work trip?"

"I'm good, but we're talking about you. It's been a rough week. How are rehearsals going?"

"Yeah. They're fine."

Nikki squinted at her. "Fine? Just fine? You spent the night at his place a bunch of times, and then all hell broke loose. Fine can't possibly cover it."

"I'm deflecting, I know. I just...I'm still processing. To make it even more confusing, Miles called yesterday."

"Oh, my God. What?" Nikki nearly choked on her juice. "And?"

"He said he wants to fix things. That he made a mistake."

Silence. Then the interrogation began. "Okay. Start from the beginning. What exactly did he say?"

"That he panicked. That we had a good life, and he shouldn't have let me go. That I was always the *sensible* one, and he wants to come out here and talk."

Nikki rolled her eyes. "He called you *sensible*? Wow! Be still, my heart." Then she softened. "Honestly, though. How was it, hearing from him?"

"It was... weird," Gia admitted. "I mean, one minute I'm drowning in everything happening here. Then, out of nowhere, there's this voice from the past offering the easy life I always thought I wanted."

"Is that what you want? I mean, Miles is *Miles*. Wealthy, handsome, good on paper."

"Great on paper," Gia added.

"Superb on paper. But he's also..." Nikki trailed off. "Kinda vanilla."

"You mean *extremely polished and professional*," Gia replied.

Nikki deadpanned, "Mmm, same-same. Look, I just can't imagine going from dancing at Sevilla with Sebastián to brunching in the Hamptons with Miles. That's not a pivot. That's whiplash. It's like trading a jalapeño margarita for a glass of aged Chianti. Both great, but only one makes your pulse race."

"I mean, red wine is fabulous."

"Sure, but you're not exactly throwing your head back laughing after two glasses. You're more...warm and sleepy."

"Okay, when you put it like that!" Gia couldn't help but laugh. "You're not wrong, though."

"*I'm just saying*," Nikki exaggerated. "So. What did you tell him?"

"That I needed time."

"Giiiiiiiiiaaaaa," Nikki threw her hands up. "That's basically a maybe."

"It's not a no," Gia corrected. "Because I don't *know*," she whined. "I mean, it's Miles. We had *three years together.* It makes sense to get back together when I go back."

"But does it *feel* right? I mean, do you even *want* to go back?"

Gia didn't have an answer for that. Her throat tightened around the truth she couldn't voice—that the thought of going back felt safe, but not alive. If she said it out loud, she'd have to admit she was choosing safety.

There was a long pause before Nikki spoke again. "Well, whatever you decide, make sure you choose what *you* want. You don't owe anyone anything." Then, softer, "And you'd be missed."

Camila folded her hands on the table, pulse ticking in her jaw. "Wait. Let me get this straight. *Miles* is back in the picture?"

Nikki nodded. "He wants to *fix things.* Gia didn't exactly shut it down."

Camila's brows shot up, then dropped into a hard line. She didn't answer right away, just reached for her water glass and swirled it, thinking about the last rehearsal. Gia's smile didn't reach her eyes. There was so much stiffness in Sebastián's frame.

"I knew something was off," Camila said finally. "But *Miles*? That I didn't see coming."

"She always planned to leave at the end of September. She was offered a promotion, and she might have to go back earlier if she takes it," Nikki said, shaking her head back and forth with disappointment. "Maybe this was a last hurrah before she settles down or whatever."

"So that's it? She just lets the guy who walked out swoop back in now that he's bored with playing around? She gives up dance, moves back East, and plays house in some brownstone?"

"Technically, she'd be on Long Island, not Manhattan. So, a house with a yard, not a brownstone."

Camila didn't even hear Nikki's joke. "Don't even start with the whole 'there's salsa in New York' thing. Gia belongs here. She's part of this family now."

Nikki raised her hands in surrender. "Agreed, one hundred percent. The last thing I want is for my cousin to hide herself again. Or leave. I'm telling you this so we can shake sense into them."

"I've watched Gia fight for this all summer. She's earned her place on stage. And my brother?" She shook her head, her throat tightening. "He's in this deeper than he knows how to admit."

Nikki's brow arched. "Are we talking about the competition or the two of them?"

"Both," Camila said flatly. She leaned back in her chair, suddenly tired. "If they don't get it together, this doesn't end well for anyone. Including me." She paused. "I know how that sounds. You get it."

"Does Sebastián know about Miles?" Nikki asked.

"I don't think so. He hasn't mentioned it, but he'll sense something is up before she says a word." Camila drummed her nails on the table. "No. We're not letting either of them give up on themselves."

"Then let's remind her who she is."

"And help him accept who he's becoming," Camila said softly. "Even if he's still fighting it."

Chapter Nineteen

Sebastián wasn't expecting company, but when the knock came at his front door, he already knew who it was before he pulled it open. Camila stood on his doorstep, arms crossed, all business.

He sighed. "Let me guess. You're here to lecture me."

"Yep," she said, stepping inside. "Where do you want it? Living room? Kitchen?"

Sebastián walked to the kitchen without answering. If his little sister was about to drag him, he might as well be near the beer.

Camila followed, assessing him as they went. That much was clear.

He grabbed a pale ale from the fridge, twisted off the cap, and placed it in front of Camila before opening an IPA for himself. He took a long pull and set the bottle on the counter.

"Can I go first?" he asked. It was more of a statement. "Club Atlético Marbella wants to make me an offer. Assistant coach."

Camila blinked. "Whoa. La Liga. Seriously?"

"Yes. More money. More exposure. More... everything."

"You're considering it," she said flatly.

"I have to."

"You *want* to," she corrected.

"I'm a soccer coach, Camila. This, Ritmo Latino, the competition—it's been fun, but it's not my life. It's not soccer."

She narrowed her eyes. "Not your life? What the hell, Sebastián? Don't even tell me you're walking away."

The look on his face said it all.

"Wait, from all of it?" she pressed.

His voice sharpened. "Don't turn this into something it's not."

"Oh? What *is* it, then?" Camila demanded.

"I'm being realistic," he snapped. "What's not realistic? Living off dancing and late-night rehearsals. Pretending this pro-am thing is anything more than a temporary high. You think I'm in *denial* about soccer, but I'm trying to be *smart*. I already lost my career to injury, but I never planned to leave the game altogether."

Camila let out a slow breath, shaking her head. "Sebas..."

"You don't understand," he cut in. "This is my *life*, Camila."

Camila softened slightly. "You think you're fútbol and only fútbol, but you're more than that, Sebas. You *found* something new. Salsa gave you back your fire. So did Gia."

His face cracked around the words. "You don't get it. I don't know who I am without fútbol. And I don't know who I am *with* her." He rubbed his face, struggling to contain everything boiling under the surface. "I have to take this offer. *Camila*."

She stepped closer and put a supportive hand on his shoulder. "Okay, I hear you. Let's say you take the job. Where does that leave Ritmo Latino? We are *ten days* away from the competition. Please don't tell me you might bail on us."

He took another sip of his beer and then rolled the bottle between his fingers.

"Andrés can cover for me in the pro-am."

Camila's eyes flashed. "Not a chance in hell, Sebastián. How can you even suggest that at this point?"

He set the bottle down a little too hard.

"When will you wake up and admit to yourself that competing with Ritmo Latino is *just as important* as soccer *used* to be? What, you're not a competitor anymore?" she pressed. "A tiger can change its stripes because of an injury? Can you *watch from the sidelines* and be satisfied?" She scoffed. "You *live* for that edge, Sebas. For the spotlight. It's in your *blood*."

"I don't even know who I am anymore, Camila. Fútbol is everything. I've always needed soccer. I still do."

"I need *you*," she continued. "*Your teammates* need you. The company needs you. This competition is our shot to put Ritmo Latino on the map at the next level. Grow the business to its full potential, with you as co-director. Continue our family's legacy. I expected you would realize that on your own through this experience, but *man*, you are so damn *stubborn*."

Sebastián dragged a hand through his hair.

"Listen," Camila said, her voice softer now. "I know what fútbol means to you. How much you miss it. I was there when everything happened. But come on, Sebas, you've built something here, too. You have a family in this world. Whether you want to admit it, you love this, and you love her."

He couldn't even summon a denial. Hopelessness flickered in his eyes when he finally looked at her, searching for an answer she couldn't possibly give. "What am I supposed to do, Camila? Blow off a La Liga contract because of a girl I've known for four months?"

"If that girl brings you to life like nothing else has in years? Then maybe, yeah."

She took a step closer, eyes locked on his. "You don't need the money. The offers will come again. But Gia?" Her voice dropped, more pointed. "She might not be here once you figure that out."

Sebastián's shoulders stiffened, but Camila didn't let up.

"And she's not 'some girl,' Sebas. She's the woman who made you show up as yourself for the first time since the injury."

"Camila, she doesn't trust me." He interrupted, defeat in his voice.

"Give her a reason to." Camila's tone was steady. "Fight for her. Let her decide if she's willing to take the risk. Don't decide for her."

She paused, reading the unease simmering beneath his silence. "Her ex is fighting for her," she added quietly. "He's coming here. He's willing to do what it takes to win her trust."

Sebastián didn't answer. He grabbed the bottle in his hand and slammed it into the recycling bin, the crack of shattering glass his angry response.

Camila flinched but held her ground. "You need to figure your shit out, Sebas. Decide what matters before the choice gets made for you."

She turned toward the door, but before stepping out, she looked back. "Congratulations on your offer. Any team in the league would be lucky to have you. We both know you won't be satisfied with coaching. That ain't enough." Then, she was all business again. "Your team needs you. Dress rehearsal is tomorrow. Don't be the one who doesn't show up." And she walked out.

Chapter Twenty

Gia had barely stepped into the studio when Camila waved her over. "Hey, lovey." She pulled Gia in for a warm hug, her air kisses light and familiar.

"You're early," Gia noted as she slipped off her flip-flops near the mirror.

"*You're* early. I said thirty minutes before practice, and you're ten minutes ahead of schedule. Overachiever."

Gia looked around. "You said we're watching footage?"

Camila gestured toward the laptop perched on the sound system. "Yep. Figured it was time."

"Time for what?"

"Time for you to see what I see."

Camila pressed play. The screen flickered to life, revealing their first performance in front of a live audience. Gia had watched plenty of phone video clips, but Camila's was shot professionally. The camera tracked their every move, gliding across the floor and catching close-ups at just the right moments. It looked like a scene out of a movie.

"I asked a photographer friend to film the sets that night," Camila said.

Gia braced herself, expecting the pinch of self-criticism in her chest, but that's not what happened. She watched herself. Gia observed the confidence in her frame and the sabor in her style. She noted how she followed Sebastián, not mechanically but naturally. Their bodies spoke the same language, even when they weren't speaking at all. It wasn't perfect, but it was honest. She didn't see an impostor. She saw a dancer.

Gia's breath caught. A single tear slipped loose, but she wiped it away before it could fall.

Camila stood quietly, holding space for Gia to process her emotions.

Gia swallowed. "I look…"

"Like a total badass."

Gia shook her head, no. "Like a dancer," her voice cracked. A dancer. Not an ex-dancer. Not a hobbyist. Not a fraud. A dancer.

Camila's smile softened. "Hell yeah you are."

The footage kept rolling. She observed the way Sebastián watched her. Not just a partner leading a follower or a coach guiding a student. There was tenderness in his eyes.

It crashed into her all at once. None of this could be denied. Not the way her body came alive when she danced. Not the rush in her chest whenever Sebastián looked at her like that. She'd fallen in love with salsa almost immediately. She'd fallen in love with Sebastián, little by little.

"You can trust this, Gia. This isn't just a temporary project. This is *you*."

"Camila."

Camila took her hand, squeezing it like she had done that first night at Casa Sevilla. The squeeze that said, *I've got you.*

"Whatever happens next with the competition, with salsa, with my brother, you can't stop dancing. I won't let you."

Gia looked down, blinking away tears.

"When I watch you now, I see the woman I used to be *right* when I talked myself into believing I could make a career out of dancing. You don't get to walk away from that. Not when you've come this far. So, once we're done celebrating after the competition, you have a permanent spot with Ritmo Latino, if you want it. I could use an extra hand teaching the beginner classes, and you'd be amazing."

"Thank you, Camila. I love the idea of that so much, but I'm heading back home after the competition," Gia said automatically. "I was offered a big promotion. It's what I've been working toward for years. I can't pass it up."

Camila sighed. "Well, congratulations. Seems like everyone is chasing promotions and moving on to bigger things." She lifted one shoulder in a half-shrug. "Still, the offer stands. The spot's yours if anything changes."

Gia turned back to the laptop, watching the last moments of the performance. On screen, Sebastián spun her into the final pose. They lit up the stage that night. What she didn't know was whether they could ever find that spark together again.

By the time she and Camila finished watching the video, dancers had started trickling in, first Andrés and Amber, then Daniel and Sebastián, then a wave of others from the training and semi-pro teams.

Gia expected an intimate practice, but she should've known better. This practice was a full-out dress rehearsal. The entire dance company showed up as a family, working toward the same goal: winning.

Daniel clapped his hands the way Camila usually did to signal a transition. "Alright, everyone knows the drill. We've got one week left until go time so let's treat this like the real thing. Today's about putting on a show. Performance over technique. No do-overs."

"You know that saying, *dance like no one's watching?*" Camila asked.

A few heads nodded.

"Forget all that. Dance like everyone's watching. Because they are. You've worked your asses off for this. It's time to show it.

Burn the floor down, and enjoy every minute of it. I mean, how lucky are we to dance?"

The team cheered in response.

"Camila and I will go first." Daniel said. "Second, Andrés and Amber. Consider it a pre-show. We want to show you what we've been working on for the San Francisco Open and get some practice in front of an audience. Then we'll move to the pro-am pieces. Camila and Johnny, you're first." His eyes moved to Gia and Sebastián. "Then we'll see the main event! Our first-ever pro-am pair where both partners are new to the division. Let's hear it for Sebastián, everybody. It's his first time."

"He's a virgin!" Andrés yelled. Everyone laughed, except Gia. She didn't even catch the joke. She was still riding the high from watching the footage. She was hopeful that during this performance, she and Sebastián might get back on solid ground, at least as dance partners.

Gia overheard a conversation behind her. Andrés practically vibrated with energy, his voice cutting clean through the pre-rehearsal noise.

"Damn, Sebas, congrats, man! Heard about the offer on the news. When were you gonna tell us?"

Gia's pulse slowed. Offer? News?

She turned her head enough to see Sebastián rubbing the back of his neck, suddenly looking like a stranger in a studio that was his second home.

"Nothing's decided," Sebastián said.

But Andrés, never one to let things drop, pushed. "Is there even a question? *La Liga!* This is huge, bro!"

Gia's heart dropped. La Liga was Spain's top division, where he used to play before his U.S. Major League Soccer days. Sebastián was leaving. She had just let herself stupidly believe that maybe they could come back together after everything.

Shove it down. Focus on the dancing. It was the one thing she could hold on to, no matter how this rehearsal went or what happened with Sebastián. Gia took a breath, steadying herself, and moved to the front of the room with the rest of the audience.

Camila and Daniel went first. Their performance to Ricky Martin's "Pégate" was fiery and filled with chemistry that looked like decades of partnership, not just one year.

"Damn, y'all made that look easy," someone called.

"That lift section? Unreal."

"Camila, you weren't kidding. Daniel's the next big thing in San Diego."

Camila flashed a playful, cocky grin. "Everyone knows I only dance with the best."

Daniel responded with a smile as he caught his breath. He knew this performance was proof that he'd earned his place at Camila's side.

Then came Andrés and Amber's whirlwind routine. Their energy was flirty and magnetic. Amber's sharp, lightning-fast footwork contrasted beautifully with Andrés' grounded, smooth control. They had just enough tricks to keep them in the salsa division instead of the cabaret category. When they finished, cheers filled the room.

"Amber, your shines were insane."

"Andrés, those body rolls should be illegal."

Amber flipped her hair, grinning. "We aim to please."

Andrés shot Sebastián a look. "Good luck following that, bro."

Sebastián smirked in response.

Camila took the floor again with Johnny. Gia hadn't seen him much since the audition. He still had the same tireless enthusiasm, but now with poise and polish. They chose Marc Anthony's cover of Hector Lavoe's "Aguanile," a classic salsa song and explosive crowd-pleaser. Their routine was designed to wow audiences and stack up points with judges, and they delivered. By the time the music cut out, Johnny was panting, flushed with effort, and the entire room was cheering for him.

"Johnny! My man, you held your own!"

"Camila, how do you make every partner look like they've been doing this for years?"

"Say hello to our next Ritmo Latino star!" Camila clapped for Johnny, proud of her youngest dancer.

Finally, she turned to Gia and Sebastián. "Alright," she called over the noise. "You two are up. Make it happen."

Gia walked toward Sebastián, lifting her chin, willing her body to let go of the tension, forcing her breath steady. She didn't trust herself to look at him and not feel like a complete idiot. In contrast, Sebastián stood relaxed, arms loose at his sides, staring straight at her.

The first beats of "¿Dónde Se Fueron?" filled the room. Every slap of the conga punctuated their body isolations. The audience leaned forward, caught in the slow, smoldering build that teased and tormented before the inevitable release. The tension became almost unbearable for Gia. By the time the percussion hit its crescendo, she was ready to shatter. Then the beat dropped. The salsa section rushed in like a storm and the floodgates blew wide open.

Sebastián took her through the cross-body lead that started their sweeping partnerwork across the floor. The way he moved told her this would not be their practiced choreography. He led differently. Rather than directing her or even inviting her into the movement like usual, he was questioning her.

Is this only a dance for you, Gia?

With every move, the pressure in his fingertips demanded answers. His frame expressed urgency, as if he were searching for something. He was pushing her to answer.

Her heartbeat pounded against her ribs. This wasn't the careful, measured practice they had done dozens of times.

Gia refused to let him be the only one making a statement. She matched his intensity and responded sharply. When he spun her, she snapped into it deliberately, resisting the urge to soften.

Sebastián's grip flexed at her back as he led her into a body roll. It was the same delicious move they had done a hundred times before. The same movement that had unraveled her the first time they spent the night together.

This time, Sebastián slowed it down even more. He made her feel every inch of it. He made her remember the night in the studio. Her back pressed against the cold surface of the steamy mirror. Tension crackled between them—hot, heavy, and impossible to ignore. His mouth hovered inches from hers.

No, Gia responded silently. She broke out of the body roll faster than necessary, giving them an unexpected half-beat where they needed to pause to keep timing. Sebastián's grip tightened as they waited through that excruciatingly long half-second.

She threw in a head whip, letting her hair fan out to hide the way she avoided his eyes and his questions. He stepped in closer.

His hands gripped her waist and said more than words could.

Is this all a performance?

When he realized he wouldn't get anywhere with this line of questioning, he tried a new tactic to reach her. He changed the choreography, breaking the patterns she'd memorized. The changes demanded her full attention to keep up. She had no choice but to tune into him.

It felt like he wasn't asking a question anymore. He was giving her the answer.

This isn't just a dance, and you know it.

She had enough. She responded by increasing the tension in their connection, adding resistance that asked, *why do you keep pulling me in when you are going to leave?*

The music swelled toward the climax before its abrupt ending.

Sebastián spun her back into his arms and pulled her flush against him.

His body was a furnace. His breath brushed her cheek. Passion fruit. Delicious.

In that split second, with the entire room watching, she wouldn't stop him if he kissed her. If he asked her to stay, she would.

But he didn't. The song ended, and he simply held her there while they and the audience caught their breath.

Applause erupted. Gia tore herself away from Sebastián and stepped back, fighting back tears. Her fingers curled into fists.

Andrés jumped up and clapped Sebastián on the back. "That was fire, man."

Camila beamed. "Yes! That's what I want to see!"

Gia barely heard any of it because her pulse hammered in her ears from their dance floor confessions.

She needed to leave, but Sebastián stood in her way. If she looked at him now, she'd break.

Camila called out over the noise. "Alright, let's all grab dinner. We need to debrief the performances."

Gia froze. After all that, she couldn't handle any small talk or join a group hangout. She planned to make a quick exit, dodging any conversation with Sebastián that lingered ahead.

He stepped closer, his voice low. "Please stay."

The crew went to one of their usual late-night spots. They grabbed a long table near the back, pushed the chairs together, ordered pitchers of margaritas, and filled the space with post-performance energy that should have been exhilarating.

Gia took a seat at the far end of the table. Sebastián took the chair beside her.

The team dissected the performances. Daniel and Camila rewatched clips on a phone, breaking down footwork. Johnny glowed with the rush of his performance, grinning as Andrés clinked a beer bottle against his.

Gia nodded and laughed in the right places, all while dying inside. Every slight press of Sebastián's leg against hers made it worse, or better. She couldn't decide.

Camila nudged Sebastián. "Alright, be honest. Did you two plan that? Not your usual chemistry, but the tension tonight? Chef's kiss."

Gia felt sick.

"Excuse me," she muttered, pushing back from the table. Her

chair scraped loudly against the floor, but that didn't slow her down. She needed one minute. One goddamn minute to breathe, to keep from drowning in her own emotions.

She shoved open the restroom door, let it swing shut behind her, and gripped the edge of the sink like it was the only solid thing in the room.

In the mirror, her reflection stared back. Her eyes were wide. Her chest rose and collapsed too fast. Her cheeks were flushed, and her jaw was tight.

The door creaked open again. A tall silhouette filled the doorway. Sebastián.

She spun toward him. "What the hell?" Her voice cracked with alarm. "This is the women's room."

He closed the door behind him without flinching. "You're avoiding me."

Gia crossed her arms and stepped back. "I'm not."

"Stop dodging this conversation. Please."

"You can't just barge in here like this."

"Gia, we need to talk."

"I don't think now's the time, Sebastián—"

"Then when? Is there any time when you're not ignoring my calls or slipping out of the room the second I get close? Any time you'll actually look at me and say what's going on?"

She shook her head, laughing nervously. "You want to talk now? In the women's bathroom?"

"I don't care where we are. I care that you're shutting me out like nothing ever happened between us."

The room was too small. His voice was too raw. She couldn't hold the wall up much longer.

"Gia." He reached for her and took her hands in his.

The words formed before she could stop them. Her arms fell heavily to her sides.

"You're leaving. What else is there to say? Were you even going to tell me? Or were you planning to disappear after the competition? Are you even competing? Or is everything we worked for already gone too? How could you do that?" She blinked hard, trying to shove the sting behind her eyes away. "I need to know, Sebastián. Because I can't keep pretending this doesn't matter. You don't get to be everywhere and nowhere in my life at the same time."

"Gia, let me explain."

The door flew open again. A woman stepped in but halted mid-stride. Her eyes widened, snapping from Sebastián to Gia, and down to the floor. She shielded her face as she recoiled.

"Oh—" Her voice pitched up as color surged to her cheeks. A wince flickered, shaky and unsure. "My bad." She edged backward, hand already fumbling for the handle. "Y'all take your time," she added with an awkward laugh, slipping out and pulling the door closed behind her a little too fast.

Once outside, her voice rang out, aimed at some unsuspecting patron heading to the restroom. "Private moment happening— do not go in there!"

Silence as Sebastián and Gia stared at each other.

The absurdity crashed into both of them all at once, and they burst into laughter, unable to hold it in.

Gia gasped for air, pressing a hand to her stomach. "If anyone filmed that, we'd definitely be trending on RedCardRumors."

His lips twitched as he tried to compose himself. "Not funny."

"Kinda funny." Gia shook her head, still laughing, wiping under her eyes.

"Come on," Sebastián said, his voice gentler now. "Let's get out of here before someone comes in here desperate." He pushed the door open and extended his hand. Gia slipped her fingers into his, letting him guide her out of the restroom and into the restaurant's glow. The laughter that clung to them broke against the silence waiting outside. Gia lifted her gaze and froze at the sight of Camila's face.

Camila sat stiffly at the table, her fingers curled around her glass, seconds from crushing it.

Gia recognized the expression in her eyes. Emilio must be there.

He approached the Ritmo Latino table as if it were filled with friends, not a crew of former teammates and students staring at him in disbelief. His shoulders were relaxed, his smile perfectly in place, and his new partner trailed like a trophy at his side. It was Vanessa from the pro-am audition. Gia stiffened.

Laughter at the table stuttered. Even the music seemed to be quiet. Daniel cleared his throat, forcing the tension to break. "Funny seeing you here, Emilio."

"Yeah, well. Some traditions are hard to let go. Camila. You look great."

Camila met his eyes. "I always do."

Gia noted Camila's effort to keep the war happening beneath the surface from exploding out of her. Sebastián must have too. He walked Gia to her seat before walking over to his sister and placing a hand on her shoulder. Camila squeezed it in silent response. *It's okay. I've got this.*

The moment dragged, weighted with things unsaid. Emilio lingered in it, his smile hopeful but unsteady. His eyes drifted with sadness across the group, as if mourning the traditions, the camaraderie, and most of all, Camila. Gia studied him, searching his face for the villain she'd expected. What she saw was something closer to heartbreak than hostility.

The usually fiery Vanessa, on the other hand, was ice cold. She shifted her weight to one hip, arms crossed, eyes fixed on Gia, then Sebastián, and then finally Camila. Her blood-red lipstick was perfectly applied to a smile too tight to be real.

"Camila, I just want to say how much I admire you. Really. It's inspiring to see someone with true longevity in the scene." Vanessa paused, letting the compliment drip like syrup. "I hope I'm still dancing when I've been at it as long as you have."

Camila let the words settle, swirling her wine lazily before finally looking up.

"Longevity isn't a miracle, querida. It's what you do with it that matters." Camila's voice was smooth and deliberate as she turned to face Emilio. "Some of us evolve. Others just orbit or reach their peak and then plateau." Camila looked back at

Vanessa. "Enjoy your moment, sweetheart. I'm glad you found a way to compete in L.A. this season."

She lifted her glass in an almost-toast, then turned her gaze away from the two of them.

Vanessa's smile faltered, the edges stiffening as color crept up her neck. Emilio went still. He managed a weak nod, eyes dropping to the floor as if he could disappear into it. Showing up at Ritmo Latino's usual spot had been a mistake, and he knew it now.

Camila shook her hands out the second they were gone, like she was physically ridding herself of the moment.

"Alright," she said, meeting the eyes on every face around the table. "We're going to crush them next week. I want everyone to visualize Emilio and Vanessa's names printed *below* mine and Johnny's. Can we all see it? Sí o yes?"

"Sí," everyone responded.

"Good. We're going to crush him. Now, let's order dessert." Camila rolled her neck left, then right, two soft cracks breaking the tension. She did a playful shimmy, shaking off the moment like dust from her shoulders. She was back to the radiant, composed, and unmistakably in-charge Camila that they all knew and loved.

The team returned to talking, and Sebastián leaned in to Gia, voice quiet enough for only her to hear.

"Are we okay?"

"I want to be."

He searched her face, as if begging permission to close the distance she'd kept between them. His hand hovered for a moment before settling over hers.

"I'd really like to talk soon. We can't leave things the way we did."

Gia opened her mouth to answer, but her phone buzzed against the table, screen lighting up between them.

Heat rushed up her neck as she flipped the phone over, pressing it face down. She dared not look at Sebastián, unsure if he'd caught the glimpse of Miles's name, or the exclamation points, or the dangerous hope tucked between the lines.

"Yeah," she whispered. "Me too."

She let her eyes fall shut, a faint, weary smile tugging at her lips. She'd wanted to feel alive again, and somehow heartbreak managed to deliver that cruelly in full force.

Gia sank into the back seat of her Lyft, her fingers twisting in her lap as the streetlights streaked across the window.

"Good night?" the driver asked, glancing at her in the mirror. He was an older gentleman with a comforting voice. He had warm grandpa energy with a hippie vibe.

"Yeah," Gia said softly. "Dance performance."

"Groovy. What kind of dance?" His tone was curious and sincere.

"Salsa. I have a pro-am competition coming up, and this was a dress rehearsal."

"Like *Dancing with the Stars*?"

"Yes, actually. A lot like that."

"Nice. I've heard dance is a shortcut to happiness. Think that's true?"

"I believe that. I've been rehearsing nonstop for months, and I've never felt more alive."

"So it was worth it then."

"More than I expected."

"How so?"

"At first, I was scared of showing up and letting others actually see me."

He nodded in the rearview mirror. "You'd be surprised how many people spend their whole lives hiding. Dancing's a risky thing. It forces you to be honest."

Gia smiled faintly. "It does. Especially when you're dancing with a partner who doesn't let you disappear."

"Sounds like a great partner to have."

"He was." She paused. "He is."

The driver's eyes flicked toward her in the mirror. "Was?"

Gia's throat tightened. "He's leaving soon. Got a big job offer. It's what he's always wanted."

"And you?" he asked gently. "You gonna chase a big dream too?"

"I thought I was. I've been chasing a promotion for years, and I finally got it. I should be happy, but lately, I don't even recognize the person who wanted it."

"Maybe that's a good thing."

Gia looked up, meeting his gaze in the mirror. "How do you mean?"

"Means you grew," he said simply. "That old dream might've fit the old you. Might've been a great dream. Doesn't mean it fits now."

Gia let that sink in as they turned onto her street. "Yeah," she whispered. "I think I outgrew the girl who needed it."

The car rolled to a stop.

"You remind me a lot of my granddaughter," the driver said. "She's in college, trying to figure out her dreams too. You know, it's okay for dreams to evolve. Maybe just keep dancing. Especially if that's what makes you feel alive. Dance partners change, but the music's always there."

Gia smiled. "Are you sure you're a Lyft driver and not a philosopher? Or a therapist?"

He chuckled. "Same thing. You have a good night."

As the Lyft pulled away, Gia took out her phone and typed: *I loved the future we imagined, but I've outgrown the girl who needed that dream. The woman I've become belongs here. I hope you find what lights you up, too.*

Her thumb hovered for a breathless second before she hit send. Relief and ache tangled as the screen went dark. She turned her phone off.

Tomorrow, she'd call Diana and ask for the promotion on one condition: it came with a San Diego zip code. When Sebastián left, she'd let herself grieve, but she'd keep dancing.

Chapter Twenty-One

Sebastián leaned back in the leather chair of his home office, absently tossing a stress ball between his hands. The coaches' meeting droned on in his earbuds. Pre-season plans were falling into place. He hadn't committed yet, but they included him on Zoom calls as part of the team.

His phone chimed. Camila.

He sighed, pressing his fingers into his temples before answering.

"Hiya. What are you up to?"

"Listening in on a call with the coaches in Spain. Can I ring you later?"

"Did you sign with them yet?"

"Not yet."

"Okay. Don't sign anything until we talk. Call me as soon as you're done."

"What's going on, Camila?"

"I have a proposal for you."

"What kind of proposal?"

"An idea that would keep you here in San Diego. I want you to be Ritmo Latino's full-time director. Partner with me. Let's continue our parents' legacy."

"What are you even talking about?" Sebastián let out an exasperated sigh. "Camila. I love you. I love dancing at your studio, but this is *La Liga*. People would kill for this chance. It's the closest I'll get to being back on the field."

"What if you stopped choosing between soccer and everything else? What if you could do something different with soccer?"

He frowned. "That's not how it works."

"Why not?"

"Because the only way to win anything is full commitment. One lane. No distractions."

"What if you built a new lane? One big enough for all your dreams? One with more, I don't know, *sparkles*."

A reluctant laugh escaped him. "Sparkles, huh?"

"Okay, no sparkles. Something way more manly. I'm serious. Take a *part-time* coaching gig here and go *all in* on salsa. Compete. Choreograph. Tour. We could host a big event and host international guests. We'll build it together."

"We?"

"You're already training dancers, even if you don't realize it. You know I don't want to run Ritmo Latino alone forever. We've got the talent. The brand. Connections. It could be so much bigger than a studio."

The stress ball slipped from his fingers and bounced to the floor.

"I need a minute to think," he said.

"One more thing. Nikki told me that Gia was offered a promotion in New York. So she's going to leave right after the competition." Camila dropped her voice into a mock Sebastián impression. "It's a chance she can't pass up because it's what she's been working for her *whole career*." Then, back to her own voice. "That's almost a month earlier than she planned."

A sharp jolt hit his chest. "I thought we had more time."

"Me too. I offered her a spot on the semi-pro team. I don't know if it's enough because if this is just about salsa, she doesn't need you. Or me. Or San Diego."

Her voice picked up speed, passion rising. "She hasn't even

scratched the surface. New York is waiting. The Bronx, Manhattan. That's the scene. Legends in every room. Gia is talented and gorgeous. She'll draw partners like moths to a flame. Partners who'll spin her dizzy in the clubs, then take her home to finish what they started. I mean, wintertime? Ha! The way men dance in New York, she'll never be cold in that city. Not to mention—"

"Okay, okay. I get it." Sebastián's jaw clenched. The image of her in another man's arms made his chest ache. The thought of her leaving and completely slipping away from him was too much. "I can't lose her."

Camila let out a short laugh. "Well, finally."

"What?"

"You've been miserable without her. Frankly, it's been embarrassing to watch."

He groaned, dragging his hands down his face. "Shit."

"Go get her like you get everything else, by refusing to give up."

He paused, voice low. "Yea. Thanks, Cami."

"Always, hermano. But damn. Sometimes you boys need a swift kick in the ass."

"Noted." A grin tugged at his lips. "Listen, you're definitely going to want to kick my ass because I need to do a press conference tomorrow before I drive up to L.A. for the festival."

"You've got to be kidding me. You're not driving up with us? Wait, is there a chance you might *miss the competition,* Sebas?

"Of course not. Don't worry."

"Sebastián. I swear—"

"I'll see you soon. Promise. I've got a few things to take care of, and I'll head over to your place."

He hung up.

Then, he called his agent. Then, his banker.

The press conference was crowded with reporters, team

executives, and league officials. Everyone waited for one thing: the official announcement from Sebastián Solano.

Sebastián stepped into the spotlight of the podium, navy suit sharp against the glare, white shirt crisp, gold cuff links catching the light like tiny sunbursts. He placed his hands on the lectern, lifted his chin, and looked out at the crowd.

He took a breath and began.

"First, I want to thank my teammates, colleagues, rehab team, and my family. The past two years have been the most challenging of my life. After my injury, I spent months figuring out where I belonged. For most of that time, I believed the only way to prove I still mattered was to go back to the world that made me."

He looked up, scanning the rows of expectant faces.

"But here's what I forgot. It wasn't only soccer that made me. It was music. It was dance too. I was raised by Antonio and Rosa Solano, living legends of salsa. I grew up with my sister in a house full of rhythm and joy. While rehabbing my knee, I kept asking myself to choose between my past and future when I should've been building the life I want."

Murmurs rippled through the crowd. Reporters leaned forward. News was coming.

"I'm staying in San Diego."

Flashbulbs exploded, and the room erupted into a shouting match of questions.

"I'm investing in the new MLS team here. I'm going to help elevate soccer in San Diego and the U.S., the way it deserves. This game is not only a sport. It's an identity. Culture. Community. I want this city to love it as much as I do. San Diego is a soccer city. Some of you just don't know it yet."

A reporter stood. "So, are you coaching?"

Sebastián smiled. "We'll see. For now, I'm investing in a future where kids in California grow up dreaming of playing *here*, not overseas. One where our culture, our fans, and our level of play can compete with the best in the world. I believe we can elevate the game in the U.S. to the global stage, and it starts right here in San Diego."

Another voice from the crowd: "What made you change your mind, Sebastián? What made you stay?"

He paused, fingers resting on the edge of the lectern.

"You all know my sister, world salsa champion Camila Solano, founder of Ritmo Latino." He couldn't help but plug her company when the opportunity arose. "She told me I was caught between two worlds but didn't belong to either. She was right. Soccer is in my blood. So is salsa. I finally stopped trying to choose between the two. I'm both."

Applause swept the room, but one question cut through the noise.

"Is there any other reason you're staying in San Diego? Is there a special someone?"

The room hushed, the silence pressing in on him as every eye waited for his answer. These reporters always brought up Sebastián's personal life. They were after something headline-worthy.

The question hung in the air like a soccer ball sailing in slow motion from midfield, everyone waiting to see if it would land in the goal or not. For a heartbeat, he considered dodging, giving the press the safe, polished answer he usually did. Then he thought of the way she looked at him, the way she trusted him with her whole body when she danced.

So Sebastián gave it to them. "Yes. She's the future I want."

Flashbulbs burst like fireworks. Questions flew from every direction.

"Who is she?"

"Is it serious?"

"Are you engaged?"

"Are you going to be a dad?"

Sebastián laughed in response. "Thank you, everyone," he said, stepping away from the podium. "I'm excited to be part of the new San Diego Football Club. I'll see you all at the games!"

With that, he waved, turned, and walked out.

Chapter Twenty-Two

At the Pacific Salsa Fest, the practice hall throbbed with percussion and nerves. Bodies in motion, sequins flashing, every dancer pretending not to size up the others.

Gia sat and watched while Johnny and Camila warmed up together. She rolled her ankles in circles, willing the adrenaline not to spike higher in her chest. Her palms were slick with sweat. The floor under her shoes felt too slippery, like it might betray her at any second. All around her, dancers stretched, fixed their costumes, and slipped into performance mode. Behind her, someone rehearsed a lift. Another couple hit the final pose of their routine with a dramatic exhale.

From across the room, Vanessa adjusted her earrings slowly, deliberately, never taking her eyes off Gia like a lioness surveying her prey. Gia's stomach knotted. She hadn't been in a competitive space in years, and everything about this moment pressed in too much, too fast.

Still no sign of Sebastián. She'd known he'd be late, but that didn't stop her pulse from quickening with every passing minute. Her thoughts spun in useless circles. Thankfully, Nikki and the rest of the Ritmo Latino pro team were there like a steady center in the chaos until Andrés' phone lit up. "Awwww, shit!"

Gia, already on edge, jumped up. "What is it?"

He turned the screen toward her. It was a live press conference. The sound was muted, but the headline screamed.

SOLANO'S SURPRISE ANNOUNCEMENT: STAYING IN SAN DIEGO FOR "LOVE AND LEGACY"

Her heart slammed against her ribs.

No. She blinked. *No way.*

Then the doors flew open. All eyes shot up at the same time and landed on Sebastián.

He strode in like he'd stepped off the podium seconds ago, in his tailored suit, shirt half-unbuttoned, tie abandoned somewhere along the way. He scanned the room until he found Gia. Her breath caught. He didn't stop until he was standing right in front of her.

Gia shot to her feet, arms crossed, gripping her elbows to steady herself. "We just saw the headline. I thought you were about to tell the world you were leaving."

His expression softened, his shoulders easing as if he'd finally stopped fighting himself. When he spoke, his voice dropped low, intimate, meant only for her. "Gia, I would cross oceans to dance with you."

Her lips parted, but no sound came. Breath caught in her throat, and her body froze.

"I don't walk out on what matters," he went on, steady and certain. "And I don't leave the people I love. And I'm sorry. I'm so sorry. For everything that happened the other night."

The ballroom dissolved, the noise dimming into nothing. All she heard was the roar of her pulse in her ears, the wild, frantic beat of her heart.

"I should've said this sooner," he added. "I don't just want the trophy. I want the life. With you. On the floor. Off the floor. Dancing all night. Take out at home. *Dirty Dancing* on repeat. All of it."

Her vision shimmered, tears threatening. She searched his face for the catch, some crack, anything to prove this was too good to be true.

Her hand trembled as she reached for his. "This is real?" she whispered.

He nodded, catching her fingers in his, pressing them against his chest where his heartbeat thundered wild beneath her palm. "Gia, say yes. We'll figure out the rest."

The tears spilled, hot and unstoppable. Her laugh broke through with a sob. "Yes. Sebastián, yes. I've never been more sure of anything."

His mouth crashed into hers before she could utter another word. A chorus of "¡vamos!" and "finally!" echoed through the room in response. Camila's voice rang out, "*¡Hermanooooo!*" while Nikki let out a piercing whistle.

Laughter and applause swelled around them like music, until it swept Sebastián in too, his laugh spilling against her mouth, his breath hot on her skin, his heartbeat drumming hard against hers. At last, they were moving in the same rhythm again.

When they pulled apart, he leaned in, forehead to forehead.

"Let's show them what we made together."

Her smile lit up the room.

"So ready."

The competition opened with the beginner pro-am division. Backstage, Sebastián and Gia stood shoulder to shoulder listening to the emcee's voice echoing faintly through the walls. Her fingers hovered for a moment on the tie of her robe, then pulled it loose. The fabric slid away, revealing sequins, skin, and muscle honed over months of sweat and constant rehearsal. Once, she would've panicked at the idea of being on stage dressed like this. Her instinct to shrink would kick in, and she'd make herself smaller. Not tonight. She lifted her chin, grounding her feet to the floor, steady and sure. Every inch of her felt earned.

When she looked up, Sebastián was watching her. He didn't move or speak. The heat in his gaze wasn't desire. It was reverence.

"You're radiant," he said.

Before she could respond, a dazzling, stage-ready Camila swept in between them. Her dragon braid was dusted with gold glitter, and the shimmer of her costume caught the light beneath her Ritmo Latino robe.

"Camila!" Gia threw her arms around her, nerves and adrenaline spilling into the hug. "We're next. We're going on next. Okay. We've got this. We're ready. It's almost time."

"Hey, Gia." Camila's voice cut her off. "Look at me. Breathe, babe."

She held Gia tight, then pulled back enough to meet her eyes. "You've worked your ass off. You are ready. Listen. I want you to throw perfection out the window. It's about *why* you dance. Show them your story. Make them feel it. Unleash on that crowd, and they won't even know what hit them."

Gia swallowed hard. Sebastián's hand found hers, his fingers curling firmly around hers like an anchor.

Camila turned to him. "Sebas." Her voice caught. "I'm so damn proud to call you my brother." She placed a hand against his cheek, quick but tender, her nails catching the stage light. "You belong here." She blinked fast, fake eyelashes fluttering, willing the tears away. No time for smudged mascara.

"I love you both," she added, stepping back. "Now go burn the place to the ground."

"We'll make you proud," Sebastián said.

"You always do." Camila winked at Gia and disappeared through the curtain, heading to the front row, where her voice would be the loudest one in the room.

"Representing Ritmo Latino, Gia DeLuca and Sebastián Solano!"

The ballroom lights dimmed, then burst into gold as Gia and Sebastián stepped onto the floor, hand in hand. They were the final couple in the beginner division. Applause swelled and faded into an expectant hush.

"Just like the first time," he whispered, voice low against her ear as they walked to center stage.

"Mmm, the first time ended with my back against a mirror," Gia teased.

He couldn't help laughing. "We can definitely make that happen again. Actually, please, can we make that happen?"

The laughter and heat between them sparked like a match, and the audience noticed. A ripple of whistles and cheers followed as they stepped apart and took their positions, the tension still crackling in the space between them.

Near the front, their crew leaned forward. Nikki clasped her hands to her heart. Daniel offered a solemn nod. Camila, Andrés, Amber and Luna shouted their names like they were courtside at a final.

Gia's pulse kicked up as she waited for the music. Her costume was Ritmo Latino's signature purple and gold. The sleek bodysuit showed off legs she'd carved from months of dancing through self-doubt. Her sparkly bronze heels, once stiff and unfamiliar, now hugged her feet like well-worn ballet slippers. Sebastián, in a sleek midnight black shirt unbuttoned halfway and even darker trousers, wore gold cufflink accents that caught the light like fire.

She glanced at the audience one last time, heart pounding.

The music began.

Sparse percussion echoed throughout the room. The staccato beats tapped into her memory of the first time they danced this piece together. Gia let it pull her under.

The rumba section was their story in motion. Every movement carried the restraint that defined their early relationship. They didn't touch, but the connection between them was obvious. They had lived a lifetime within this one dance. Their passionate love story was told in this one song.

Dance, the part of her she thought she'd buried forever, now pulled her into the light. In finding her way back to it, she had found Sebastián, the man who challenged her, steadied her, and saw her. Tonight she embraced her first love and her forever love. The dream she'd never dared speak aloud and the life she once thought impossible were now in her hands.

If rumba was the flirtation of their beginning, and salsa the chaos of falling in love, the cha-cha-cha was the surrender and everything after.

The crowd clapped along. Camila's voice rang out, "¡Eso!" The judges leaned forward, captivated by the story Gia and Sebastián wove across the stage.

Every step surged with intensity, building toward the final beat that abruptly ended the song. A spin, a catch, the dramatic dip...and then, silence. The music finished, but no one moved. Time seemed to freeze.

Sebastián kissed her. Right there in the heart of the ballroom, holding her suspended in the dip. His lips met hers like it was the only possible ending.

The room erupted. Their friends were the first to jump to their feet. Camila let out a scream, brushing away tears. Andrés and Nikki stood on their chairs, howling.

Sebastián pulled her up gently, and they bowed together. He leaned in, voice barely a breath. "Whatever happens now, we already won."

Spectators lined the ballroom walls. There was standing room only by this point in the evening. "Welcome to the advanced student division, where dancers with three or more years of salsa training are paired with California's top professionals," the emcee said. This was the moment everyone had been waiting for.

At the judges' table sat a formidable lineup: Gabriela Ramos, the legendary salsa champion from Miami, Pedro Vasquez of the New York Salsa Company, and Luis Cortez, a world-class choreographer from Puerto Rico.

Gia and Sebastián wove through the crowd toward their team, where Nikki waved them over to two empty seats. When Gia sat down, Sebastián slipped an arm around her shoulders. She leaned into him, letting the warmth of his body and the hum of relief settle through her. The hard part was over. They could finally just breathe and enjoy the night.

Offstage, Camila and Johnny stretched in the shadows. Gia caught Camila's eye and grinned. Camila flashed her a smile, radiant even under pressure.

"Next up, representing San Diego, Emilio Cruz and Vanessa Lennox!"

Gia's gaze snapped back to the floor. The sight of them together on the stage with Camila in the wings made Gia's stomach turn. She glanced sideways at Sebastián and whispered, "Is it bad that I hope they fall on their faces?"

He chuckled. "Nah. But Camila's hoping they crush it."

Gia frowned, confused.

"She wants to beat them at their best."

"That's kinda badass."

"That's my sister."

The moment "Aquí Traigo Mi Montuno" by Ismael Quintana began, Emilio and Vanessa hit an overhead lift, Vanessa arching mid-air like a flame caught in the wind. The technical difficulty only increased from there. As the music picked up, their footwork sped up too. Their execution was flawless.

The final combination comprised a rapid series of dips and lifts, ending in a dramatic drop with Vanessa's head nearly brushing the floor as Emilio held her suspended by one arm. The crowd roared, clearly impressed. Emilio's first major show without Camila went perfectly.

"Technically excellent," Gia whispered.

"And emotionally flat," Sebastián replied.

The announcer's voice cut through their commentary. "Next up, representing Ritmo Latino from San Diego, Camila Solano and Johnny Ruiz!"

The crowd surged with cheers. Gia's heart skipped as Camila and Johnny stepped on stage. Camila scanned the room, her confidence radiating, and blew a kiss in their direction.

Then the music hit. "Aguanile" burst to life, percussion thundering, pulling everyone into its pulse. From the first beat, the energy was electric.

Camila moved across the stage like she owned every square inch of it. Her moves were crisp and sensual all at once. She played with the crowd, inviting them in with a glance, a flick of her wrist, a daring sway. Gia leaned forward, breath caught, as Camila, arm in arm with Johnny, walked straight towards the audience. Suddenly Camila leaped into the air, tucking her knees, flipping in a clean rotation before landing perfectly on beat. She never let go of Johnny's hand, so the flip seemed to come from nowhere.

The audience gasped and then roared. Gia's skin prickled, goosebumps racing up her arms. She remembered that first night at Casa Sevilla when she watched Camila dance and felt something inside her spark alive. That same wave crashed through her now, stronger than ever. "They're amazing," Gia breathed.

"Ca-Mee-La! Let's go!" Sebastián shouted.

The routine crescendoed with a series of fast shines and closed with a dramatic, forward-facing dip. Camila stretched long and straight, her chest angled toward the floor, with only the tops of her toes kissing the ground. She seemed to defy gravity once again, held up by Johnny, sure and steady, but about to lose his mind with excitement.

Gia clapped until her palms stung. A few weeks ago, this might have sent her spiraling into jealousy or doubt, convinced she'd never measure up. Tonight, it was all inspiration. Gia let herself wonder, *how far can I go with this?*

The announcer stepped up to the microphone. "Good evening, everyone." His voice echoed across the ballroom, pulling every eye toward the stage. "We're ready to announce the results of the beginner level pro-am salsa division."

The room held its breath, the hush so complete it was as if the walls were listening.

"In third place... Stephanie Vale and Sam Carter."

Applause rippled, polite but thin, and Gia's chest pinched as she watched Stephanie and Sam take their trophy. Their smiles looked too bright, stretched tight to cover the heartbreak she recognized all too well.

"In second place... Gia DeLuca and Sebastián Solano."

Gia blinked, stunned, the words taking a moment to land. Second place. *He's going to be so disappointed.* She felt Sebastián free her hand so she could take the trophy from the judge, who brought it over to them. Their teammates leaped to their feet, jumping and chanting in rhythm, "Ritmo Latino! Ritmo Latino!"

The announcer glanced down at the card in his hand, then back up with a smile.

"And in first place..." The announcer's grin stretched wider, his pause deliberate, pulling the entire ballroom into the moment. The room leaned in, holding its collective breath.

"Francesca Donato and Leo Evers!"

Shouts and cheers thundered around her. From the stage's edge, she spotted Camila and Johnny, both beaming, their joy a balm against the knot in her stomach. The announcer moved on to the next division, but Gia barely heard him. All she could think about was Sebastián and what second place might feel like for him. "Are you disappointed?" She steeled herself for impact. For heartbreak, anger, or worse.

He stopped mid-stride, turned fully to face her, and waited until her eyes met his.

"Disappointed?" Her chest tightened in anticipation of the blow that was coming. "Gia, I won the whole thing."

The ballroom noise faded, all of it blurring to the edges as those words settled into her heart.

"I have an entirely new respect for competing on this stage. Plus, I've got some serious training to do if I ever try this again." His grin went crooked, boyish charm breaking through his sweat and exhaustion. "You know, if you started teaching classes, you could be the pro and I could be the student next year. Technically, I have under two years of salsa training."

Gia laughed. "Only if you promise to behave and do every-thing I say."

He leaned in, mischief sparking in his eyes. "No chance on the first thing, but it would be my pleasure for the second."

Gia slipped her hand into his as they walked offstage. In her best imitation of his low, serious tone, she teased, "Just so you know, I don't go easy on my students. I need more than potential. I need commitment."

Sebastián's fingers closed firmly around hers. "Gia, I'm yours. Committed. For as long as you'll have me."

Tears stung her eyes, but this time she didn't hide them. She let them fall, every one of them proof of how far she'd come, including how far they'd come together.

She whispered, voice breaking, "I was so scared to hope for this."

He brushed his thumb across her cheek. "Then let's call this what it is. Not the end of a routine. The beginning of everything."

Gia's laughter spilled through her tears as he kissed her again, slow and sure, sealing the promise between them. They were offstage, but the audience still had all eyes on them. For once, she didn't care who was watching. She wanted the entire world to see.

The peak of the celebration had passed. Awards were clutched, photos snapped, and congratulations exchanged while everyone waited for the next ballroom to open for live music and social dancing.

Sebastián surveyed the room, smiling at the sight of Johnny holding court at the center of their crew, describing the lift from their final routine for the fifth time. Camila wasn't with them.

He spotted her near the edge of the room, half in shadow, perched on a folding chair, stretching her neck up and down, staring at the floor like she was somewhere far away.

Sebastián crossed the room, keeping quiet until he was close enough for her to notice.

"You're gonna miss the victory lap," he said softly.

Camila lifted her head, offering a half-smile. "Figured I'd let Johnny soak it up for a minute. He deserves it."

"You okay?"

She leaned back, her shoulders slumped in a way he didn't recognize. "My hands won't stop shaking."

He stayed quiet, giving her time to fill the space.

"I almost didn't do it this year." Her voice was stripped of its usual edge. "Too much pressure. Too many people waiting for me to fall on my face." She gave an exhausted laugh. "Emilio's words in my head, louder than my own."

Sebastián continued looking at his sister. He didn't interrupt.

"I kept telling myself it was about showing him up. Proving to Emilio and everyone else that I'm still on top. The truth is, I needed to prove it to myself."

Sebastián dropped into the chair beside his sister. "Did you? Because there was never a doubt in my mind. Or anyone else's."

Camila's eyes glistened, but she smiled, shaking her head like she wouldn't let the tears fall. "Man, I hate when you go full softie on me."

He bumped her shoulder with his. "Yeah, yeah. Don't get used to it."

She chuckled, wiping one eye with the heel of her hand. "I forget what it feels like to dance when I have nothing to lose. Not to win or prove anything, just to dance."

Sebastián nodded. "You're still the best damn dancer I know, Cami."

"Don't you forget it."

"Not in this lifetime."

She stood up, straightening her spine like armor slipping back into place. "Come on. Let's go before Johnny gives himself an injury showing off that lift again."

Sebastián followed, watching her move ahead of him, her shoulders a little lighter and her steps a little freer.

He felt grateful to his sister for helping him see what mattered and reminding him where happiness lived. He wondered how he might do the same for her.

The grand ballroom glowed warm and golden, the air rich with music and laughter. A live band brought the dance floor to life. Competitors, now in their social best, shed the day's fierce energy for a night of effortless play with world-class salsa dancers.

When Camila and Gia slipped into the room, they were greeted by the roar of their crew. "Reina. Camila. Reina. Camila," they chanted.

"I'm first with the queen!" Daniel announced. Camila threw her head back, laughing as he swept her into a social bachata frame.

Andrés, all swagger, approached Nikki with a grin. "You know," he said, offering his hand, "I can't let the night end without getting at least one dance with you."

"I thought you'd never ask."

He spun her onto the floor like they'd done it a hundred times. "You're exactly who I need for this song. By the time we're done, Camila's going to beg me to start a bachata team."

"Oh, so this is a mission now?"

"Operation: Win Over the Queen," he whispered. "And you, Nikki, are my secret weapon."

"Okay, you have my attention." The music folded around them as they melted into the groove. "Tell me all about it. Or better yet, show me."

It took seconds for Amber and Luna to be whisked away by partners ready to dance with San Diego's top followers.

Sebastián held Gia in a slow dance on the edge of the floor. "What's next for you, Gia? I heard something about a promotion in New York…" He smiled like he was happy for her, but the ache in his eyes gave him away.

Gia smiled, fingers brushing the back of his neck. "Actually,

I'll be opening a San Diego office with the publisher. It's official as of this morning."

His hand tightened at her waist, drawing her in.

"You're staying!" he shouted.

"I'm staying!" she yelled back and laughed.

He spun her out, then back in, wrapping both arms around her.

"We're both here in San Diego for a while. What should we do first?"

"Let's dance."

Epilogue

Gia slipped the band of her hair tie off her wrist and twisted her ponytail higher as she scanned the studio. The mirrored walls caught rows of nervous faces, a few couples shuffling their feet while others chatted too loudly.

I remember this feeling, she thought. *All nerves, sweaty palms, and second-guessing your shoes.*

She cued up a slow-tempo salsa track and turned toward them with a smile.

"Alright, everyone, welcome to Ritmo Latino's beginner class. I'm Gia, and I'll be subbing for Camila tonight."

A few students exhaled audibly, smiles breaking the tension.

"I promise we're going to have fun, mess up, and get better together. Sound good? Sí, or yes?"

"¡Sí!" a few voices shouted. "Yes," came from others.

She smiled. "Perfect. Basics first. We'll start with one, two, three, five, six, seven."

Her own laugh bubbled up as she told them about the time she stepped on her own foot, earning chuckles from the room. Bit by bit, she coaxed them into the rhythm until the music started sinking into their bodies. She borrowed a volunteer to demonstrate, then separated them into two circles, leads on the outside, follows on the inside.

She teed up "La Cura" by Frankie Ruiz and when it poured through the speakers, Gia stepped back to take it all in. She loved to catch the moment when the steps finally clicked for a new dancer.

Her smartwatch buzzed.

CAMILA

The tango lesson starts in 10 minutes! Didn't realize how badly I needed this vacation. You're amazing. Thank you!!!

Gia responded with a heart emoji. She would type a message later, but for now, she was in dance class and fully present.

The studio door opened, and she didn't need to look to know who it was. Sebastián's energy filled the space before his footsteps did. A ripple of whispers passed through the group. His soccer star aura never quite dulled, even here.

He leaned against the wall near the speaker, arms folded, watching her like she was the only one in the room.

"Rotate!" she called, then walked over, pulse rising from the way he looked at her.

"What are you grinning at?" she asked.

"The love of my life."

Her heart warmed, and she leaned in to kiss him hello.

"Agent meeting is off till tomorrow," he said. "Think I can steal you when class is over?"

"Only if you dance through the last few rotations. Eli and his wife made it, and I promised him I'd make sure she has a good first experience."

"Easy, yes."

Gia pressed her mouth to his once more, then turned back to the class waiting for her. Time to dance.

Acknowledgments

Christine, Diane, Janette, and Tris: Thank you for devouring this book, sending immediate and thoughtful feedback, and celebrating this story with such enthusiasm. Your support meant more than you know. I'm incredibly lucky to have such audacious, badass women in my life.

Courtney, Liz, Jenna, and Julie: Thank you for the encouragement, creativity, and constant reminders that this work matters. Every writer should have a group like ours. The world would be more magical for it.

Mom, Stephanie, and Samantha: Thank you for all your feedback and quick opinions every time I texted you with a random idea, title, or cover idea. I love you to "humidity" and beyond.

Francesca and Leo: You inspire me to dream bigger. Of all the dancing, writing, and creating I have done, you two are my greatest masterpieces.

Hussein: Thank you for your limitless support, encouragement, and love—for being my tech support, my design artist, my anything-else-I-needed, and my biggest fan. I love you endlessly.

To my dance teachers and friends, from ballet to salsa, from childhood to now: Life is richer because of you.

Also by Jessa Leads

**Don't miss the next books in
the San Diego After Dark series.**

Coming soon!

Visit www.jessaleads.com for updates and sneak peeks.

About the Author

Jessa Leads writes contemporary romance and women's fiction from a desk near the beach. Her work brings together sensual dance worlds, heartfelt character journeys, and sun-soaked San Diego magic.

Friends know her as the author of seven children's books, an executive ghostwriter, and a startup marketer. She uses this pen name to explore the more passionate side of her writing.

A graduate of the University of California, San Diego with a B.S. in Cognitive Science, Jessa has spent her career exploring how people think, communicate, and connect. Her fiction writing grows out of that curiosity, too, and is inspired by the way dance can stir emotion and awaken desire.

Stay in touch at www.jessaleads.com.